SECRETS AND HISTORY

Rachel McLean writes thrillers that make your pulse race and your brain tick. Originally a self-publishing sensation, she has sold millions of copies digitally, with massive success in the UK, and a growing reach internationally. She is the author of the Dorset Crime novels and the spin-off McBride & Tanner series and Cumbria Crime series. In 2021, she won the Kindle Storyteller Award with *The Corfe Castle Murders* and her books regularly hit No1 in the Bookstat ebook chart on launch.

ALSO BY RACHEL MCLEAN

The McBride and Tanner series

Blood and Money
Death and Poetry
Power and Treachery
Secrets and History

RACHEL McLEAN

McBRIDE AND TANNER 4

SECRETS
AND
HISTORY

ACKROYD PUBLISHING

Ackroyd Publishing

ackroydpublishing.com

Printed and bound in the UK by CPI Group (Uk) Ltd, Croydon CR0 4YY

CHAPTER ONE

Angus Wallace trudged through the damp grass, his boots squelching with each step. The early morning mist clung to the village of Lochranza, obscuring the loch's edge.

"Kylie! Heel!" he called, his voice gruff from disuse. He lived alone these days, and barely spoke to anyone except his dog.

The black terrier ignored him, straining at her lead. Angus sighed. He should never have let his daughter name the dog.

As they neared the loch, Kylie's excitement grew. With a sudden jerk, she slipped her collar and bolted towards the castle.

"Kylie! Get back here!" Angus shouted, but the dog had vanished towards the ruins.

Muttering under his breath, he followed. The castle loomed before him, its stone walls eerie in the mist. The dog had gone into the structure, through the lone opening. He followed with a grimace.

Inside, the air was cold and damp. Angus's footsteps

echoed as he trudged up the steps to the left of the narrow entrance, calling for the damn dog.

"Where are you, you daft mutt?"

A bark echoed from deeper within the ruins. Angus turned to follow the sound, rounding a corner into a large chamber and then a smaller, darker one off to one side. The old prison. He shivered.

Kylie stood a few meters in from the entrance, rigid, staring in at something. Angus followed her gaze.

His breath caught in his throat.

An object sat in the centre of the chamber, its shape becoming distinct as his eyes grew accustomed to the darkness. It was... it was a rowing boat.

A boat? In here? There was no water in here.

He edged forwards, wondering if it was wise. This dark chamber had given him the creeps ever since he was a child, his pals daring him to come in here.

He gasped as he saw what was inside.

A man.

Kylie gave one short sharp bark, then drew closer to Angus, leaning into him.

"It's alright, girl. Nothing to be scared of."

He was trying to reassure himself as much as the dog.

The man lay sprawled on his back, his limbs at odd angles. His face was pale, almost grey in the dim light. Dark hair clung to his forehead, matted with what looked like blood.

Angus didn't know him, but he'd seen the man around the village. One of those bloody cult members, the ones staying up at the campsite. He'd seen them all in the pub, at first chatting with the locals like normal people, but then becoming increasingly isolated the longer they'd stayed.

But what was he doing here?

The man's eyes stared blankly at the stone ceiling, lifeless and glassy. His mouth hung open in a silent scream.

Angus's gaze travelled down the man's body. His clothes were soaked through, as if he'd been pulled from the loch. But how had he ended up here, in this boat, inside the castle ruins?

Angus swallowed. Kylie was gone now. He hoped she'd run out of the castle. She'd wait for him, she was a good dog.

Angus took a step forward, raising his phone to shine the light more clearly onto the dead man. A deep gash ran across his throat, the skin around it ragged and torn. Blood had pooled beneath him, staining the wooden boards of the boat.

Angus swallowed hard, fighting the urge to be sick. He'd seen bodies before, but never like this.

Kylie whined from somewhere, breaking the silence. Angus shook himself out of his daze.

"Get out of here," he muttered. Bloody fool, disturbing what was probably a crime scene.

He turned and headed out of the old prison, crossing himself and muttering a short prayer. Kylie was in the main chamber, her gaze on him, her head cocked. The mist had seeped into here, and with it an air of menace.

"It's alright, girl." He bent and ruffled her head, and she whined.

Yeah, me too.

Hands shaking, he pulled up his mobile and dialled. PC Sam Henderson. He didn't envy the lad, having to deal with this.

"Sam? It's Angus Wallace. You need to come to the castle. Now."

CHAPTER TWO

Jade sipped her coffee, watching the loch. The sun was beginning to rise, casting a pink light over the water. Birds swooped and dived, their shapes silhouetted against the sky.

For the first time in three years, she could appreciate the beauty of Loch Lomond. It didn't make her want to cry.

She'd had another date with Fraser last night. She'd asked her mum to take Rory for the evening, and Fraser had driven up from Glasgow. He'd arrived at her house just as the sun was setting, and they'd walked along the loch, talking.

Or rather, she'd talked and he'd listened. She'd told him about Dan, about her work, about her fears for the future. She'd told him about the A82 and how she couldn't bear to drive along it, and how that sometimes made her job difficult. She'd told him about her team in the Complex Crimes Unit, and how proud she was becoming of them. She'd told him about her son, Rory, and how he was the light of her life.

Probably too much to tell your boss. But not too much to tell someone you were falling for.

She'd told him all these things and, remarkably, she

hadn't felt self-conscious. She'd felt as if she could tell him anything and he wouldn't judge her. Maybe it helped that he'd known Dan, that the three of them had spent time together. She'd worried that might make it feel odd. But it didn't. It made it feel right.

And then they'd come back to the house and he'd cooked dinner. He'd made a risotto, one of her favourites. After eating, she'd opened a bottle of wine and they'd sat on the sofa, talking some more. And then they'd ended up kissing.

All in all, it had been a perfect evening.

Her phone rang and she felt her chest clench: Fraser.

She picked it up. "Morning."

"Morning, Jade. I hope you don't mind me calling you at this time."

She looked at the clock. It was 7am. "It's fine. Rory's still asleep." She'd have to wake him soon, get him ready for school.

"Good. I just wanted to let you know that we've had a call from Police Scotland. A body's been found on the Isle of Arran."

No mention of last night. His voice was formal, professional.

Had she misjudged things?

She pulled the phone closer to her ear. "OK. It's good to hear your voice."

"Yours too." A pause. "Jade, I want you to lead the investigation. I've already spoken to Petra and she's happy to come on board. There are aspects of the crime that I think a forensic psychologist can help with. But I wanted to make sure you were OK with it."

She swallowed. *Have I got this all wrong?*

A sound came from Rory's room; he was awake. She shook herself out, mentally.

"Thanks, Fraser." She couldn't call him *Sir* anymore, not when it was just the two of them. It was a habit he'd been trying to encourage her out of for a while, anyway. "When do you need me there?"

"It needn't necessarily be you. In fact, you might be better off directing things from the office. But brief your team and let me know what your plan is."

"Right. Will do, Sir." Was the 'Sir' a dig? She wasn't sure, but she couldn't resist.

"Fraser," he said. "You always call me Fraser."

She smiled. "So I do." There would be time later to continue where they'd left off last night. For now, she needed to do her job. "I'll call you later this morning."

"Thanks, Jade. And thanks. Thanks for last night."

He hung up. She held the phone out and stared at it, torn between personal confusion and professional excitement.

CHAPTER THREE

FREYA OPENED her eyes to a blanket of grey. The cold had seeped through her sleeping bag during the night, leaving her stiff. She rubbed her hands together, her fingers numb, her breath forming clouds in the damp air of the tent.

She really needed more sleep.

But the thought of Erik – wherever he was, probably already up, making sure everyone had what they needed – tugged her out from the thin warmth of her bag. The group. *Always the bloody group.* Always Erik, organizing everything, thinking he could take care of her just because he was a couple of years older.

She struggled to her feet and unzipped the tent, wincing at the freezing air on her skin. The campsite was quiet. She pulled on her boots and squelched over to Erik's tent. The grass was wet, as always.

Empty. His sleeping bag was a crumpled heap inside, but there was no sign of Erik.

A gust of wind whipped across the campsite, rattling the pegs of the older tents. Freya tugged her jacket tighter around herself and looked over at the yurt, the one Astrid slept in. The ties opened, and Astrid stepped out, hair perfectly straight despite the damp air.

She spotted Freya and hesitated. Something flickered in her eyes: worry?

The truth was, Freya was scared of Astrid. The older woman had a way about her that brooked no disagreement, and made Freya feel like she'd acquired a second mother. And not a benevolent one.

Ignore it. Don't let her see what she does to you.

Freya stepped forward. "Have you seen Erik?"

Astrid looked around the campsite, her gaze passing over the tents, the trees, then back to Freya.

"We need to talk," she said, ignoring the question. "Come inside, it's cold."

Freya frowned. "I'm fine here. Where's Erik?"

Astrid sighed, a long, exaggerated breath. She ran a hand through her hair, fingers twitching. "The local plod called."

Freya felt bile rise in her throat. "What?"

Astrid raised an eyebrow. "I told you to come inside my yurt."

"Astrid." Freya clenched both fists. "Has something happened to Erik?"

Astrid blinked, then took a step forward, reaching for her. "Freya—"

Freya flinched, dodging the embrace. "Tell me." Her voice shook.

Astrid lifted her head, staring back into Freya's eyes. "Someone found him. Some old fisherman. At the castle."

"What do you mean, found?"

Astrid raised her hand again. This time, Freya didn't stop her putting it on her shoulder.

"I'm sorry, Freya. Your brother's dead."

Freya's chest hardened. She stared at Astrid, waiting for her to keep talking, to explain the joke. Astrid's sense of humour was... Well, it could be cruel.

"I'm so sorry, Freya. But he really is dead."

Freya screamed. She shot out her arms, shoving Astrid so hard the other woman stumbled, gasping for air. Freya didn't wait to see if she got up. She turned and ran.

The campsite blurred behind her, the muddy path skidding under her boots. She didn't care. The only thought she had was Erik.

It was a joke. It had to be a joke. If it was, she was getting out of there, and taking Erik with her. She didn't care if she had to drug him and drag him out.

Her throat was raw by the time the ruins appeared ahead of her. Mist hung low behind the castle, covering the surface of the sea loch. A flicker of yellow – a police cordon – flapped listlessly at the entrance.

Oh God. It's not a joke.

She barely slowed as she ducked under it, boots crunching on the gravel.

After a few steps, she slammed into a chest. Strong hands grabbed her arms, holding her back.

She blinked, heart thundering. A uniformed police officer was holding her, his face grim. His expression said this wasn't the first time he'd stopped someone from doing something stupid.

"Let me through," she croaked.

"You can't go in."

She shoved him, yanking her arms free. "I need to see him!"

"No. Are you his sister?"

She nodded. The castle beyond the man was blurring. She wiped her eyes and held down another scream.

She strained against his hold. "Let me *see* him!"

He steered her away. "You don't want to do this."

"Freya."

She turned to see Astrid behind her, watching. Freya's stomach twisted as she looked at her.

Go away. Leave me.

"I'll take it from here," Astrid muttered, stepping forward.

The policeman glanced at Astrid, then nodded, letting go of Freya.

Freya felt Astrid's hand on her back. Her legs gave way, sending her crumpling to the ground. She folded in on herself, shaking, the cold creeping back into her bones.

She wanted to scream, but nothing came out.

What the hell was she going to do without him?

CHAPTER FOUR

JADE STOOD by the window of the CCU offices, staring out at the grey drizzle. The view over this part of the city was dismal at the best of times, but today, in late March, it was like looking at a watercolour someone had given up on because they couldn't find colour paints. The wind rattled the thin windows, and the radiators on two walls were making clicking sounds but not giving out much heat.

She shivered, wishing she'd brought a jumper.

She took a breath and turned away from the window to face her team.

Mo was slouched at his desk, gazing at his phone. Stuart was already deep into a sandwich, a half-eaten mess of cheese and pickle. Patty was pacing, her footsteps heavy on the thin carpet. She held a coffee mug from which she'd swig from time to time.

Jade could feel Patty's eyes on her now and again, flicking briefly over, then away. Did she know about her and Fraser? Or was it just that the two of them had worked together for so long, Patty could read her mind?

Get on with it. You've got a murder investigation to lead.

"Right," Jade said, clapping her hands together. "We need to allocate responsibilities. First there's—"

"I'll go," said Stuart. "You need people on the scene, right? I'll go."

Jade raised an eyebrow. Stuart was keen and ambitious. The Isle of Arran wasn't exactly the sort of place he'd be able to showcase his talents. But maybe he wanted to gain some more varied experience.

"Good," she said. "We'll need two of us out there, and two of us back at base."

"I'm happy to do background here, boss," Patty said. "Not the best time for me to go off on a jolly, what with my mum being ill."

Jade gave her a look. This wasn't a jolly.

"Patty," Mo said, "I'm not sure—"

Patty spun to face him. "Sorry, Sarge. I didn't mean it. A man died. I shouldn't—"

Mo nodded. "Where is the Isle of Arran, anyway? Somewhere up north?"

Jade shook her head. "It's actually not that far. Off the west coast, short ferry ride from Ardrossan."

"Sorry, boss. I'm none the wiser."

Patty grinned. "Ardrossan's a shithole. It's basically a ferry terminal and a bunch of pissed off seagulls. You've not missed much."

"Right. But where is it?"

"South west of Glasgow," Jade told him. "Arran's away to the west from there. You can get the northern ferry though, from—"

"That's bloody miles to drive, though," said Patty. "You're surely not thinking of going that way?"

Jade sat down at one of the empty desks. They had a murder to solve. How had they ended up discussing driving routes?

"It's very beautiful," Stuart said, looking at Mo. "I went there with my folks when I was a wee kid. Didn't appreciate it much then, but I've seen the photos."

"Aye." Patty nodded, then looked across at Jade. "Maybe the sarge should go with Stuart, boss?"

Jade pursed her lips. She had Rory to think of; a trip to the Isle of Arran wouldn't exactly be convenient. But when she'd taken leadership of this unit, she'd known what that would entail.

"Beautiful, you say?" Mo said.

"Gorgeous," Stuart replied with a grin.

Mo nodded. "OK. Boss, I'll run operations on the island. It'll do me good. That is, if you're happy for me to."

"I'm more than happy for you to do that, Mo. It'll be useful experience for you. You'll need to go home first though, let your wife and—"

He was shaking his head. "I always keep a change of clothes in the boot of my car, just in case."

"You'll need more than one," Patty snorted.

"I was speaking figuratively," he told her. "I'll be fine."

Patty shrugged. "Fair enough. Boys on Arran it is, then. Us girls back at base."

Jade frowned. She hadn't meant for the investigation to split on gender lines. But then, there were all sorts of ways she could split the team. This was as good as any.

"OK," she said, striding to the meeting room they used as an incident room. These offices were spacious, even more so when there were only the four of them to occupy them. Fraser had said it was to keep them away from potential conflict if they ended up investigating fellow officers. Given that that had never happened, she thought the more likely reason was that other units weren't all that keen on the existence of the CCU, and had no desire to share a space with them.

The others followed her in, and she started writing on the whiteboard at the end of the space. A large meeting table dominated the room, with eight chairs around it that were rarely used. Mo leaned on the desk and Patty and Stuart sat.

Jade wrote Erik Haldane's name on the board. A photo would come later. And they'd have to use the digital systems, what with the four of them being separated.

"What are the names of his friends at the campsite?" she asked, looking at Patty. She knew the DC would have done the research as soon as she'd heard about the existence of the group.

Patty pulled out her phone. "I've spoken to PC Sam Henderson at the local station, and he's sent over the names. We've got a Freya Haldane. She's Erik's sister."

Jade wrote Freya's name on the board, drawing a line to Erik and the word 'sister'. "Who else?"

"Astrid Thorsen. She's the ringleader."

"Ringleader?" That sounded ominous. "What kind of group is this?"

"Some of the locals think they're a cult. Apparently Astrid said they were a research group. But there've been reports of weird stuff at night. Chanting, some kind of ceremony at the castle."

"Sounds like a cult to me," said Stuart.

"Let's not jump to any conclusions until we get there," said Jade. "Who else?"

"Erik, of course. Two more: Morgan Douglas and Alistair MacLeod. All I have for them is names."

Jade wrote the names on the board. "Mo and Stuart, you'll need to interview each of them separately as soon as you get there. They've already had long enough to confer on their stories."

"We think one of them did it?" Mo asked.

She shook her head. "We don't think anything yet. But they're all potential suspects. Patty, your mate Sam. What did he say about the group's relationship with the locals?"

Patty snorted again. "Not good, boss."

Jade wasn't surprised. Arran might have been an island, but it was still Scotland. Chanting and weird rituals weren't always welcome. "Any specific incidents?"

"Nothing serious. Sam said nothing he'd had to get involved in, anyway."

"Right. We need to find out who Erik might have had contact with. Is there anyone he might have pissed off? And of course there's the possibility someone from his home might have travelled to the island. Where did he come from?"

"Still not sure, boss," said Patty.

"The name sounds Norwegian," Mo pointed out.

Jade sniffed. "There are plenty of folks with Norwegian names in the Highlands and Islands. Doesn't necessarily mean anything. But it's another thing we'll need to establish."

"I'll look at official records," said Patty.

"Good. Mo and Stuart, you find out what you can from the group and the locals. Especially this PC Henderson."

"No problem, boss." Mo was taking notes in his pad.

Jade pushed out her chest. This was looking more positive. Sure, there were far too many potential suspects, and she had no idea what the significance of the body being found in a boat could be. But she was hoping Petra could help with that.

"Petra will be joining you," she said. "The super's already called her in."

"Good," said Mo.

Jade suppressed a smile. Since when were Mo and Petra pals?

"She'll meet us on the ferry?" Stuart asked.

"She's making her own way. Expect her sometime today or tomorrow. I gather she has work commitments to clear up."

She placed the whiteboard marker down on the table. "Right, folks. Let's get to it."

CHAPTER FIVE

Mo SAT in the driver's seat, gazing down at his phone. The smiling faces of his family stared back at him, frozen against the backdrop of his back garden in Birmingham.

He traced a finger over the image, his shoulders slumping. The memory of that house in Northfield – nothing special, but home – left him feeling empty.

He needed to get past this. Learn to appreciate Scotland. Catriona was happy here, and the girls loved their new school. And his old team had broken up and gone their separate ways. There was nothing back there for him now.

But he missed it, still.

The phone buzzed; a voice call from Cat. They hadn't spoken this morning; she'd had a 7am meeting and slid out of bed before he was even awake.

"You alright?" Her tone was soft, concerned.

Mo blinked away the photo, still in his mind's eye. "Yeah, fine. Just tired."

"You sure?"

He nodded. She waited for him to speak, silent.

"Yeah," he said with a sigh. "I'm sure." It wasn't fair on his wife, him moping around like this. They'd moved north to be closer to her parents, who needed them more than his did. He should be happy for her.

His gaze drifted out of the car, to the bleak industrial estate surrounding him. Grey buildings against a grey sky.

He berated himself. *Birmingham isn't exactly the Costa del Sol, is it?*

A tap on the window made him jump. Stuart stood outside, ready to go.

"I've got to go, Cat. I'll let you know when we get there."

"You take care, love. Talk to me if you're feeling low."

He felt his chest dip. *I shouldn't be burdening her with this.* "I will."

"Good. Hope the journey's smooth, love."

He nodded and plastered on a smile as Stuart climbed into the passenger seat. "Time to hit the road."

With one last glance at the low building of the CCU, Mo pulled out of the car park, hoping the Isle of Arran would be an improvement.

CHAPTER SIX

DR PETRA MCBRIDE fumbled with her keys, struggling to unlock the door. The hallway light flickered, casting shadows that were familiar but eerie nonetheless. She climbed the stairs to her flat and flicked on the light, sighing.

The living room was a mess. Dust sheets covered the furniture, half-painted walls their backdrop. Paint tins cluttered the floor. And the smell of fresh paint hit her nostrils.

Petra felt her body slump. She'd spent a fortune on doing up this place after inheriting it from her Aunt Lydia. For what? She still felt unsettled, hating the constriction of being tied to one place.

She dumped her bag on the sofa and a cloud of dust rose. She blinked.

Envelopes lay scattered on the floor. She bent to gather them up: bills and junk. An unmarked envelope.

She pursed her lips. It could be anything.

But she knew it wasn't.

She tore it open.

The handwriting was shaky, barely legible. She scanned the words, feeling bile rise in her throat.

You were wrong. He should have stayed behind bars.

She let her fist unclench and the letter fluttered to the floor.

That case. The young man whose liberty she'd helped win. The murder he'd committed afterwards.

Blood rushed in her ears. She cast her gaze around the flat, and found herself wishing she'd never moved in here. She should just have sold it, used the money to keep moving, taking on cases wherever she found a place that took her fancy, then moving on again.

Running.

"It's nothing," she muttered. "I can deal with it."

She'd had therapy, or one session at least. A psychiatrist her ex-girlfriend Aila had hired.

The relationship with Aila had ended over her decision to stop after that single session. Petra was a psychologist. She didn't need bloody therapy.

"Physician, heal thyself," she barked, stomping back to the front door.

She double-checked the locks. Triple-checked. Ignored her shaking fingers.

She sat down on the bed, the one piece of furniture still uncovered. The bed was cold; she'd been away for two weeks, for a job in London. Aila was long gone.

This flat.

Petra had tried to love it. To see it as a continuation of the life of Aunt Lydia, her most eccentric aunt, perfectly suited to Glasgow's West End. But she wasn't Lydia.

She crawled into bed. The sheets felt damp, clammy. She tossed them off then pulled them back up, shivering.

She'd turned the bloody heating off when she'd left. It would take days to bring this flat back to a comfortable temperature. And she had no plans to hang around. There were plenty of job offers, plenty of opportunities to travel.

But she'd promised Stan. Dr Stan Rushton, to give him his full title, manager of the community psychiatric unit she worked at now. She'd taken a leave of absence to take the London job. She owed it to him to return to the job she'd started six months ago, a job she was enjoying, in spite of herself.

Could she do it? Or was running preferable?

She stared up at the dark ceiling, willing sleep to come.

The words echoed in her head. *You were wrong.*

She knew her testimony had influenced the probation board. But she'd only said what she believed to be true. Stated her professional opinion.

Could she be blamed for that?

CHAPTER SEVEN

Mo STEPPED out of the car, his legs stiff from the long journey. The loch stretched before him, its surface reflecting the brooding sky. Lochranza Castle loomed in the distance, a silent sentinel.

He took a deep breath. The air was crisp, tinged with salt.

"Quite a sight, isn't it?" Stuart said as he got out of the car and stretched his neck.

Mo nodded. "Different from what I'm used to."

As they approached the cordon, curious locals huddled nearby, whispering. Mo felt their eyes on him.

"Stuart," he said. "Start canvassing the locals. See if anyone saw anything unusual."

Stuart nodded and moved off.

Mo ducked under the tape. A uniformed officer approached, arm outstretched.

"PC Sam Henderson. You must be DS Uddin."

Mo shook his hand. It was large, the skin rough. *Island*

life, he thought. "Pleased to meet you. You been here all day?"

A nod. "I've been keeping an eye on things. As far as police goes on the island, I'm it."

Mo raised an eyebrow. He couldn't imagine working like that. Although, he had to admit, he secretly envied the guy. "Anything you can tell me?"

Sam turned and gestured towards the castle. "Young man found this morning by a local fisherman. Victim is Erik Haldane, part of a group staying at the campsite just down the road there—"

Mo nodded. "We drove past it."

"Did you see their section?"

"They have a whole section?"

"Yurt and a few tents. Yurt belongs to their ringleader. The locals aren't all that enamoured of them."

Mo wondered what Sam meant by 'ringleader'. But then, living in a remote spot like the Isle of Arran was different from Glasgow, Stirling or Birmingham.

"Why not?" he asked.

"They're... well, I'd rather not colour your judgement before you meet them. I can take you to Angus, he's the old fella who discovered the body. He's given me a statement, but I imagine you'll want to find out more from him."

"I'll read the statement you took first."

Sam gave him a sidelong glance. Was that the flicker of a smile?

Trust people, and they normally live up to it.

"Where do you suggest we start?" Mo asked. "I've already got Stuart – DC Burns – talking to the gawpers."

Sam sniggered. "Oh, you'll get plenty of that here. This is

the most interesting thing that's happened since... well, since before I joined the force, that's for sure."

"Well, hopefully we'll keep the drama to a minimum."

Sam paled. "Sorry, I didn't mean to—"

Mo put a hand on his shoulder. "I didn't mean to infer anything."

Mo felt the shoulder tense below his hand. "No, Sarge," said Sam. "I'm sure." He cleared his throat. "Anyway. I'll take you to see the body."

"Have Scene of Crime been?"

"Not yet. We're expecting them in the morning. I was actually quite impressed you made it here so quick."

Mo smiled. He wanted to get this done with so he could get home to his family. That was the only reason he'd got here so soon. "Let's go see this body, yes?"

Sam led him to the castle. "It's inside, in the old prison."

"It was a prison?"

"Had a prison. Lochranza Castle was built in the thirteenth century. The prison's got a bit of a reputation locally. I've had to clear vagrants out of it from time to time. But never..."

Sam led Mo through a narrow doorway in the castle's tall, featureless stone wall. The building was square, imposing against the backdrop of the sea loch and the hills beyond. Mo shivered.

Inside was an empty space, some sort of old chamber. Sam turned right and led him through another archway into a space which had been lit by floodlights.

At its centre was a boat, a small, wooden vessel that was barely more than a collection of planks of wood.

"That's not a usable vessel," said Sam. "Maybe one that was abandoned. It reminds me of a knarr, but smaller."

"Knarr?"

"Viking boat, relatively small. Well, compared to the longships. Although, I'm not so sure it's the boat that's making me think that, or the way he's sitting up."

"I've never seen a body arranged like that before," Mo observed. The body was propped up in a seated position, its back against one end of the boat. There was something Mo couldn't make out behind the man's back, holding him in place.

Sam nodded. "It's how Viking burials were sometimes done."

Mo sighed. He really was going to have to become an expert. "Who's been in here?"

"Just me, and old Angus Wallace, who found him. And Angus's dog."

"The archetypal dog walker finding a body," Mo said. "No idea what we'd do without dogs and their keen noses."

"I think this'd have been found pretty quickly."

Mo looked at the space around them. "Can you turn these lights off?"

"Sure." Sam strode towards a control switch and extinguished the lights, plunging them into darkness.

It felt like the temperature had dropped by five degrees. The chamber was at an angle to the main part of the castle, meaning little light reached them.

How the hell had someone got a boat in here, and a body?

That boat had to be important.

"Viking burial," Mo murmured.

Sam nodded. "A simulacrum of one. I'm not sure about the boat. And there's no grave goods, of course."

"How d'you know all this stuff?"

"My wife works at one of the tourist sites. I sort of pick it up by osmosis."

"So whoever did this wasn't an expert."

"Nope."

Mo nodded. "And you identified the victim?"

"Wasn't hard. Erik Haldane, one of the folks down at the campsite. His sister, Freya, is also at the camp. She'd been told. Tried to get in here but I stopped her." Sam had turned on the lights again and Mo could feel his breathing return to normal.

"No one I've spoken to saw anything," Sam said. "But there's talk of strange goings-on near the castle lately."

Mo frowned. "What kind of strange goings-on?"

"Lights at odd hours. Chanting, some say."

"Some?"

"Locals."

Mo exchanged a glance with Sam, who shrugged. "I know."

A group of outsiders. Locals who weren't keen on them being here. And plenty of rumours and talk.

Just another day at the office.

CHAPTER EIGHT

PETRA CLUTCHED her bag as she boarded the morning ferry for Brodick. The wind whipped her hair, threatening to pull it out of its neat arrangement on top of her head, and she squinted against the salt spray.

After the dreary walk through Ardrossan, the grey sky matched her mood. Boarded-up shops and peeling paint. Not exactly a tourist hotspot.

Her stomach lurched as the ferry pulled away from the dock. She gripped the railing, willing herself not to be sick.

"First time?" An elderly woman smiled at her.

Petra shook her head. "Just been a while."

She fumbled for her phone, desperate for a distraction. No signal. Of course.

The boat lurched. Petra's knuckles whitened on the rail.

She should've asked about transport on the other side. Surely someone would meet her? The thought of navigating an unfamiliar island made her queasy. Or maybe that was just the motion of the boat.

Maybe if she went inside...

She turned away from the roiling sea and headed inside. There was a lounge, with a canteen-style serving area at one end. All she could smell was fried food, and the low ceiling exacerbated the movement of the boat.

She swallowed and turned back to head outside, making her way down a flight of steps to a quieter area where there were bench seats.

She settled in, pulling her coat tight about her, glad she'd worn hefty shoes. Water sloshed around the deck, making its way towards her corner every time the boat tilted.

If this was what it was like in March, what would it be like in December? She'd once had a girlfriend whose brother commuted across here every day, rain or shine.

Poor bastard.

The sky cleared a little and birds swept down from the clouds. The Isle of Arran was nearing, its crags and peaks ominous against the sky. She had no idea where Lochranza Castle was.

Should have done some research. But Fraser hadn't exactly given her much notice.

At what felt like an eternity, she looked up to see they were coming into port. She brushed down her coat, which was damp from the spray, and stood to find the exit.

The sooner she could get off this boat, the better.

As she clambered down a steep flight of steps, wind pushing her back up, her phone buzzed in her pocket.

Whoever it was, they could wait. And hopefully it was someone from Police Scotland, telling her a car was waiting in Brodick.

Safely at the bottom of the stairs, she pulled it out.

It wasn't Fraser. Or Jade. Or anyone else from Police Scotland.

Her neighbour in the flat below, Tom. They barely knew each other, but they'd exchanged numbers, just in case.

Saw someone outside the building this morning. Looking up at your flat. Probably nothing but thought you should know.

Petra's breath caught. She read it again.

Maybe it was someone from the contractors who were doing the place up.

Yes, that would be it.

Or at least, she hoped so.

CHAPTER NINE

JADE SAT AT HER DESK, the office eerily quiet with just Patty typing away nearby. Her phone buzzed: Mo.

"What've you got so far?" she asked.

Mo's voice crackled through the speaker. " Just calling to confirm what we already know, really. The victim's name is Erik Haldane. He was part of a group camping half a mile away from the castle. Locals think they're some kind of cult, and I'm not sure they're wrong."

"A cult? You think this might be ritualised?"

"His body was arranged in the boat in a way I haven't seen before. Viking, apparently. No idea if it signifies anything, but when Petra arrives I can ask her if she knows anyone who can help us with that."

Jade wrinkled her nose. Last time Petra had brought in one of her colleagues, he'd turned out to be the killer.

"Yeah, leave that with me, why don't you?"

"You sure?"

"Yes. We don't want another Anthony Urquhart."

A pause. "No," he replied, finally. "OK, let me know if

you get anywhere. Stuart and I will be questioning the rest of the group members. Locals really weren't keen on them. I think we've got half a dozen people at least with motive."

She nodded. Haldane's group being unpopular was one thing; that being a motive for murder was entirely another.

"What about cause of death?" she asked.

"It's pretty obvious, by the looks of it, although he hasn't been taken away for the PM yet. There's a vicious stab wound in his neck. Jagged, I'm hoping it'll lead us to the weapon, it could be distinctive."

"Well, that's something. SOCOs there yet?"

"They got here about an hour ago."

"Good. What about Petra? She should be on the ferry by now."

"Sam Henderson's gone to pick her up, that's local Uniform."

"What kind of presence do we have over there?"

"Just the one guy."

"Wow. OK, he'd better be good, then."

"He's like a kid in a candy shop, boss. Never seen anything as exciting here in all his time on the force."

"Right. Well, make sure he has clear instructions."

"Will do. I'll let you know if we get anything more."

"Thanks." She hung up and leaned back in her chair. An image from last night appeared in her mind; Fraser leaning in to kiss her. She smiled.

"Boss."

Jade closed her eyes. If she tried really hard, she could almost smell him...

"Boss?"

Jade blinked her eyes open. Patty was staring at her, pointing at her phone.

"Your phone's ringing, boss. You OK?"

Jade gave the DC a smile. Patty had known her for years; she could probably read her mind.

Let her.

She picked up the phone. "DI Tanner."

"My name's Elizabeth Drummond. People call me Liddy."

Jade gave Patty a look. *Liddy? Who the hell was Liddy?* But Patty's gaze was back on her screen.

"Er, hello, Ms Drummond. How can I help you?" She resisted the urge to ask how the woman had got her mobile number. She didn't sound like a cold caller. Too agitated.

"I've got information about Erik Haldane. The man you found dead at Lochranza Castle this morning."

Jade straightened in her chair. She waved at Patty to get her attention and put her phone on speaker.

"Ms Drummond, I have a colleague with me. DC Patty Henderson. She can hear too."

"I've got nothing to hide."

"I'm not suggesting you do, Elizabeth. How do you know about Erik Haldane?"

"I want to come and speak to you, in person."

"OK." Jade stood up, the phone still on her desk. She gestured at Patty, who was already searching for the name Elizabeth Drummond. Police systems, social media, Google.

"OK," Jade repeated. "Our office is at—"

"I know where you are. I'll be there in an hour."

"Can you tell me—"

"Not over the phone." The woman hung up.

Jade looked at Patty. *What the hell was that?*

CHAPTER TEN

Mo RUBBED his eyes as he entered the lounge bar at the back of the pub. Sam had told him this doubled as a community hall; the bar was shuttered and the tables had been cleared to allow them to use it. Someone had pulled a group of tables together along one side, by the long windows that afforded glimpses of the loch.

Fluorescent lights buzzed above him, casting a harsh glow on this makeshift incident room. The group of tables was covered with a map of Arran, and photos of the crime scene were scattered on its surface.

He looked back towards the door, wondering who had access to this room. He'd speak to Sam, make sure it was secured.

Stuart yawned beside him. "Rough night?"

"Seagulls," Mo grumbled. "And other birds, not sure what they were. Woke me at dawn."

"Same here. Didn't help that the pub's mattress felt like concrete."

Mo considered, thinking back to the first half hour of his

day. Lying awake with the curtains open, listening. "I quite liked the birdsong, actually. Reminded me of camping trips with the kids." He smiled. "God, *that* was a long time ago."

The door swung open, and Petra hurried in, shaking raindrops from her coat. Sam followed, looking grim.

"Morning, all," Petra said. She approached Mo and Stuart in turn and shook their hands. Formal and professional, even though this was their fourth case together.

She turned back to the PC. "Thanks for the lift, Sam."

Sam shrugged. "No problem."

Mo spotted a tea urn at one end of the room and poured himself a mug. He sipped at it, ready to grimace. But it was surprisingly good.

"How was the ferry?"

"Don't ask," said Petra. "Me and water don't mix."

He smiled. Petra was one of those people for whom everything was either perfect or a disaster. But he was glad to have her here.

"And the drive?"

"Wet," Sam said. "But we made good time."

They gathered around the table, each of them looking over what they had so far in silence.

"Fraser told me it might be ritualistic," Petra said. She picked up a photo of the victim and turned it one way, then the other. "Viking symbolism?"

She looked over the picture at Mo, who shrugged. "The DI is looking into it. What we need from you is input into the psychology of a killer who might do this. Also I want to understand the dynamic between the group Haldane was part of and the locals. It seemed they don't much appreciate the newcomers—"

"Bloody hated them," said Sam.

"—but I'm not sure that's sufficient motive for murder," Mo continued.

Petra nodded. "You'd be surprised." She turned to Sam. "What can you tell me about this group?"

Sam shrugged. "I'm based further south, past Brodick. Haven't had call to interact with them until this happened. But they've got a ringleader. Astrid Thorsen. She's got a scruffy looking yurt in the campsite while the others have to slum it in tiny little tents."

"Astrid Thorsen," she said. "Norwegian?"

Sam nodded. "According to her passport, yes."

Petra sniffed. She sat down in one of the chairs surrounding the table with the map, deep in thought.

Mo examined the map. "I want to look at logistics, too. Erik was placed in a boat."

"A boat that wasn't wet," added Stuart, "so it didn't come from the loch."

"Either that or it dried out," said Petra.

Mo shook his head. "Have you experienced the weather here? If it's not raining, it's thinking about it. The grass is permanently wet. If that boat came out of the sea loch, then it would be damp. It was dry as a bone."

Petra cocked her head. "Brand new?"

He shrugged. "No idea. But how did it get there? There must be CCTV. You don't bring a brand new boat into a place like this without someone noticing."

"No CCTV along there," said Sam. "Sorry, this isn't Glasgow. And I've already been talking to the locals. Want me to go again, ask them about the boat?"

Mo shook his head. "I want to get more from the SOCOs first. Let's go back to potential witnesses when we've got a bit more information, so we can ask informed questions."

"Fair enough. Just point me in the direction you want to go."

Mo nodded at the man. Sam might have seemed almost overexcited yesterday, but he was proving reliable now. It was good to work with local Uniform who didn't think they knew his job better than he did.

"So," he said, "we've got logistics. How'd that boat get there? And then we've got the weapon, or lack of one. A weapon like that, you don't hang onto. We need to mount a proper search for it, cover the whole of the area around the castle."

He was annoyed with himself about the weapon. They should have done a fingertip search yesterday, but they'd only been sent one small SOCO team, and the one Uniform they already had, so he was hoping there wouldn't be too many locations to examine.

How were you supposed to run a murder investigation like this?

"OK," he said. "Maybe we can get the locals involved. Sam, find half a dozen people you can trust to do exactly what you tell them. We'll begin a sweep of the land around the castle at 11am. If that doesn't bear fruit, then we'll start along the beach."

"Plenty of places to hide a weapon along there," Stuart said. "Bushes, dunes, all sorts."

"And plenty of wildlife to damage it," Petra pointed out.

Damn.

"OK," he said. "In that case, we'd better get to it."

Stuart cleared his throat.

Mo turned to him. "Stuart?"

"As you know, I've been talking to locals. Apparently,

there've been some odd gatherings at the castle lately. Astrid Thorsen leading some kind of chanting."

"And they think that's related?"

Stuart shrugged. "Might point to a ritual."

Mo narrowed his eyes. If this had been performed by the whole group, with the others watching on...

Petra was shaking her head. "I don't think it is."

"Why not?"

"He was found in a chamber. An old prison, right?"

Mo nodded.

"Too secluded," she said. "Too small. Whoever killed Erik didn't want to be seen. A ritual would have been done in the open, or at least in a larger chamber, open to the sky. That way, his soul would have been able to escape."

"That's part of the ritual?" Mo asked.

"From what I can remember of my reading of *Beowulf*, yes. But I'll do some background research, see what I can find out."

She hadn't specifically said she'd contact a colleague at Dundee University. And lightning couldn't strike in the same place twice, surely.

"OK," Mo said. "Meanwhile, I want to focus on interviewing the other members of the group in detail, and on the search for the weapon."

"Sarge," said Stuart, gesturing for Sam to follow him out of the room.

Mo looked at Petra. "You'll come with me, to do the interviews? Observational capacity only."

She gave him a mock-salute. "I know my job. Let's get on with it."

CHAPTER ELEVEN

JADE SAT BACK in her chair, fingers tapping on the desk. Her office was as sparse and functional as the rest of the building the CCU was based in, but it was the only private space, so this was where she'd brought Liddy Drummond.

Outside, Patty sat in silence at her desk, investigating ritualistic killings on the Scottish Isles and the history of Viking burials. Opposite her sat a nervous-looking Liddy Drummond.

Liddy's hands clenched tight in her lap and her face glistened with sweat. She looked like she didn't get much sleep, or at least hadn't lately: messy hair, a nervous twitch in her left eyebrow, pale cheeks. Every time she ended a sentence, she bit her lower lip. It was starting to bleed.

"Thanks for coming in," Jade said. "My first question is, how did you know Erik had died?"

Liddy stopped fidgeting. "What do you mean, how did I know?"

"Who told you?" The man had been dead just over twenty-four hours and no formal statement had been released. But on the way up the stairs, Liddy had talked about being involved with the group at Lochranza campsite. Jade wanted to know which of them had told her.

"It was Freya."

Jade nodded, waiting for more.

"She sent me a WhatsApp," Liddy said, chewing down on her lip. "We kept in touch, after I left." She looked up. "Freya's OK. I was worried about her."

"Why?"

Liddy pulled back and shook her head. "That's..."

"Liddy, I know this is hard. But I need you to tell me everything you know about Erik and the people he was with. If—"

"You think one of them killed him? It wasn't Freya. They were close. Very close. Maybe..."

Maybe too close? If that was what Liddy had been trying to say, what was it supposed to mean?

Jade relaxed in her chair, trying to appear as unthreatening as possible. "What did Freya tell you?"

A shrug. "Just that he was found at the castle. Murdered."

"That's not been officially—"

"He was in a boat, wasn't he? You know what that means?" Liddy leaned forward. "Ritual. Just the kind of thing you'd expect from Astrid."

There was something in the woman's voice. Not dislike. Something stronger.

Jade licked her lips. "Tell me about Astrid. There's another member of the group, isn't there? Morgan. Tell me about him."

"Them. And there's Alistair. He's... Well, he's complicated."

Jade nodded. What she wanted to know was why Liddy had left the group, and why she seemed to hate Astrid so much. But that would come.

Liddy nodded back at her, a jerky movement like she wasn't quite in control of her own body. "I... I don't know where to start."

Jade leaned forward, elbows on the desk. "Start with Astrid. On the way up here, you said she was taking control."

Liddy had talked nonstop all the way from the door to the unit to Jade's desk. And then as soon as she sat down, she'd clammed up. She'd told Jade that she'd been a member of the group until two weeks ago, and then there had been an argument and she'd left.

"She..." Liddy swallowed, a thin sheen of sweat on her upper lip. "She always had control. She just didn't show it straight away. You know? She'd... she'd let everyone think they were equal. Even Erik. But then things changed."

Jade nodded, watching. Liddy was short, with square features and mousy blonde hair. She looked nothing like either Freya or Astrid, both of whom seemed much less conventional, from the photos Jade had seen. "When did they change?"

"There was a conversation between Erik and Astrid. In her yurt. She'd been drinking. He'd – well, I think it was just beer, with him. I heard them shouting at each other, and then the sound of him hurrying back to his tent. The next morning, he was meek as you like. Did anything she said."

"Did the rest of the group witness this?"

Liddy shook her head. She wiped her palms on her corduroy trousers, her breath shaky. "Astrid got weird. There were late-night summonses, she'd ask me to speak to her in her yurt... She had a way of threatening you, without threatening you. You know the kind of thing?"

Jade had seen plenty of bullies in her time, but she needed specifics. "No, I'm sorry. I don't."

Liddy swallowed. "She'd say things about my mum. She's sick, in a home in Galashiels. It was like Astrid knew all about her. I think she was threatening her."

Jade narrowed her eyes. "Did she make specific threats?"

"Of course not. Astrid's not stupid. But it was implied."

Implied didn't mean a crime had been committed. "Tell me about Erik and Freya's relationship."

Liddy's eyes were wide as she looked at Jade. "You don't understand – she made it sound like if you didn't follow her, you wouldn't survive."

Jade's vision blurred for a moment. She blinked, then rubbed the bridge of her nose. She could feel a headache creeping up the back of her neck.

"Erik and Freya?" she prompted.

"Close. Separate tents – of course – but they spent lots of time in each other's tents. Talking. Sometimes just hanging out. Like they wanted to escape from the rest of us. Or from Astrid."

"Was there any tension between the two of them?"

Liddy shook her head. "They were solid. But you need to know about the ritual Astrid was planning."

"What ritual?" It felt like this interview was veering all over the place. But maybe that was just Liddy's mind.

Liddy shifted in her seat, her expression pained. "Erik..." Her voice shifted, and she bit her lip again. "He told me bits of it. That's how it started. He couldn't stop talking about it – Astrid wanting more control. More loyalty. She wanted him to lead some kind of... of sacrifice."

Jade's headache throbbed. She rubbed her eyes again, harder this time, wondering how much sleep she'd actually got last night. She could almost feel the exhaustion pooling at the corners of her vision. But she had to focus.

"What kind of sacrifice?"

Liddy's face paled. "He said... He said it wasn't what you might think. Not human, for starters. Astrid asked him to find someone who'd sell us an animal. A goat, or something."

Jade felt her nose wrinkle.

"But Erik refused," Liddy continued. "That's when she snapped. She started telling the rest of us things about Erik. Said he was... That he was abusing Freya."

Jade peered into the woman's eyes. There was something about her body language and the incoherent nature of her story that made it hard to believe. But this was a murder inquiry, and they had to follow every angle.

"Did you believe her?" she asked.

Liddy's mouth dropped open. "No. Not for a moment. It just... It just wasn't like that."

But you're no expert. Jade made a mental note to ask Petra about Freya's state of mind.

She pressed a hand to her forehead, finding herself blinking against another wave of blurriness. *Dammit.* Stress, that was all it was. *Don't lose focus.*

Liddy sobbed. "He didn't make it out. I got out, when I realised what a crazy woman Astrid was. But Erik. Poor Erik." She leaned forward and stared at Jade. "You have to arrest her. She's dangerous. You have to protect the others."

CHAPTER TWELVE

THE RAIN HAMMERED against the windscreen as Mo drove them out of Lochranza. Petra clung to a styrofoam coffee cup she'd got at the community centre, her fingers toying with the lid, her mind working over the details they'd gleaned so far. Erik Haldane's death was certainly gruesome. It might be related to ritual, it might not. Maybe someone was playing them.

Either way, this rain was a pain in the arse. She hadn't brought a brolly and she knew what it would do to her hair.

Mo shifted in his seat. "I hope the protection the SOCOs have put up at the scene will hold."

Petra grunted. "This is Scotland. You take what you get."

He smiled, peering up at the hills ahead of them. Goatfell, Arran's highest peak, loomed in the mist, barely visible. The rain blurred the outlines, but it was beautiful, she had to admit. Maybe not her natural habitat, but stunning from time to time.

"You're right," he muttered. "I'm surprised by the landscape. I didn't expect... this."

The island had a bleak magnificence, all moody greens and greys. But experience had taught her to focus less on the scenery and more on the people. She was running over what she'd learned so far about the group at the campsite, and what she could expect from them. She had a feeling that Astrid would try to prove herself smarter than Petra.

"Right," said Mo, breaking the silence. "We need a plan. You can't interview them, bu—"

"I've done this plenty of times with Jade. You, too. I know my role. Watch, listen, report back. Don't worry." She cast him a smile.

He smiled back at her. There was a brightness to him she hadn't seen before. During their last case, on Loch Long, he'd looked like he was almost jealous of the victims.

"We don't want to push any of them too hard," he continued. "Especially not Astrid. We need background. More on Erik, more on the group dynamic."

She tapped her nose; *I know what I'm doing.* "And the tension between them and the locals."

"You think any of them will talk about that?"

"I think it's highly likely. Throws suspicion on the locals, surely."

Mo nodded as they took a left turn into a generous campsite on a flat patch of land flanked by hills. The site was empty save for a cluster of tents as far from the road as it was possible to get; one large, tidy-looking yurt and three smaller, more conventional tents. One of them had its porch open but the other two were zipped up. A campfire, or a site where one would doubtless be lit later, was outside the yurt, with logs surrounding it in place of chairs.

As they drove along the gravel roadway towards the group of tents, a woman emerged from the yurt. She wore a large raincoat, hood up, along with red wellies. Mo drove slowly, anxious not to splash or get the car stuck.

To one side of the yurt was a wooden sign: *Celestial Circle Retreat*. Petra raised an eyebrow and snorted.

"OK, so not academics researching Viking history, then."

Mo gave another smile. "Let's not jump to conclusions."

Petra pursed her lips. She'd dated a hippie five years earlier, and it hadn't ended well. The woman had changed her name from Ruth to Rainbow-Sunrise while they'd been dating, and had become angry when Petra had used the wrong name once too often. She'd also not approved of Petra's science-based approach to psychology, preferring to examine people's chakras, whatever that meant.

This place would be right up her alley.

But Mo was right. Petra needed to push away her preconceptions and prejudices and focus only on the evidence.

Which so far, consisted of a young man meeting a brutal end in circumstances that looked very much like a simulacrum of Viking ritual.

Let's see if that's the kind of thing these people are into.

She got out of the car, following Mo towards the woman, who was standing in the rain with her arms folded, staring at them. She zipped her waterproof right up to the neck and hoped Astrid would invite them inside the yurt.

At the sound of a zip she turned to see a slim, red-haired woman emerging from one of the smaller tents. Freya, perhaps.

She waited. It was Mo's job to kick things off.

Mo held out a hand which Astrid ignored, her arms still folded. He cleared his throat and brought out his ID.

"DS Mo Uddin, Police Scotland," he said. "This is my colleague, Petra McBride."

Astrid eyed Petra. "You don't look like a cop."

"I'm an advisor."

Astrid cocked her head back. "What kind of advisor?"

Petra sighed. "A forensic psychologist. My role is to help the police understand the motivations behind th—"

"Oh, I've seen *Cracker*. I know what you are."

Petra resisted a flicker of irritation. It wasn't as if she hadn't had that one thrown at her before. Short, Scottish, and a psychologist. But there the resemblance to the fictional TV character ended.

"We need to ask you some questions about Erik," Mo said. "Find out more about him and the people he spent time with, whether there might—"

The woman barked out a laugh. "You want to know if we ganged up together to kill him." She widened her stance, ignoring the rain. "No, of course we fucking didn't. That do you?"

Petra watched as Mo forced himself not to react.

"We will need more than that, I'm afraid." He gave the woman a smile which she didn't return.

"Fine." She turned on her heel and strode into the yurt. The redhead watched, her face pale.

"Mo," Petra muttered. "What about...?"

"I know." He approached the younger woman. "Sorry, but am I right in thinking you're Freya Haldane?"

She nodded. Her eyes were red-rimmed, with large grey circles beneath them. She was skinny as a baby foal, pale as a ghost. She didn't look like she'd have had the strength to kill her brother, much less set him up in that boat.

But looks could be deceptive. And she had friends who might have helped.

"Freya," Mo said. "We need to speak with Astrid briefly, and then I'd like to talk to you, if you don't mind. Get some background on your brother, help to piece together a picture of the man he was."

She sniffed, nodded, and wiped her nose with the back of her hand.

"You want me to help?" Petra asked.

Mo shook his head. "I need you with me while I speak to Astrid."

To be a witness as much as anything else, she thought. Astrid seemed like the kind of woman who'd be quick to make accusations of police harassment.

"Sure," she said. "Freya, do you mind waiting in your tent? It's freezing out here."

Another nod. Freya turned away and crawled back into her tiny tent. Petra wondered if she'd shared it with her brother. She hoped not.

Inside the yurt, Petra swallowed a grimace. The air was thick with the smell of damp and something herbal bubbling on a stove. Astrid handed them two cups of tea, the pale yellow liquid looking more medicinal than appetising. Petra took hers with a nod and sipped. It was bitter. She forced down a second mouthful.

To one side was a vast bed, strewn with blankets and quilts. At its end was a low table, with two stools. Mo indicated towards them and Astrid nodded. He and Astrid sat on the stools, and Petra looked around for another perch.

"Sit on the bed," barked Astrid.

"Thank you." Petra pulled herself up onto the end of the

bed and attempted to make herself comfortable, leaning back with her arms out behind her for support.

Mo faced Astrid across the low table. "I believe you've already spoken to PC Henderson and told him a little about Erik. I gather you're in charge of this site, so I hope you can provide some background for us."

Astrid's gaze flicked to Petra. "Does she have to be here?"

Mo didn't hesitate. "She does, yes."

Petra offered yet another smile. Again, it wasn't returned. She resisted a roll of the eyes.

"Can you tell us more about Erik's role here?" Mo asked. "How long had he been camping here?"

Astrid shrugged. "He was just another member of the group. We don't have the kind of hierarchy you lot seem so desperate to impose."

Petra cast her eyes around the cosy, spacious yurt and thought of the tiny tents outside. *Yeah, right.*

Mo offered a non-committal nod. "Mmm-hmm. But regardless, every group has dynamics. Relationships that influence things."

Her lips pursed. "He worked for cash, foraged for food. Participated in group gatherings and celebrations. Same as everyone else."

Petra let her gaze wander over the yurt's interior as Mo kept talking. Patchwork blankets, oil lamps, a stove that looked handmade. It was busy and well-used, cluttered with personal belongings and clothes in random piles. To one side, water dripped down the inside wall.

"I understand there were tensions between yourselves and the locals," Mo said.

Astrid's eyes narrowed. "We're doing nothing wrong here. We pay for these pitches, and we cause no trouble."

"That's not what I asked. Do you think someone might have wanted to hurt one of the group?" Mo paused. "It's important we know if that's the case, because the rest of you might be at risk."

Astrid sniffed. Petra looked at her, wondering. The woman was defensive and clearly hated authority. But had Erik been at more risk from her and her group than from the locals?

It was too early to tell.

"We're fine," Astrid said. "Don't need police protection, if that's what you're thinking." She laughed. "Can you imagine?"

"It's normal when a relative dies in traumatic circumstances to provide a family liaison officer. Freya might benefit—"

"Spy, more like. No thanks. Look, get on with it, will you? I've got work to do."

Petra wondered what kind of work Astrid meant.

Mo nodded. "Very well. I assume you've been told where Erik's body was found? And the circumstances?"

"It's not a Viking burial, if that's what you're thinking. I know this stuff. You know my name, you'll have worked it out. Whoever killed him was trying to make it look like a ritual killing. But it was clearly faked."

"What makes you say that?"

Astrid stood up. "I suggest you speak to his little sister. She'll be happy to talk to you."

The younger woman had done nothing but stare silently since they'd arrived. Petra hoped Astrid was right.

"Now," said Astrid, "I suggest you get on with your jobs and work things out for yourselves. If you know anything about anything, you won't need me to join the dots."

She pulled up the hood of her raincoat and strode out of the tent, leaving a cloud of water drops behind her.

Mo turned to Petra. "What did you think?"

Petra wrinkled her nose. "I didn't like her. But that's no reason to think she killed him."

"You think she's a potential suspect?"

Petra shook her head. "She might be, she might not. We don't have enough to go on yet. But I'm confident she's hiding something."

CHAPTER THIRTEEN

STUART CROUCHED near the grey stone wall of the castle, scanning the ground. Sam was around the other side of the structure and the SOCOs were inside. He and Sam had marked out the area on a virtual plan and were now working in a spiral, starting at the walls.

Towards the village, a group of locals and tourists was standing on the other side of the cordon, watching. This was probably the most entertainment they'd had in years.

A man was dead. And in the most brutal way possible. How was it they could just stand there, gawping?

But this wasn't Glasgow. People weren't sufficiently jaded to glance across then carry on about their business. And communities like this spotted things, noticed when something was out of the ordinary. They didn't ignore their suspicions or dismiss the unusual. These gawpers might be helpful.

He paced the ground, heading in a broad sweep away from the castle wall. The rain had stopped, for now at least, although dark clouds over the hills behind him threatened more.

If they stopped for rain here on the Isle of Arran, they would never get anything done. And they needed to find any remaining evidence before the rain ruined it or washed it away.

Something caught his attention: a scrap of white.

He took a step forward and leaned over.

It was a scrap of paper, wedged under a stone.

He leaned in further to get a good look, careful not to disturb it. It was probably nothing, but it had rough edges and what looked like ornate writing. It could be relevant to whatever ritual Erik's death had followed. Or it could be nothing.

He stood up and walked into the castle, careful to remember where he'd seen the paper.

Wendy Douglas, the senior SOCO in charge of the site, was inside, leading her two colleagues in collecting evidence from inside the old prison. They'd rigged up bright lighting and it felt like broad daylight in there, despite the darkness and blustery conditions outside.

"Wendy," he said. "I've found what might be a note. It could be nothing, but just in case..."

She stood up, placing her palms in the small of her back and stretching out. "No problem, mate. I could do with stretching my legs, anyway. This boat's confusing."

"Confusing? How?"

"Oh, I don't know. Bits of it seem old, other bits new. I'm sure if we get an expert in, they'll make sense of it all." She gave him a grin as they walked through the narrow door leading out of the castle. "I'm just the woman who collects the evidence. I don't need to understand it."

Stuart wasn't so sure about that, but he didn't contradict her. He led her to the stone under which he'd found the paper, relieved it hadn't been blown away in the blustery wind.

"Hmm," she said as she bent over for a better look. "Let's get this bagged up."

She picked up the stone then grabbed the scrap of paper with tweezers, placing it in an evidence bag. The stone went into a second bag.

She held the paper up for Stuart to get a closer look. It was a creamy colour, its edges blackened and curled. He frowned.

"What've you got there?" Sam was approaching from beyond the castle.

Stuart looked up. "Some kind of note or document. Looks like it's been burned."

He squinted at the faded markings. It wasn't writing after all, or not any writing he'd seen before – all angular lines and strange symbols.

Sam peered at it. "Looks old." He looked at Wendy. "What d'you reckon?"

"No idea, not without a proper analysis. If it's been burned, it might just *look* old. It's been shoved halfway into the earth there, so it can't have been there all that long, or it'd have disintegrated."

"Hang on." Sam took out his phone and snapped a photo of the paper. "I'll do an image search."

Stuart waited while he scrolled through his phone.

"I'll get this safely stored away if you don't mind, gents." Wendy took the two evidence bags and headed for her van back by the road.

"OK," said Sam, stopping his scrolling.

"What?" said Stuart.

"It's not writing."

"What is it, then?"

Sam looked up. "Well, according to Google... And Google could be wrong, of course. It's runes."

"Runes?"

"Yup." Sam looked at Stuart, who nodded.

"What are runes?"

Sam laughed. "You never heard of runes?"

"I've heard of them. But I'm from Glasgow, mate. We don't get that kind of thing there."

Sam shrugged. "Symbols, from ancient languages. Like an alphabet, of sorts. Some people think they've got mystical properties. People like your hippies up at the campsite there."

"We're not calling them hippies."

"No. Sorry. But d'you think this could be relevant?"

Stuart nodded. This was something to tell the sarge. He looked back towards the castle, considering the boat, the way Erik had been arranged.

"You reckon this was a ritual killing?"

Sam was pulling off the hood of his forensic suit, which was soggy from all the damp in the air. "No idea, mate. But it's definitely worth considering."

CHAPTER FOURTEEN

FREYA HALDANE STOOD at the edge of the firelight, just far enough not to be noticed but close enough to watch. The faint smell of damp earth and burning wood clung to the cold air. She pulled her jacket tighter, even though she knew the shivers running down her back had little to do with the cold.

Alistair was at the centre of it, moving around the ring of stones they used for the rituals. Freya had seen him lead ceremonies before, with steady hands and a low voice that calmed the group. But tonight, setting up before the others arrived, he looked different. Twitchy.

His movements were faster, more erratic. His eyes, usually focused and serene, darted around like they were tracking something only he could see.

Freya shifted back, her foot crunching on a stray twig. She froze.

Alistair didn't notice. He was muttering to himself again, his voice too quiet for most to pick up on. But Freya had been concentrating, inching gradually closer when no one was watching.

"Purification... it had to be done... Erik... filthy," Alistair's voice broke, then came back stronger. "He didn't believe... didn't *deserve*..."

Freya held her breath, straining to hear. Her head throbbed as she tried to understand what she was hearing.

She was mishearing, surely?

Alistair was odd. He had a way of commanding attention, from everyone except Astrid, at least. The two of them had clashed plenty of times, power battles Freya preferred to keep well out of.

But... this? Erik, *filthy*? *Purification*?

She swallowed, her mouth dry. Confronting him could be dangerous. The others still trusted him. And what if she was wrong?

Worse, what if she was right? Would she end up propped in a boat in the castle's old prison, like her brother?

Her chest felt empty.

Those police, the ones who'd come before.

Astrid had told the group not to speak to them. They were the oppressors. Not to be trusted. They would invent lies about Erik's death and find a way to blame it on the group, simply because they didn't fit into the ways of the conventional world.

Would they really do that? Or did they just want to find out who'd killed her brother?

Freya pressed herself into the shadows, blending into the dark. Her heart hammered. She watched Alistair more closely, focusing on each movement. He was pacing faster, his shoulders tense. His lips kept moving, and although she couldn't make out every word, the ones that reached her made her feel sick.

"Erik's weakness... filthy, had to *cleanse*... no choice..."

Had he done it, then? Had Erik's death been a ritual? A punishment? Or more honestly, nothing of the sort, just one man deciding he'd had enough of another?

If she was wrong, she'd be cast out. Without Erik, she had no one.

She was wrong. Surely she was wrong.

In which case, there was no point in saying anything to the police. *Don't bring more trouble onto the group.*

A figure moved, breaking her line of sight. Astrid had joined Alistair, lighting candles. Her laugh echoed through the camp, too loud, too normal for the situation they were in.

Astrid would never believe her. Nor Morgan, who hung on Astrid's every word. Astrid might despise Alistair, but they stuck together. *Us against the world.* Always.

Freya was wrong. She had to be. Imagining things. She'd smoked some weed earlier, it had messed with her head.

The locals resented them. They didn't want them here.

It would be one of them. And if she did anything that cast doubt on that in the minds of police, justice would never be done.

She turned towards her tent.

"Freya?"

Astrid's voice.

Freya froze, then turned, plastering a smile on her face.

"Freya? You OK? Where are you going? It's time."

Freya nodded. She flicked a glance at Alistair, who was giving her an odd look.

Stop it. You're making things up.

"On my way," she said, and walked towards the flames.

It would be OK. Astrid, and the group, would protect her. They'd ensure that Erik's killer was punished.

CHAPTER FIFTEEN

Mo LEANED against the edge of the desk, scanning the evidence board. Petra and Stuart sat nearby, both looking as tired as he felt. Sam was sitting a couple of tables away from them, rubbing his eyes.

"Right, let's go over what we've got," he said. "Right from the top. Stuart, you want to start?"

Stuart shrugged. "Angus Wallace found Erik's body in a boat inside the castle. That in itself is odd. I mean, who puts a body in a boat far from any water?"

"Exactly," Petra said. "And then there's the deep gash across his throat. The arrangement of coins over his eyes suggests a ritual element. Either that, or that's what someone wanted us to think."

Mo looked at her. "You think we're being fed false evidence?"

A shrug. "I don't think anything yet. Just entertaining possibilities, formulating hypotheses."

He nodded. "We've had reports from the locals of strange

lights and chanting. All tied to the cult that Erik was a part of."

"I'm not sure I'd describe them as a cult," said Petra.

"If it looks like a duck, and it quacks like a duck..." said Sam.

Mo frowned at the PC. "I know the locals aren't keen, but they've been no trouble. You said that yourself."

"I did. And I'm not saying they were trouble. But they're not exactly... normal, are they?"

"Normal is highly subjective," said Petra. "Let's not even try to define it."

"Isn't that your job?" asked Stuart.

She shook her head. "I work with the not-normal. I'm not calling it abnormal. My focus is people who don't behave in the ways mainstream society expects them to."

"Which is exactly the way the Celestial Circle Retreat would describe themselves, I imagine," said Sam.

"OK," said Mo. They were going round in circles, and there were too many assumptions being drawn. "Let's move away from the group and what we do or don't think of them. Focus on the evidence. We've got the coins, whatever they may or may not mean, and then there's the parchment Stuart found."

"Which may not even be parchment," Stuart pointed out.

Mo resisted an eye-roll. Why was everyone so determined to ignore the evidence in this case? Was it a Scottish thing?

"Whatever it is, we'll know more when we get those symbols translated."

"Runes," said Petra.

"Runes. What exactly are runes, anyway?"

"Ah, now that I can help you with," said Sam. "My wife's sent me some stuff." He pulled out his phone and read. "The runic alphabet used by the Vikings is known as the Elder Futhark, which contains twenty-four characters. Runes were used for writing, inscriptions, and" – he looked up – "for magical and divinatory practices."

"Divinatory practices?" asked Mo.

"Telling the future," Stuart explained.

"I know that. Do we think the group's into that kind of stuff?"

Petra snorted. "If they are, they'll not get anywhere. I wouldn't worry about all that. It's the people we need to think about. The individuals. The way Erik was killed... ritual or not, it was brutal, but not visceral. There's the one wound, as far as we can tell, and it's deep. This person was confident, and they intended to kill."

Mo nodded. "No practice wounds."

"Indeed." Petra chewed on one of her long pink finger-nails. It looked like the Arran weather was getting to them.

"How much strength would have been needed?" Stuart asked.

"To inflict the fatal wound," said Mo, "not very much. But to get Erik into that boat..."

"That depends if it was done pre- or post-mortem," Petra pointed out.

"Good point. And if it was pre-..."

"Then his killer told him what to do," said Stuart. "Which indicates either fear or trust."

"Not much difference between those then, eh?" said Sam with a thin smile.

Mo looked at him. Their resources were tight here on Arran. He was reluctant to involve a member of local

Uniform in their deliberations, but he didn't have all that much choice. He'd just have to hope that the man's natural inclinations, away from the group and in favour of the locals, wouldn't cloud his judgement too much.

"Freya's reaction to her brother's death was genuine," Petra said. "She's distraught."

Mo looked at her. "Not an act?"

She shook her head and dropped into one of the chairs, placing a hand over her mouth to stifle a yawn. "No."

"What about Astrid?"

Petra smiled. "Now she's much more interesting."

Mo nodded. "Didn't take to us."

"Doesn't take to anyone, from what I can tell. I saw the body language between her and Freya. That is not a mother substitute."

"We don't have any evidence to point to her as a suspect."

"We have tensions with Erik," Petra said. "When we spoke to Freya."

Mo nodded. After speaking with Astrid they'd gone to Freya's tent and managed to get a little more from the woman. She'd referred to Erik having some sort of conflict with Astrid, and resenting the older woman's control over the group. Then she'd realised what she'd said and clammed up.

"Astrid certainly exercises power over Freya," he said. "And she had reason to be pissed off with Erik."

"I'm not sure it's enough for murder, though," Petra observed, her nose wrinkling. "I don't know. I just think Astrid is too obvious. She's a textbook suspect. Hates authority. Rules that group with a rod of iron. Won't tolerate any dissent, and could persuade the others to help her if she wanted to bump one of them off."

"Even his sister?" asked Stuart.

Petra turned to him. "You didn't see the way the two women looked at each other. Freya would do anything Astrid told her to, in my estimation."

"But still you don't think she's suspicious?" Mo asked.

The psychologist shook her head. "Like I said, she's too obvious. She's clever, clever enough to hide her true self if she had a murder to hide as well. I'm not ruling her out, but I'm not keen on her either."

"What about the others?" Stuart asked. He peered at the board. "Morgan Douglas and Alistair MacLeod."

"They weren't there," said Mo. "We need to go back in the morning, see if we can pin them down."

"Good luck with that," muttered Sam. He glanced at his watch. "I need to get off now, Sarge, if you don't..."

Mo gave him a thin smile. "Of course, Sam. Thanks for all your help today." It was long since dark, long since the end of Sam's shift. "See you tomorrow."

"Yeah." Sam gave the others a little wave as he headed for the door. "See you in the morning."

Someone was standing outside the door as Sam opened it. Mo felt his breath catch, wondering if they'd been overheard. But it was only Wendy Douglas, the forensics officer they'd been assigned.

Only one senior SOCO, he'd noted. A murder case, but only one person capable of understanding the relevance of key evidence.

"Hey, Wendy," he said. "I didn't know you were still up."

"I figured if I could get finished today I'd be able to get off home," she said, patting her hands together for warmth. "Bloody hell, it's freezing out there."

"Anything new?" he asked her.

She shook her head. "I've sent the paper Stuart found off to the lab in Glasgow. Still waiting on results, but it's not old."

Stuart's eyebrows shot up. "Faked?"

Wendy shrugged. "Maybe copied."

"That's what we need to find out," Mo said, pushing himself off the desk. "Good work, everyone. I need to update the DI. Get some rest, yeah? We'll pick this up in the morning."

He watched the team disperse, wondering how long they'd all be stuck out here. And secretly hoping it'd be a while.

CHAPTER SIXTEEN

THE EVENING FELT thick with the storm gathering outside Jade's lochside house. Shadows stretched across the walls, distorted by the faint flicker of the candles she'd lit for the first time in months, if not years.

Fraser sat back on the sofa, his wine glass held loosely in his hand, his legs crossed casually like he'd spent his whole life sitting on this sofa. He'd accepted the glass Jade had offered him, neither of them saying the obvious out loud. That once he'd drunk it, he wouldn't be able to drive home. Jade could feel her stomach flickering with nervous excitement.

She perched on the armchair opposite him, one knee tucked up, the other foot on the floor. She was trying to relax, but her mind kept straying back to the case. To the photographs of Erik Haldane's body, propped up in that boat.

Fraser broke the silence. "You alright? You look tired."

"I'm fine." Jade swirled the wine in her glass with more

force than she intended. She winced when it splashed onto her hand. "Just the case, y'know."

He tilted his head, watching her. "You sure? You seem like there's more."

She tightened her grip on the glass, suddenly worried she might drop it. Had he noticed? Her vision was blurring again. She was blaming it on the wine, but she knew she was lying to herself.

She didn't have the time for this.

She took a sip of the wine, forcing herself to enjoy the feel of it travelling down her throat. "I'm fine, really. It's just weird, being so far away from it all."

"You could always go over there. Ferries run a few times a day. Especially the northern one."

She nodded. She'd thought of that, looked up the sailing times from Claonaig. But she'd put Mo in charge, and she didn't want him to feel like she was breathing down his throat.

She shook her head. "It'll be fine."

He smiled and patted the sofa next to him. "Talk to me. I'm not your boss now, Jade. I'm me."

She swallowed and put the glass down on the coffee table as she slid across to the sofa. She leaned into his side, and he put an arm around her. The skin on the back of her neck bristled. She blinked, feeling like a teenager again.

Rory was asleep in his room. He'd enjoyed seeing Fraser, always did. But she wanted to give the relationship time to breathe before she brought her son into it.

Fraser kissed her ear. "I've known you a long time, Jade Tanner. Since before you were Jade Tanner."

She felt her mouth go dry. Jade Thomson, she'd been,

before marrying Dan ten years ago. Always JT. It had made it easier to get used to the new name.

She smiled. "I'll always be Jade Tanner."

He squeezed her shoulders. "I know that. And that's not what I'm talking about. You look... exhausted. Beautiful," he stroked her cheek, "but exhausted. Pale."

She put a hand to her face. "It's the winter. I haven't seen the sun for months."

He raised an eyebrow, getting the message. Whatever he thought was going on, she wasn't about to talk to him about it. Not yet.

They weren't that serious yet.

She turned to him and kissed his cheek. He turned his head, and her mouth moved to his lips. She closed her eyes and let herself sink into the kiss. Her stomach felt like jelly and her legs like fire.

It felt good.

Pulling away, he smiled. "I think I might be falling in love with you, Jade Tanner."

She gasped, realising she was blinking back at him. "Oh."

His face fell. "Sorry. Too soon?"

"No." She put a hand on his shoulder. "I... I don't know." Her gaze flicked to the door. "Rory... I can't..."

He pursed his lips. "I understand. You have to be sure of yourself. Of me."

"I know what kind of man you are, Fraser. I know how much you mean to Rory. But you're my boss. It complicates things."

"I don't have to be your boss."

She stiffened. "I'm not leaving the CCU."

He laughed. "I'd never do that to you, Jade. I'm talking about me. I can get a transfer to Edinburgh. Stirling."

"You'd be miles away."

Another laugh. "Edinburgh isn't exactly the North Pole, you know?" He hesitated. "And you've often told me you'd rather not stay in this house."

Had she?

"A new... a new relationship and a new home, both at the same time. It would be too much for Rory."

"I understand." He lifted her chin and kissed her forehead. His lips were cool on her skin. "I don't mean to rush you. I'm sorry."

She grabbed his hand and kissed his fingers. "You're not doing anything wrong. I appreciate your honesty. I just need some time."

He nodded. "I know. And I'll give it to you." He kissed her again. She leaned back as he bent her over the sofa cushions, letting the kiss wash over her.

When she came up for breath, she was smiling again. "Let's go to bed."

His eyes widened. "You're sure?"

She nodded, her gaze on his. His eyes were sparkling.

Forget the case. Forget whatever's happening to my vision. Just enjoy it.

"Sure," she said.

"What about Rory?"

"He's five. He'll just think you had to stay over because of a case or something."

"Or I had a sleepover." He winked.

She chuckled. "A sleepover. Yes, let's call it that."

CHAPTER SEVENTEEN

DARKNESS DRAPED itself over Lochranza like a cloak. Mo stopped on the raised terrace outside the pub and community centre, gazing out towards the water.

It was beautiful. So quiet, like nothing he'd experienced before. He heard a bird of some sort shriek from somewhere far away, and the distant sound of a boat engine. The water was still, and the road that ran alongside it was quiet. He still couldn't believe that this was the island's main road. It was smooth and clearly well looked after in a way roads like that never would be in the city. And at almost every point on the way up here from the ferry, there had been that view of the sea to his right, and houses staring out towards it to the left.

It was idyllic. A nightmare in a storm, he imagined, but possessing a wild beauty that took his breath away.

He pulled in a deep breath, zipped his coat right up to the neck, and took the steps down to the road, his senses alert for traffic from either direction.

Nothing.

He heard rustling from up ahead and crossed the road, pausing to look both ways then cursing himself.

There was a deer on the beach. A huge specimen, antlers the length of his forearm. It was grazing on some bushes.

He stopped on the edge of the road, wary. Would it feel threatened by him? Should he withdraw?

The creature stopped, stilled for a moment, then looked up. It stared right into his eyes.

Mo held his breath.

The animal stared back at him for a few moments, then let out a snort-like breath and resumed its grazing. Mo put a hand to his chest, trying to still his heart.

Was he in danger? Or was he just being a foolish city dweller?

Either way, he wasn't going to get any closer.

He turned right, heading towards the hulking shadow of the castle. The old prison inside was still lit and the light shone dully from the doorway which was the only way inside.

He shivered. Had Erik Haldane been alive when he was brought here, or already dead? Had this view been the last thing the young man had seen?

Stop it, he told himself. You're being morbid. It wasn't as if he hadn't investigated his share of murders.

He stuffed his hands into his pockets and walked alongside the road, noting a wooden chair that someone had left at a bus stop and pausing to frown, then smile. *Practical.*

At the pathway leading off to the castle, he paused and took in the view. Behind him, all was quiet. The village slept, houses huddled together beneath the shadow of Goatfell, lights off, curtains pulled tight against the night.

But he wasn't the only person out here. There was someone moving about, near the castle.

Wendy?

He shook his head. Wendy had left in her van after the briefing, bound for the ferry and her home in Kilmarnock, her team following in the other van behind her. And the rest of *his* team had made their way up to their rooms above the pub.

He squinted, trying to see better. But the faint light coming from the doorway in the side of the castle wasn't enough.

He had every right to be here. And so did the person moving around near the water, most probably.

Unless...

He stepped forward, his heart picking up pace along with his strides. The path here was well made and his footsteps weren't too loud, but he knew that in an environment like this, he would be spotted.

As he neared the castle, he realised the figure was carrying a torch. Either that, or they were using the light from their phone.

He was in darkness. If he stayed quiet, he had the advantage.

Should he call for backup? Sam? The man was probably in front of his TV by now, feet up and enjoying an evening in with his Viking expert wife.

Sam would take an age to get here.

Stuart?

No. Not yet.

Mo clutched his phone in his pocket as he crept towards the shore. He had all of the team on speed dial and could summon Stuart in a matter of seconds, if he had to.

For now, he just wanted to see who was out there.

He shuffled across the grass, leaving the path behind and glad he'd brought sturdy shoes. He knew there were muddy patches, but as long as he kept his footing, that wasn't an issue.

He was nearly at the castle now. The figure had stopped moving. It was sitting on a bench facing out towards the loch, next to the castle.

Suddenly, the light went out.

Mo froze.

He turned to see what was behind him. Was he silhouetted by lights from the village, making him visible against the new darkness?

But the village itself was dark.

He bent his legs, unsure whether making himself smaller would help. He couldn't see if the figure was moving anymore, but he could hear them, wherever they were.

Sobbing.

A woman's voice, sobbing.

The sound intensified, echoing across the empty ground between him and the castle. A woman, sobbing.

Probably not the killer, then.

Or was that a stereotypical assumption?

Nothing he could do now. If he moved, he'd draw attention to himself.

The light came back on, and Mo let himself breathe again. The figure's face was illuminated.

He bit his lip, daring to take a few steps forward. He moved in the direction of the castle, hopeful that it would disguise him, if necessary.

He could make out the face now.

Still sobbing. Freya Haldane sat on the bench, her cries shaking her body as they moved through it.

Mo felt his insides tighten. Poor girl. She'd come to the spot where her brother had died, to mourn for him.

Or was she returning to the scene of her crime?

He took a few more steps towards the castle until he was standing right by it. He leaned against its bulk, breathing heavily. Surely she'd hear him?

But Freya was too wrapped up in her grief.

He watched as she lifted herself off the bench and walked towards the water.

He gasped. *Don't.*

She turned, extinguishing the light.

Shit.

She'd heard him.

He leaned into the wall of the castle, forcing himself to move along it until he was hidden from her. He waited, expecting her to shine that light in his eyes at any moment.

Footsteps. She was moving again.

She appeared around the wall of the castle, but she wasn't closing in on him. She was heading back towards the road. Almost running. The light was on now, its beam arching in front of her.

He'd scared her.

"Sorry," he whispered.

The light receded and gradually disappeared as she headed towards the camp site. Mo swallowed and stepped away from the castle, half expecting to be accosted by one of the other cult members at any moment.

He picked up pace himself, not running but walking as quickly as he could in the darkness. Back to the pub.

It was dangerous out here. Or it could be.

But was Freya a threat, or was she in danger herself?

CHAPTER EIGHTEEN

JADE SAT at the head of the table, laptop open in front of her, the camera facing her and Patty from the far wall. The conference room always felt empty, the sound seeming to sink into the grey carpet and get lost in there, never to return.

Mo, Petra, and Stuart's faces were blurred on the screen, the signal from the Isle of Arran not what they'd have liked. Wendy was in another corner of the screen, patting down her curly hair and smiling awkwardly.

Patty shifted in her seat beside Jade, a thick folder in front of her. She looked agitated, like she wanted to get on with things.

Jade smiled. Patty always wanted to get on with things.

"Right, let's get started." She glanced at Patty's folder. "We've been digging into the cult—"

"The *Celestial Circle Retreat*," interrupted Patty, making air quotes with her fingers.

"That's the one," Jade said. "It's definitely bloody weird."

"When's it ever not?" asked Mo. He leaned in towards the camera, silhouetted by the window behind him. Jade could just about make out what looked suspiciously like blue sky.

Patty nodded. "Obviously their name means nothing. Typical hippy nonsense. But they seem to be more than just a bunch of incense-burning space cadets. Got about a dozen or so members in all, give or take a few, depending on how many they've brainwashed recently."

Jade frowned. "Surely we shouldn't be jumping to conclusio—"

Patty slapped a sheet of paper in front of her. "I'm not doing that, boss. That Astrid's a bad 'un. She recruits people to her group, convinces them she can access spirits or chakras or something or other, then gets them to give her money."

"Which?" Petra asked over the video link.

"Sorry?" asked Patty.

"Which? Spirits or chakras? They're different. Different belief systems."

Patty shrugged. "All the same, far as I can tell."

Petra shook her head. Jade sighed. "Let's tone down the hippy bashing, eh, Patty?"

"Fair enough, boss. But that Astrid Thorsen... We need to look into her."

"What have you managed to find out about her? Her bio, I mean, not her ideologies."

Patty pursed her lips. "Norwegian, lives on an island called Sula. Owns half of it, as far as I can tell."

"Her own private island?" asked Stuart.

Another shrug from Patty. "*Half* her own private island. Either way, the woman's wealthy. And I've found photos of her online dressed in business attire. She's a con artist, pure and simple."

"That doesn't mean she's a killer, though," said Petra.

Patty looked at the screen for a few moments, then sniffed. "No. It doesn't."

Thank God for that. Jade had worked with Patty for years. She was a good copper. Sure, she had opinions on things, and sometimes she didn't hold back. But she hadn't let her assumptions about a suspect get in the way before. Jade hoped she wasn't going to do it now.

At least she's not at the scene.

"Anyone else notable?" Mo asked. "Is it just the people at the campsite, or...? You said there were a dozen of them."

Patty rifled through her file, making Jade wonder why she'd bothered printing everything off. Maybe the hippy vibe was rubbing off. "There's a man called Marcus who seems to be her second-in-command. He's running another retreat, according to their website, in Ireland. But she's the one in charge."

Jade looked at Mo. "What's your take on Astrid?"

He shrugged. "When we spoke to the others, they mentioned her a lot. Freya seems to be scared of her. Morgan, too. Not Alistair."

"Which one's Alistair?" asked Patty.

"He's an academic. Specialises in early Norse history. Astrid hired him as a freelancer to give credibility to the retreat."

"How long's he been with them?" asked Jade.

"Two months, give or take a week. He doesn't say much, but there's an intensity to him. Makes me think we should keep an eye on him."

Patty scoffed. "I think we should keep an eye on all of them."

"What about the other one? Morgan?"

Stuart cleared his throat. "I interviewed them."

"There's more than one of them?" asked Patty.

Even over the screen, Jade could tell Stuart was giving Patty a look. "Non-binary," he said. "Vulnerable, I reckon. They seemed scared of pretty much everyone, but at the same time hero-worshipped Astrid and Alistair."

"What's their background?" asked Jade.

"Student. Recruited by Alistair. Professor Alistair MacLeod, to give him his full name."

Jade nodded. "I'd like you to get formal statements from all of them. As soon as we have an estimated time of death, I want alibis."

"Of course," said Mo.

"Anything to add yet, Petra?" she asked.

"Not formally, no."

"Informally?" Jade knew that Petra liked to collect her thoughts before giving advice. She was a scientist, not a copper; thoroughness was her bread and butter.

"Informally, I think Astrid's too obvious. If she had something to hide, she'd be less abrasive."

"Maybe she's just like that," said Patty.

Petra nodded. "Well, she certainly behaves that way. But people tend to have more to them than the surface they present at first. I'd like to sit in if she's interviewed again, try to find out what's underneath that surface." She looked at Mo. "With all of them."

"Of course," Mo replied. He looked at her, then the screen. "Boss?"

Jade nodded. "Makes sense. And then there's Liddy."

Mo leaned into the screen. "Of course. What did she tell you?"

"Not much, I'm afraid. Not much of any evidential

value, anyway. She hates Astrid, thinks she's a crook. But that doesn't mean she's a killer."

"Did she give anything concrete?" Patty asked.

Jade shook her head. "Well, she did talk about some kind of ritual. Animal sacrifice, she claimed, but she didn't give any detail. I'd like to know more about that. Apparently Astrid and Erik fell out over it."

"How so?" Mo asked.

"Erik refused to participate. Astrid, it seems, has a system when people displease her. Their tents get moved. To the edge of the group, doorway facing away."

Patty wrinkled her nose. "She can't make people move their tents, surely."

"And it all sounds pretty childish," added Mo.

"Bullies often are childish," said Petra. "And Astrid Thorsen seems to fit the description of a bully. But that—"

"I know," Mo said. "It doesn't mean she's a killer."

Petra turned to give him a smile. "You're catching on."

He laughed. "I certainly am." He turned back to the screen. "Have you heard any more about the paper Stuart found? Wendy said she'd sent it to the lab."

Jade shook her head. "It's too early. No results yet. I'll tell you as soon as we do, of course."

Mo, Petra, and Stuart nodded in unison.

"OK," Jade said. "What else do we know about the way Erik was arranged in that boat?"

Stuart waved a hand. Jade resisted the urge to remind him it wasn't school. "Stuart."

"I spoke to Sam's wife. She works at a local tourist attraction. She put me in touch with another guy, a Kyle Fairbanks. He's an expert, advises various sites."

"What's he said?"

"I haven't had a chance to speak to him yet, but he did send me an email saying he thinks it was faked."

"Of course it was faked," Patty pointed out. "This isn't prehistoric times."

Stuart shook his head. "Not faked. That's the wrong word. The details are inaccurate. Whoever put him there, if they were trying to make it look like a Viking ritual, they got the details wrong."

Which could mean anything.

"OK," Jade said. "Next steps. Mo and Stuart, go back to the group members. Get each of them alone, preferably away from that campsite. Petra, you attend. I want more background, more on the relationships."

"Boss," said Mo, who was writing in his notepad.

"Don't assume anything," she said. "Even Freya... she seemed distraught, you said. But she could be hiding something."

"I doubt it," said Mo. "I saw her last night, near the castle."

"What?" Jade said. "Doing what?"

"Just walking. Sitting. Crying, mostly."

There was a moment of silence.

"Did she see you?" Petra asked. "Did she start crying after she spotted you?"

Wow, that's cynical, thought Jade. But it was Petra's job...

Mo shook his head. "I'm pretty sure she didn't spot me. If she did, it was after she'd been crying, anyway. And she didn't seem to be attempting to access the crime scene itself."

"We've finished with forensics," said Wendy from her corner of the screen. "And the victim and the boat were removed yesterday. No reason to keep it cordoned off anymore."

"Are you saying it's no longer cordoned off, or that we should remove the cordon?"

"It's already been taken away," Mo said. "At close of play yesterday."

Jade rubbed her eye. The picture in front of her was blurring. She was tired; too many late nights with Fraser.

"So even if Freya did go inside, it wasn't trespass," she said. "Has anyone checked inside the castle, in case...?"

Mo raised an eyebrow. "In case she's the killer and she took another body there?"

Jade sighed. It was a ridiculous idea. "I don't know." She yawned, hoping no one could see it behind her hand.

"I went down there last thing, before I left," Wendy said.

Mo shook his head. "It's OK. I was there, first thing." A smile flickered on his lips. "I'm enjoying the early morning and late night walks."

"Good. Right then, let's focus on those detailed interviews," said Jade. "And have a word with Sam. There must be more light that local police can shed on this. Are there any locals we should be looking into? Anything the locals have seen and aren't telling us about?"

"On it," said Mo. He was still smiling.

"Good," she said. Her head was throbbing. "Let's hope we start making progress soon."

CHAPTER NINETEEN

THE AIR inside Astrid's yurt was stifling. Not just from the memory of burning incense, or the layers of fabric hanging against the walls (if 'walls' was the right word), but from Astrid's demeanour, too. The group leader sat across from them, arms relaxed, back straight, eyes far too calm for those of a woman being questioned in connection with a murder.

Petra shifted on the rough-woven cushion beside Mo, who'd been given a pouffe and consequently sat about six inches above her. He was still as a stone, jotting down notes with barely a glance around the room since they'd first entered.

But then, it was her job to take in Astrid's surroundings. To observe her body language. To get the measure of the woman.

She still wasn't close to having a full profile for the killer. The nature of Erik's arrangement in death was important, sure, but did that importance lie in something real, or in something imitated? If it was real, then the killer had made mistakes. Petra's experience had taught her that those who didn't know something intimately, but were trying to imitate it, were more likely to be exact.

So, there was a possibility that the killer had invested Erik's death with symbolism. The same kind of symbolism she could see scattered across this yurt? Petra wasn't so sure.

"Tell me about Erik," Mo said, his gaze on the notepad balanced on his lap, his tone neutral.

Astrid smiled, that thin smile Petra had seen on her lips far too often given the circumstances. Was it some kind of spiritual reaction, or was it smugness?

"Erik was... intense. Passionate, in his way. More interested in his work than in people, but I'm sure you already know that."

Petra certainly didn't know that. She waited for the follow-up question from Mo. It had taken her a while to get used to working with Mo; on their first case he'd been new to Police Scotland and hadn't coped all that well. On their most recent case, he'd seemed on the verge of some kind of depressive episode.

Sometimes I just wish I could ask the bloody questions.

She said nothing; not a cop. Not allowed to question witnesses.

"What do you mean?" Mo asked. "How did that show itself?"

"Well, you know the work we're doing here. A mix of spiritual celebration and research." That smile again. "Erik was almost fanatical about the research. He was determined to uncover the secrets of this magical isle."

Magical isle. Did she always talk like that? Was that how she convinced people to stump up the money to join her group, with vague mysticism?

"So Erik didn't have much interaction with the rest of the group?" Mo prompted.

Astrid shrugged. "I wouldn't put it like that. He wasn't... unfriendly. Just preoccupied. Whenever I spoke to him, he was perfectly affable."

"And what about his sister? What was his relationship with her like?"

"Close."

Mo paused his writing, waiting for Astrid to go on. Petra looked at Astrid, trying to mirror that smile. Was the woman attempting an impression of the Mona Lisa?

After a few moments' silence, Mo said, "Close?"

Astrid shifted in her chair. It was a deep, wing-backed chair, upholstered with a floral fabric that Petra thought would be more at home in her Aunt Lydia's sitting room.

Her sitting room now, she reminded herself. And the chintz was on its way out.

Astrid shrugged. "He was protective of her. She joined our circle after him, you see. He was worried about how she would settle in. He—"

"He told you that?" Mo asked. "That he was worried?"

"Of course not. But I watch my children, you see. I feel a responsibility to them."

They're not your children. Was that really how Astrid considered them?

"Did you feel responsible for Erik?" Mo asked, his gaze rising to meet Astrid's for the first time since they'd begun talking.

She leaned back. "Of course. Although I hope you're not suggesting that makes me somehow culpable." She gave a light laugh. "I'm not a prison guard."

"No," Mo said. "Can you tell me where you were on the night before last?"

"The night Erik died? Of course. I was here, counselling Morgan."

Mo raised an eyebrow. "Counselling? About what?"

Morgan Douglas was a member of the group, one Petra hadn't met yet. She wondered where he or she was.

Astrid cocked her head. "Confidential, I'm afraid. I'm sure the content of our session isn't pertinent to the provision of an alibi."

"No."

But it might be relevant to motive, Petra thought.

"Good," Astrid continued. "Morgan, as I'm sure you're aware, identifies as non-binary. They have been struggling with their family's reaction to this, and I've been helping them to understand that a family that rejects you is no family at all."

"Morgan's family rejected them?"

"Not as such, no. But..." Astrid waved a hand in dismissal. "As I say, confidential. I'm sure you'll be speaking to Morgan too. And Alistair."

Mo nodded. "We will. So you were here on that evening with Morgan. In your tent?"

"Of course." Astrid's nose wrinkled.

"Until what time?"

They still didn't have a time of death for Erik. But it didn't do any harm to gather the information.

Astrid frowned. "Midnight. No, I lie. Four minutes after midnight."

"That's very precise."

"I'm a very precise woman, when it comes to the passing of one day into the next." Astrid clasped her hands together and held them out, almost as if she wanted Mo to join her in prayer. Petra pushed back a smile.

"Very well," said Mo, flipping through his notes. "And what can you tell us about your other member? Alistair MacLeod?"

Astrid raised an eyebrow. "Professor Alistair MacLeod. He brings the circle its credibility. Academic heft, if you would."

Mo nodded, looking down again. Petra wondered if he was as cynical about the idea of this lot having academic heft as she was.

"Professor MacLeod is another researcher?" Mo asked. Astrid had leaned forward in her chair and was cradling her hands in her lap, almost like she was protecting them.

Was that something to do with her feelings about MacLeod?

Astrid nodded, her lips tight. "He was researching the history of spirituality on the Isle of Arran and its impact on the history of the island. *Is*, sorry. He *is* researching."

Petra narrowed her eyes. Talking about someone in the past tense was one thing. Catching yourself doing it and flushing bright red in the way Astrid had done was another.

"He's been a part of your group for a while?" Mo asked.

Astrid had regained control over her face. "Yes."

Mo sighed. "How long?"

"Since we arrived twenty-four days ago."

"He came with you?"

"He did."

"So is he another leader of the group?"

Astrid looked up. "No, Detective. Alistair is – was – my husband. That's why we came together. But as you'll see, we don't share a tent."

Petra scanned the yurt for signs of male inhabitation. There was nothing; no clothes, no shoes, no toiletries. In fact, there was no sign of any toiletries at all. Maybe Petra kept them in the shower block at the back of the campsite.

"You separated while you were here on Arran?" Mo asked.

"Don't be ridiculous. We've been separated for a while. But Alistair is a..." She licked her lips. "He has a role to play in the circle. He continues to make his contribution as our historical expert, and we stay as far apart from each other as we can."

Petra looked at Mo. How had they not picked this up from local police? Did the other members of the group know that Astrid and Alistair were married?

And was it relevant to Erik's death?

CHAPTER TWENTY

STUART STEPPED out of the community centre, squinting to adjust his eyes to the sun reflecting off the surface of the water. He was a city boy, most at home in Glasgow. He wasn't used to the shadows of the hills and the openness of the sea; it made him uneasy. The village stared out over the sea loch, its stone cottages and quiet streets exuding a quaint charm that Stuart knew he'd tire of within days.

He approached the first house, rapping his knuckles against the weathered wooden door. An elderly woman answered, her eyes narrowing with suspicion.

"Good morning, ma'am. DC Stuart Burns." He held up his ID, shivering and wishing he'd thought to bring gloves. "I'm investigating the death at the castle. Mind if I ask you a few questions?"

The woman hesitated, then gave a curt nod. "Suppose I've no choice, do I?"

Stuart pulled out his notebook. "What can you tell me about the group up at the campsite? The"—he checked his notes—"Celestial Circle Retreat?"

She scoffed. "Bunch of troublemakers, if you ask me. Barely speak to the villagers, do all their shopping in Brodick, strange comings and goings at all hours."

"Did you have any direct interactions with them?"

She shook her head. "Steered clear, we all did. Nothing good comes of meddling with that lot."

"And did you see anything unusual on Monday night or early Tuesday morning?"

She shook her head. "I go to bed when it's dark. Warmer under the eiderdown."

Stuart jotted down her comments, thanked her, and moved on to the next house. As he walked, he took in the scenery – gloomy hills to the south, the loch's surface sparkling in the sun like nothing untoward had ever happened here.

After several more interviews, he met up with Sam near the path that led to the castle.

"Any luck?" Stuart asked.

Sam shrugged. "Not much. People are hesitant to talk. You?"

"Same. But I'm getting a picture of a community that actively avoided the group at the campsite. Seems there was a fair bit of fear and distrust."

"Aye, I got that impression too," Sam agreed. "Fits with what I've seen over the last few weeks, too. There's a sense of 'told you so' from some folks."

Stuart shuddered. Whatever Erik Haldane had done to piss these people off, he didn't deserve what had happened to him. "D'you think that's enough to put one of the villagers in the frame for the murder? Maybe someone's had enough and taken matters into their own hands?"

Sam frowned and shook his head. "Nah. No way, Stu.

These are good people. They might not have liked those cult folks, but murder? That's not their way."

Stuart felt his shoulders slump. "You're probably right. Still, we can't rule anything out just yet."

They stood in silence for a moment, watching as a group of children ran down to the lochside.

"Did you get any reports of trouble?" Stuart asked. "Any altercations between the group and the locals?"

"I hear grumblings. People worried they were causing damage, that they'd ruin the campsite. But truth was, they kept it cleaner than most."

Stuart nodded. "So do we think the two groups interacted with each other at all?"

Sam shook his head. "Maybe in a cursory way. But nothing significant. I reckon it's one o' your hippies that did it, Stu."

Stuart smiled at the PC. "Don't jump to conclusions."

"I know," replied Sam. "We'll see."

Stuart resisted the urge to sigh in frustration. Sam was a police officer, and a good one, as far as Stuart could see, but he wasn't immune from bias.

CHAPTER TWENTY-ONE

THE YURT SMELLED of incense and damp fabric. Mo ducked through the low doorway, emerging face-to-face with an altar covered in crystals, feathers, and a stack of dog-eared books with titles like *The Energies of the Earth*. He'd ignored all this while they'd been talking to Astrid, but now he'd been outside and come back in again, the place seemed even more claustrophobic.

Candles flickered in glass jars. Astrid perched on the edge of her comfortable chair, her arms crossed, gaze sharp as flint. A young person dressed in a purple hoody three sizes too large and green trousers made of something that looked like cheesecloth sat on a floor cushion, fiddling with a loose thread on their sleeve, knees hugged to their chest.

"Morgan," Mo said. "I assume you're Morgan Douglas?"

The young person looked up and nodded. Their skin was pale, their eyes wide. They glanced at Astrid, who nodded and smiled. Morgan's eyes remained wide.

Scared of Astrid, or scared of him? It wasn't the first time Mo had needed to calm a terrified teen.

He felt movement behind him as Petra entered, stopping before she collided with him.

"Sorry," she muttered.

"It's OK." He nodded towards the low cushion she'd sat on before. She gave him a look – *really?* – then took the low seat he'd occupied himself.

Fair enough.

He toyed with remaining standing. It would be more comfortable on his knees, but it wouldn't give the right impression to the clearly terrified Morgan. Too intimidating. He sighed and sat down on the cushion, giving Petra a look. She flashed him a smile in return then sat back, arms folded, taking up as little room as possible in the circular space.

"This is sacred," Astrid said, her voice clipped. "I'd rather not—"

"And I'd rather not conduct an interview in a draughty tent," Mo cut in, glancing at Morgan. "If you don't mind waiting outside, I'll make it quick."

Morgan's gaze flew up to Astrid's face. Mo frowned.

"How old are you, Morgan?" he asked.

A sniff.

"Morgan is fifteen," Astrid said.

Fifteen, and stuck on this island with this lot. How had that happened?

Mo sighed, sensing Petra tensing beside him. "OK," he said. "Morgan, would you prefer it if Astrid stayed with us?"

Morgan nodded. Mo shook his head. It wasn't ideal, but he would make sure Astrid didn't intervene, and it wasn't like he had much choice. It wasn't as if there was a trusted villager they could bring in.

He threw Morgan a smile. "This won't take long. We're

just trying to understand how Erik interacted with the rest of the group. And where you all were on—"

"Monday night," Morgan interrupted. "When he died. That's easy." They looked at Astrid, who nodded.

Mo pursed his lips. If this ever needed to be used in evidence...

"I was here," Morgan continued. With Astrid."

"And you were talking?" Mo decided to pick up his pen and look down at his notes. Less intimidating, maybe.

Or more. He needed to get better at reading teenagers. But Morgan was very different from his two, safely at home with Catriona.

Morgan nodded, still tugging at the thread in their sleeve. "Yeah... I needed some advice. Astrid's been helping me. It's... been hard. My family doesn't..." A sniff. "They haven't been great. About me. About who I am now."

Astrid looked at Mo, then Petra, her expression sharp. "They don't deserve Morgan's energy," she said. "Some ties aren't worth mending."

Morgan flinched a little but didn't argue. Mo kept his gaze on the teenager. So much for not letting Astrid intervene. "I see," he said. "And you, Morgan? What do you think?"

Morgan shrugged, shoulders hunched. "I don't know. That's why I'm here. Trying to... figure it out."

"Morgan has a beautiful soul," said Astrid. "I'm helping them to nurture their potential as their new self."

Petra snorted quietly from her corner. Morgan looked up, catching the sound. Their face twitched.

Mo flicked his hand towards Petra without looking. "What did you and Astrid discuss?"

Morgan swallowed. "It's hard to explain. Stuff about

finding peace. Letting the island's energy, I dunno, guide me. Heal me."

"Right," Mo said. He wrote down the words: *energy, island, heal*. "What time did you finish talking?"

Morgan's brow furrowed. "Midnight. Yeah. I remember because we went outside after, me and Astrid. Did another ritual thing. Welcomed the new day."

Mo leaned forward, resting his elbows on his knees. "Anyone else with you? Or was it just the two of you?"

"Just us." Morgan's face tightened further. "Well, Freya came out too. For a bit. She's... she's been helping me here."

The silence was broken by the discordant chime of Petra's phone. Everyone turned at the sound, and Petra fumbled to grab it from her pocket. The glow of the screen reflected on her face for a moment before her expression froze. Her face paled.

Mo straightened. "Everything alright?"

"Fine," Petra muttered, shoving the phone into her pocket. She squared her shoulders as if daring him to push it further.

Mo set his notebook down. "Right. I think we're done here, Morgan. Thanks for your time."

Morgan nodded stiffly, almost bolting for the door. Astrid grabbed their hand as they passed, gave it a squeeze, and murmured something Mo didn't catch. The two of them left the tent together.

Astrid wouldn't be gone long.

"Petra." Mo stood, stretching his calves, and looked at the psychologist. "What was that about?"

"Nothing," she snapped. Her hand hovered over her pocket, where her phone was.

Mo frowned. "Doesn't look like nothing. You're pale as a sheet."

She met his gaze, her lips a thin line. After a moment, she asked, "What do you know about... stalking laws?"

Mo felt his frown deepen. "Plenty. Arrested enough on suspicion. Why?"

She stared at him for a moment longer, her jaw tight, her foot tapping once against the rugs on the floor of the yurt.

At last she shook her head. "Ignore me."

He opened his mouth, but she turned away, ducking out of the tent before he could ask more.

He stood there for a moment, wondering. Stalking? Did that mean Petra had someone stalking her, or she was being accused of stalking someone else? And what did it say about him, or about her, that he was even considering the latter option?

He heard a shout outside the tent, and tensed. A man's voice.

Mo swallowed, pushing aside his worries about Petra, and hurried out of the tent. The shouting was intensifying; the man, and Petra's voice.

Outside, a thin, reedy man dressed in an ageing water-proof jacket and a pair of leather shoes that looked wholly inadequate for the situation, was leaning into Petra, jabbing his finger into her face. She flinched each time, his finger coming close to hitting her, but seemed to be standing her ground.

"What the hell?" Mo asked.

The man turned to him. "Get out!"

"What?" He'd met the campsite owner back in the village; a rotund man in his sixties who didn't want any trouble. Was this MacLeod?

And where was Astrid?

He scanned the campsite, but there was no sign of her. At last he spotted her next to another tent, standing with Morgan. The two of them were watching the man, saying nothing.

"Alistair MacLeod?" he asked, raising his voice.

The man looked at him, and Petra took the opportunity to take a few steps back. "Yes," the man snapped. "And I know what you want. But you're trespassing. You need to leave."

"Sir." Mo stepped towards him, ignoring the *trespassing* nonsense. The man spun and put a hand on Mo's chest, holding him still.

Shit.

"Sir," Mo said. A potential suspect in a murder investigation and now...

Certainly impeding their enquiries, even if not yet actually assaulting a police officer.

"Sir," he repeated. "I suggest you stand back. My name's—"

"I know who you are." The man's hand thrust further into Mo's chest. "And I want you off this site. *Now*."

CHAPTER TWENTY-TWO

STUART'S RINGTONE cut through the sound of the shower, a sharp trill that bounced off the tiled walls of his tiny ensuite bathroom. He froze, shampoo running down his face, cursing under his breath.

It was almost eleven in the morning, not the time he'd usually take a shower. But the pub, community centre, whatever it called itself, wasn't used to full occupancy at this time of year, and this morning, there'd been no hot water.

He grabbed a towel from the railing, draped it around his waist and dashed into the bedroom. The phone buzzed against the bedside table, the screen lit up with Sam's name. He dried his hands on the corner of the towel before swiping to answer.

"Sam? What's going on?" He sat on the edge of the small, lumpy bed, his voice echoing through the eaves bedroom.

There was muffled shouting on the other end.

"Hang on, give me a sec—" Sam's voice came back louder, more focused. "It's DS Uddin and Dr McBride. At the campsite. Some fella's trying to kick 'em out."

Stuart rubbed his temple with his free hand, pacing across the tiny room. Through the half-closed curtains, he caught a glimpse of the Lochranza morning: damp grass, blue skies that had now turned grey, the eerily still loch.

After doing door to door this morning, he'd returned to the situation room downstairs, and when he'd found it empty, nipped up here for a shower. No one knew he wasn't working.

"Kick them out?" he said, hoping Sam couldn't hear what a small space he was in. "Why? What's going on?" He frowned. "What fella?"

"One of the group," Sam said, his voice tight. "Don't recognise him, but he's kicking off. Screaming at your sarge."

Stuart stopped in his tracks, the towel slipping precariously lower on his hips. "Screaming? Is the sarge alright?"

"Doesn't seem too fussed, to be honest. Giving as good as he gets."

That stopped Stuart cold. He leaned against the wardrobe, frowning. "The sarge? You're joking."

"Wish I was." Sam gave a faint chuckle. "Quite impressed, to be honest. Not the kind of copper I had him pegged as. He's holding his ground."

"You're not talking about Petra?" Now that, he could imagine.

"Oh, she's joining in alright. First time I've heard her speak. But it's... well it's turning into a bit of a slanging match. And the three remaining cult members are watching. I'm worried things might turn nasty."

Back at home, there would be a simple response. Call Uniform. Get backup.

But here, Sam *was* the Uniform. And Stuart was the backup.

Before he could say any more, there was a rustling sound and a new voice crashed onto the line. "Stuart! It's Petra."

He pulled the phone back and stared at the screen for a second. Flipping heck, she was loud. "Petra? Where's Sam?"

"I nabbed his phone. Listen, this chap – tall fella, but skinny. One of the group. Doesn't look the type for this, but then that's a murder investigation for you – he was throwing his weight around, shouting at me." Her breath came fast, like she'd been running. "Started yelling about trespassing, warrants and the like. Astrid didn't argue with him. She just grabbed Morgan and scarpered. Honestly, she looks... Well, this isn't a professional assessment, right, but I'm watching her now, she's half a field away and if I had to put a word to it, I'd say she looks terrified."

"What?" Stuart glanced out at the loch again, trying to picture Astrid being scared. "Hang on, back up—are you telling me Astrid just... backed down?"

"Proper rattled. That's the thing though, Stu. This fella. Alistair MacLeod. He's her husband."

Stuart almost dropped his phone. "Husband? So he's not one of the group?"

"Oh, he is. He's the 'expert', apparently. An academic. Never heard of him, myself. But they're married. Legally if not emotionally."

Stuart knew what that meant; he'd spent enough years with parents who slept in separate beds and barely spoke to each other.

He composed himself. He had the wardrobe door open now and was pulling out a pair of trousers.

"Do you need me?"

"All hands on deck, pal."

He looked down at himself – bare chest, towel hanging loose, still dripping from the shower. *Brilliant.*

"Right," he muttered. "I'm coming. Just give me—"

"Hold up – where *are* you, Stuart?" Her tone shifted, half-teasing now. "Sitting on your bum?"

Heat climbed up his neck. "I'm in Lochranza, alright? I'm..." He hesitated to admit the obvious. "At the community centre. Sorting some stuff out."

"Well, sort faster," she snapped. "You've got a good young pair of legs on you. Put 'em to use." She hung up.

Stuart stared at the phone. With a short laugh, he tossed it onto the bed.

Ridiculous. It wasn't like he could just magic himself over there. But it was... what? A mile? He could run it. As he threw on some clothes, he ran through what Sam and Petra had told him. Astrid scared? The sarge shouting? And a husband...

He'd better get over there. And quick.

CHAPTER TWENTY-THREE

THE WIND CUT across the water, sharp and damp. Freya watched the Claonaig ferry chug towards the tiny Lochranza terminal, a white hull against grey waves. Seagulls soared above it, their shrieks echoing off the hills.

It was the second time she'd watched the ferry come in. The same blinking lights. The same shuffle of people disembarking, weighed down by their bags. She imagined herself among them. Stepping onto the mainland, walking away. But where? Norway? It wasn't home anymore. Home was Erik, and Erik was gone.

Her hands gripped the metal railing by the water's edge. The cold bit at the skin of her hands; in her eagerness to leave the camp behind, she'd left her gloves in her tent. She glanced back towards Lochranza Castle, dark and brooding beneath the overcast sky. She'd avoided looking at it when she'd passed on her way here, but she'd felt its weight. There was no escaping the damn thing.

The thought curdled into a familiar ache in her chest.

She wanted Erik. She wanted to sit beside him on the uncomfortable cushions in Astrid's yurt, his leg pressed against hers, the warmth of him an unspoken comfort. He'd always looked after her. He was the younger, but the more confident. The one who'd found this camp, and brought them here, telling her how much they'd both benefit from it. How much they'd learn.

The ringing of her phone broke into her thoughts. Freya fumbled in her coat pocket and pulled out the phone. *Withheld number*. Her heart slowed.

It could be the police. Her thumb hovered over the screen, then connected the call.

"Hello?"

"Freya? It's me."

Another voice from the past.

"Liddy?"

Freya's throat tightened. She hadn't spoken to Liddy for weeks.

"Liddy," she repeated.

"Yeah, it's me. How are you holding up?"

How was she supposed to answer that? The wind whipped her hair into her eyes and dug into her coat. She was crying, she knew, but didn't raise a hand to wipe away the tears. She said nothing.

"Freya?" Liddy said, quieter, but insistent. "Are you there?"

"Yeah. I'm... I'm here."

"You sound awful. Look... I know it's probably not what you want to hear, but you've got to get out of there."

Freya stared out over the water, shaking her head. "I can't."

"Listen to me, sweetheart. You can't stay there, not with them. You're not safe."

"Stop." Freya clutched the phone tighter. "Don't."

"I mean it. Come to mine – you can stay as long as you want. I've got a place in Glasgow now. Plenty of space."

A lifeline?

No.

"I can't leave," Freya whispered. "There's nowhere else."

"You've got me."

"It's not just that." She swallowed, the words heavy at the back of her throat. "Erik... he's still here. I can't leave him."

"I get it," Liddy said, her voice soft. "I do. But Freya..." Her tone shifted. "I told that police detective woman—"

"What?" Freya felt her breath catch. "You've spoken to the police?"

"Yeah."

"Why? About what?"

"Because I'm worried about you."

"Liddy—"

"You're not safe there, Freya. Erik won't be the last."

The air seemed to freeze. Freya stumbled back from the rail, the phone shaking in her hand.

"You're lying," she croaked. "How can you say that? How can you—"

"I need you to tell me what's going on," Liddy pressed. "What's been happening since... since Erik? Is Astrid being weird?"

Freya let out a short, bitter laugh. "Astrid's *always* weird."

Liddy didn't laugh with her. "What about Alistair?"

Freya said nothing. She stared out at the water, her breath shallow.

"Freya. For God's sake. Get out of there. *Now*. While you still can."

CHAPTER TWENTY-FOUR

Mo stood with his arms crossed, his gaze on Alistair. The man was pacing, fists clenching and unclenching, his wiry frame taut with agitation.

"You need to calm down, sir," Mo said, his voice carrying just enough authority to stop Alistair mid-stride.

Alistair's laugh was sharp, almost hysterical. "Calm down? We've got coppers sniffing around, thinking one of us killed Erik, and you expect me to breathe easy?"

"We're not 'sniffing around'," Mo replied. "We're investigating Erik's murder. And Astrid has been cooperating with us."

He caught movement off to one side and flicked his gaze sideways, so quickly that Alistair would barely notice. Stuart was on the other side of the trees at the edge of the campsite. Running.

He smiled. *Good lad.* Then he smiled again, at himself this time. *Going native.*

Alistair was staring at Astrid, who lingered near the edge of the campsite, arms wrapped around herself. She had the look of someone who'd rather sink into the ground than be part of this. Morgan was behind her, beyond the furthest of the tents.

"Astrid?" Alistair called. "Is that true? You happy having this lot here?"

Astrid hesitated, biting her lip, before giving a small nod. Mo frowned; what had happened between this pair, to make her flip from defiant leader to meek follower?

Alistair's mouth tightened into a thin line. He glared at Mo. "So what, you're here to pin this all on me?" He held out his hands, wrists up. "Come to arrest me?"

Mo sighed. "I could arrest you," he said, keeping his tone even. He raised a hand, palm out, as if offering an olive branch.

Alistair scoffed, crossing his arms. "I know my rights."

"In that case," replied Mo, "you'll know I'm doing you a favour by not taking this any further. Right now, I just need to talk to you. In your tent. Please."

Alistair let out an incredulous laugh. "My tent?" He jerked his thumb over his shoulder. "Have you bloody seen it? I can barely fit in it, not since she kicked me out." He looked at the yurt, a sneer on his lips. "No way you and your bloody questions will fit in there too."

Mo took a breath. "Fine. We'll talk in your wife's yurt." He turned towards Stuart, now standing a few feet away and breathing hard, watching like a bouncer at a dodgy nightclub. "Meanwhile, my colleague will have a quick look inside your tent."

Stuart coughed, looking at Mo. Seeing Mo's nod, he squared his shoulders before walking over to the tent Alistair had indicated.

"Not a bloody chance," Alistair snapped, stepping closer.

"You're not going near it without a warrant. Do you hear me?"

Mo tilted his head. He put a hand to his chest, a reminder. "And when I tell my senior officers what you just did, I'll have no problem getting a warrant. May I remind you – this is a murder investigation. Where were you on Monday night, anyway?"

Alistair barked a laugh, his fists returning to his sides. "What is this? Everyone else sorted out their alibis, have they? None of your fucking business."

Mo pinched the bridge of his nose. *Don't rise to the bait.* He exhaled slowly. "And this was all going so smoothly."

Before he could follow up, Morgan moved out from behind the tent they'd been standing behind, and approached Astrid.

"Your husband?" they asked, brows knitted. "But you told me you were a lesbian."

Astrid sighed then smiled. "*Sapphic*, sweetheart," she said. "It's different."

The silence that followed could have filled an entire field. Morgan stared at Astrid. "You lied."

Astrid shrugged. "I was trying to help."

Stuart's voice broke the tension. "Sarge?" He gestured towards the tent. "Want me to make a start?"

Mo nodded. Alistair's jaw tightened, but Stuart simply repeated the nod. Mo watched the DC approach the tent, crouch at the entrance, then shuffle inside until only his boots were visible.

"You going to search the others too?" Astrid stepped forward, keeping her distance from Alistair. She was still folding herself up, her arms tight around her body.

"We might," replied Mo. "We might not need to."

His phone rang. The DI. *Not now.*

He pulled it out with a grimace. "Can I call you back, boss?"

"I heard you've got trouble."

Mo felt his cheek twitch. "It's all under control."

"Really?"

He frowned. *Don't you trust me?*

He cast a quick glance towards Stuart's boots sticking out of the tent like a half-drawn pencil. "Stuart called you?" he asked.

"He thought you might need backup."

Backup was miles away, over the sea. Backup, in reality, had been Stuart. Not that he'd been needed.

"Thanks," Mo muttered. "But really, it's all under control."

A moment's silence. Then the DI said, "Good. Well done."

Mo felt the tension in his shoulders ease. "Give me an hour and I'll call you with a full update."

"Thanks. I'd appreciate it." The call promptly cut out, with an abrupt cough from her end.

Mo pushed the phone back into his pocket. He turned his attention to Alistair, who was watching him with a raised eyebrow.

He blinked a few times, pushing the breath deep into his abdomen. He forced himself to look up, from this field and the people in it – he wasn't about to think of them as weirdos, at least not if he could help it – to the hills beyond.

The hills. The hills grounded him. The sea did too, and the sky.

Even miles from backup.

"Right," he said, stepping forward and indicating the yurt. "Let's get started."

CHAPTER TWENTY-FIVE

JADE ENDED the call to Mo with a sigh. He'd done his job, defused the situation at the campsite. No one hurt, no tempers flared, or at least, not too much. Mo was good at remaining calm in a crisis, and had years of experience in both Uniform and CID. But he'd been behaving strangely during recent cases. She was worried about him.

Worry about yourself, instead.

She tucked her phone into her bag and looked around the doctor's waiting room. No effort had been made to make it feel welcoming. Pale green walls, scuffed lino that would never look clean, and a cheap table piled with magazines and pamphlets Jade didn't have the energy to read. The only personal touch was a mug with a faded NHS logo, full of lidless pens. Even that looked battered.

She heard her name and looked up. A man – the doctor, or a nurse? – stood in a doorway, giving her that smile.

She knew that smile. She'd seen it when Dan died.

Oh, hell.

"Jade. I'm Dr Hartley. Come inside."

The doctor. So it *was* bad.

Oh, hell.

The doctor sat down behind the desk, indicating for her to take the chair diagonally across from him. He pulled his chair in and cleared his throat.

Her mind went to Rory, at her mum's house right now. He'd be eating the Jammie Dodgers she'd bought for him, watching some kid play video games on YouTube. He'd graduated from *Hey, Duggee*.

The doctor wasn't meeting her eye.

What am I going to tell him?

"Tell me," she said. "I can tell by the look on your face..."

His mouth opened. "I'm sorry. I'm not very good at facial leakage."

I don't care.

He smiled. "Most of your test results are back now."

Jade crossed her legs, then uncrossed them. Her hands folded and unfolded themselves in her lap. She pulled in a shaky breath.

Dr Hartley continued, his words measured but flat. "The symptoms you've been describing – blurred vision, the loss of sensation in your hands, the fatigue – it could be caused by a number of things. And we'll need to run more tests. But—"

"But what? It's bad, isn't it?"

He swallowed. "The most likely scenario, from what you're describing, plus the results so far, is multiple sclerosis. Based on the scans we've reviewed..." he paused, "I'm not prepared to make a diagnosis just yet. But I think you need to be aware that it's likely."

She sat still, staring past him at the wonky blinds covering the single window in the room. They shifted slightly, letting through a weak winter light that turned everything grey.

Multiple sclerosis.

The doctor was still talking, but the words blurred into a drone, not unlike the tinnitus Jade sometimes woke up to in the middle of the night. Her gaze honed in on his mouth. None of it made sense.

"... it's not definitive yet. We'll refer you to a neurologist, get a full work-up. There are treatments available, particularly if we've caught it early..."

Caught early? What difference did it make? She tried to wrestle her mind out of the fog, to focus. But his words were like water.

"My work," she said. "My son."

"What do you do?"

"I'm a Detective Inspector. Police Scotland."

"Ah."

"Ah."

"You will have to tell your employers. I imagine there are certain risks, with your symptoms..."

Risks.

"What about my son?" She cleared her throat and looked at him. Properly, for the first time. "Doctor, am I going to die?"

He shook his head. "Yours is most likely to be relapsing-remitting MS. Which means—"

"What's that?"

"It means your symptoms will come and go. Properly managed, you could maintain a decent quality of life for decades."

Properly managed. She was a copper, for God's sake.

"And improperly managed?"

"Ah. Now, I wouldn't recommend that."

No. Of course not.

Oh, hell.

She'd have to tell Fraser. But in what capacity? As her boss, or her... partner? Boyfriend? What were they, anyway?

And would they be anything, once she'd told him this?

Don't be ridiculous. Fraser is a good man.

All the more reason to be honest with him. But not with Rory. Not until the rest of those tests.

"I've already made the referral," the doctor said, straightening in his chair. "The Western General in Edinburgh has a dedicated neurology department with specialists in multiple sclerosis. I'm hoping we'll get you in there."

Edinburgh. She lived on bloody Loch Lomond.

He fixed his gaze on her. "Any questions?"

She blinked. Her tongue felt like lead. She opened her mouth, closed it again, and shook her head.

He dipped his body, softening a little. "Anything specific concerning you? Your vision's still an issue?"

She frowned. "It's bad when I try to focus. Reading paperwork's been hell. A few times I've..." she couldn't find the words, "...everything's just gone doubled up."

He nodded. "Carry on with the reading glasses for now. Let your team know—"

"No," she blurted. "They don't need to know."

His brow furrowed. "Alright," he said. "But you'll need to take it easy, Jade. Fatigue can be one of the hardest symptoms to manage."

She held back a bitter laugh. *Take it easy? Fat chance.*

The consultation wrapped up quickly after that. He handed her some bloodwork requisitions and a standard referral leaflet that she knew she'd never read. She stuffed them in her bag, stood, and tried to regain control of herself.

Her legs had other ideas. The faint tremor in her right knee was back, making her steps uneven. She forced herself to walk normally, hoping the doctor wouldn't notice.

Out in the corridor, she dug her phone out and dialled Patty.

The phone rang once.

"Boss," Patty answered. "You've got messages stacking up here. What's going on?"

Jade swallowed hard. "Can't come in just yet," she said, leaning against the wall for balance. "Last-minute thing. Family issue."

"Family? Is the bairn OK?"

"He'll be fine." Jade forced her voice to be steady. "I'll be back later. Keep things ticking over, alright?"

"Alright. Of course," Patty said, before hanging up.

Jade sighed and pocketed her phone. She pushed on the door to the car park, stepping into the cold air. The light hurt her eyes, brighter than it had seemed earlier. She squinted against it, her unsteady legs carrying her to her car.

She reached the driver's side, then stopped. The keys rattled in her hand.

Multiple sclerosis.

What the hell was she going to do?

CHAPTER TWENTY-SIX

STUART DUCKED out of Alistair MacLeod's tent, squinting in the bright daylight. The search had been quick – there was barely anything inside to look through. Too little, in fact; the guy seemed to keep nothing with him other than some toiletries and no more than three days' worth of clothes. Stuart wondered where these people washed their clothes. Did they wash their clothes, even?

The sarge had emerged from the yurt and was outside waiting. He bent down as Stuart struggled out of the tiny tent. "Anything?"

"Nothing. Just a sleeping bag, torch, and some clothes. Fella travels light."

"Right." The sarge's jaw tightened. He glanced back at the rest of the group. Astrid and Morgan were standing on opposite sides of the field, with Alistair as close to Astrid as she'd let him come. Freya had appeared, and was standing near Astrid's tent, looking confused.

The sarge sighed. "We need to search all the tents. By the book, though – get permission first."

Stuart nodded and followed him towards the group members. Each of them looked like they'd rather run a mile than spend any more time in one another's company.

"We need to search your tents," the sarge said to Astrid. "Part of our investigation. But we need your consent."

MacLeod stepped forward. "You need a warrant."

Stuart felt his jaw tense. Not again.

The sarge ignored him. "Ms Thorsen, do I have consent to search your tent?"

She eyed him. MacLeod was gesturing at her, muttering. She gave him a look, then folded her arms across her chest.

"Yes," she said. "I've nothing to hide."

"Good." The sarge looked at Morgan and then Freya. "Does the same apply to you?"

Freya shrugged. "What's going on?"

"They've got it into their heads that one of us killed Erik," Astrid said. "Police intimidation nonsense, but we don't need to hide anything from them, do we?" She turned to Freya with a raised eyebrow.

Freya chewed on her lip. "Er. No. It's fine." She scratched at her forehead, making Stuart wonder if they'd find anything suspicious in her tent.

But she was his sister. Surely...?

"Morgan consents too," said Astrid. "Don't you, sweetheart?"

Morgan let out a small noise, something between a grunt and a squeak. They closed their eyes for a moment, then opened them. "Mm-hmm."

"Is that a yes?" the sarge asked.

Morgan nodded then muttered, "Yes."

"Good. Stuart, you take the two smaller tents. I'll take the yurt, with Sam's help."

"You want...?" began Petra.

"Sorry." The sarge shook his head. "It has to be us." He looked around at the group. "If you could all stay away from the tents until I tell you we're done, please."

Freya frowned then turned her back on the group and started walking towards the edge of the campsite. Alistair MacLeod grunted a laugh and sat down on the grass. Astrid approached Morgan, who looked as if they were about to run away, then allowed the older woman to enfold them in a hug. A murmured conversation started up between them.

Stuart approached the tents. Morgan's was small and blue. Freya's was only slightly larger, a pale yellow.

Freya was the sister. Morgan was clearly troubled. He made for Morgan's first, snapping on a fresh pair of plastic gloves.

Inside, the air was heavy with the smell of stale sweat mixed with the remains of incense. Nothing was burning in here, so he imagined Morgan must have brought the smell in from visits to Astrid's yurt.

No one would burn anything in here. That canvas was too close.

He scanned the tent. The space was cramped – he could barely move without brushing against the canvas sides. A small rucksack sat in one corner, clothes spilling out. A sleeping bag was rolled in front of it, a pillow in the centre of the space on a sleeping mat. Beside the rucksack lay several notebooks.

He picked up the first one, flicking through pages of scrawled handwriting. Notes about the island's history, folklore, ancient settlements. The next book was filled with quotes, all followed by Astrid's name:

The old gods still walk these shores...

We must honour the sacred spaces...

The turning of the wheel brings renewal...

Stuart shook his head. New Age nonsense.

The sleeping bag was rolled tight at the far end. As he lifted it, something solid shifted inside. He unrolled it carefully, finding a package wrapped in layers of brown paper.

Stuart frowned as he peeled back the wrapping.

A knife. About eight inches long, the blade slightly curved. The handle was carved and ornate.

He turned back towards the doorway to the tent, blinking. They were all still out there.

He turned back to look at the knife, trying to remember what the pathologist had said about Erik's wounds.

Was this the murder weapon?

Was it even Morgan's, or had one of the others hidden it here or given it to them?

Only one way to find out.

CHAPTER TWENTY-SEVEN

THE WIND TUGGED at Petra's updo as she waited for the searches to be carried out, observing the inhabitants of the campsite. She shoved her hands into her coat pockets, watching tension spread through the group. She'd seen it all before, grief and pressure twisting people up until they unravelled. That didn't stop it being unsettling.

Astrid and Alistair stood about ten feet away, backs half-turned towards her. *Married.* But now they weren't speaking so much as hissing. Low and urgent, their voices barely carried over to her, but Petra caught snatches.

"... should've said something sooner," Astrid muttered, her tone sharp.

"You don't know what you're talking about," Alistair snapped back.

Astrid leaned closer, jabbing a finger just above his waistband. Her voice was lower this time, inaudible. Alistair's head jerked back, a flush creeping up his neck.

Morgan sat on a camping stool a few metres off, their face pale and body hunched. They had their arms wrapped protectively around their knees, staring at Astrid and her husband. And that hoodie... they were still picking at it, tugging on loose threads, twisting the hem.

It would be easy to walk over and reassure them. In her other job, that's just what she'd have done. But her job here wasn't to fix things. She was supposed to observe, not to intervene.

At the edge of the site, half-hidden beneath the shadow of some birches, Freya sat hunched on a log. Her phone was clutched between her hands, her shoulders trembling with soft, repeated sobs. Even from here, Petra could see streaks running down her cheeks, catching the glow of the phone screen.

Freya couldn't have been older than twenty-two, maybe twenty-three. Too young to be caught up in this kind of mess. Too young to lose her brother. But Petra couldn't assume that grief was entirely genuine. It seemed genuine, but until Petra had spent time working through her observations, collating her notes...

And there was a question. *Had these people been like this before Erik died? Or was it his death that had ripped them apart?* From what locals said, they'd seemed close. Well, close enough to shack up together on this freezing cold bloody campsite in the back of beyond. She shivered.

Her phone buzzed in her pocket, breaking her thoughts. She fished it out and checked the screen: Jade.

"Petra." Jade's voice was clipped. "What's the situation? Is everything under control now?"

Petra turned slightly to shield herself from the eyes of the campsite. Why hadn't Jade called Mo to ask this? Or maybe she had.

"As much as can be expected," she replied. "Mo and

Stuart are searching the tents. No arrests yet, no evidence to speak of."

Jade exhaled, the sound sharp and uneven. "You've got the group in your sights, though. No one's wandered off?"

"They're still all here," Petra said, glancing at Astrid and Alistair again. The argument had simmered down, but their body language was stiff. "Is everything OK with you?" Jade sounded tense.

There was a moment of silence, then: "I'm fine." Jade's voice cracked on the last word.

Petra frowned, moving a few steps further from the group. "Are you sure? Is it Fraser?"

A longer pause this time.

Finally, Jade spoke. "No. And I'd appreciate it if you didn't ask about Fraser. Personal stays personal. Let's focus on the crime, shall we?"

Petra swallowed. "Understood. I'm sorry."

"What's your take on them so far? Any of them capable of committing a ritualistic murder?"

Petra let out a breath. *Focus on what you're good at.* "They're an odd bunch. Astrid, well I had her pegged as the leader. Delusions of grandeur, greatly assisted by the way that Freya and Morgan look up to her. Especially Morgan, poor kid."

"You had her pegged?"

"The other guy here, Alistair MacLeod. Turns out he's her husband. And he just strides in and starts bossing her around like she's some kind of kid. I've seen it before, Jade, but I'm not quite sure what it means for the case. Truth is, I need some more time observing them."

"Any chance someone outside the group did it?"

"The locals weren't keen on them, but there's no evidence pointing to anyone, far as I'm aware. I'm sure Mo will be—"

"I know. Thanks, Petra. Let me know once you have a full profile, yes?"

"Of course. Take care."

A moment's silence, then the line went dead. Petra frowned; something wasn't right.

All she bloody needed, with what her neighbour had texted her this morning. *They're back.*

She caught movement from the corner of her eye and looked up to see Stuart emerging from one of the tents, his body hunched and expression tense. She glanced at the group members then walked over to him.

"Where's the sarge?" he asked, breathless.

She pointed. "Astrid's yurt."

"Course." He turned away from her with a grunt and hurried inside. Petra followed, quickening her pace to catch up. She'd worn practical shoes for once, and her heels weren't sinking into the grass.

Inside the yurt, Stuart stood near the far side, one hand on his hip, the other holding up an evidence bag. Clearly visible inside it was a knife, its serrated blade pressed against the plastic. Even in this low light she could make out blood.

"They're not gonna like this," Stuart muttered to Mo.

Mo stared at the bag. "Where did you find it?"

"Morgan's tent. Rolled up inside their sleeping bag."

"You're sure?" Mo cocked his head, gaze still on the bag.

"Dead sure. I unrolled it myself, nearly nicked my fingers on it." Stuart looked grim. "Should we arrest them?"

Mo sucked in a slow breath, then clapped Stuart's shoulder. "We should. Possession of an offensive weapon's reason enough. Wendy needs to see this straight away."

Stuart frowned. "She's gone back to the mainland."

Mo's shoulders dipped. "Someone's got to take it to the lab. Ask Wendy if she'll come back for it. If she can't, we'll send Sam."

Petra stepped forward, gaze still on the knife. "Am I right to assume this makes Morgan your prime suspect?"

Mo glanced at her, then back at Stuart. "Makes sense." He gestured at the bag. "Erik dies from a stab wound, and this shows up in Morgan's tent."

Petra folded her arms. "It could've been planted."

"Planted," Stuart echoed. "That's what I thought."

"Think about it," Petra said. "You were questioning Morgan and Astrid at the same time earlier, weren't you? That left the others unobserved, and Morgan's tent empty."

Mo looked at Stuart. The determination in his face had left him.

"Shit," Stuart said after a moment. "You reckon Alistair might've done it?"

Mo shook his head. "I've no idea. But if one of them's playing us... right, we're locking this down before it gets worse. We're taking the lot of them back to the station at Lamlash. We need to close off this campsite, search all the tents for evidence of the blood from that knife, or fibres from the paper it was wrapped in."

Petra followed as the men left the yurt, her mind racing. They had evidence now, real evidence. But she had the sense that even with the knife, this wasn't as simple as it looked.

The wind gusted through the campsite again, and she glanced back at the group. Morgan still looked ready to crumble. Freya was drying her face on her sleeve. Astrid had turned away from Alistair and was staring at the ground, her jaw tight.

Petra's stomach churned. This was not going to be easy.

CHAPTER TWENTY-EIGHT

Mo RUBBED his temples as he pushed open the doors to the station. His mind raced through everything they had to sort. The campsite was a mess – potential evidence everywhere – and then there was the knife and what lay ahead for the suspects they'd dragged back with them. He'd barely stepped inside when he caught sight of the suited figure standing near the desk.

"Ah, shit," said Sam, from right behind Mo. He'd brought Morgan and Alistair in the back of his squad car, while Mo had driven Freya and Astrid.

Mo turned. "What's up?"

"Name's Charles McIntosh. Criminal lawyer, based in Brodick. Only one on the island, most of his work's over the water. But he's a right pain in the arse."

Mo scanned the four suspects. Which of them had hired him?

His question was answered when the lawyer approached Alistair Macleod and muttered to him. Mo gave Stuart a look and the DC stepped between the two men.

McIntosh turned to Mo with a thin smile. He wore a suit that looked expensive, and an air of smugness that didn't bode well.

"Detective Sergeant Uddin, isn't it?" he said, his tone clipped.

Mo held his head up, despite being at least two inches shorter than the lawyer. "That's right."

"My client Mr MacLeod tells me he's here voluntarily," McIntosh said, raising an eyebrow, "so I assume no arrest has been made?"

"Not yet."

"Then I expect you'll be letting him go."

Mo folded his arms. Behind the lawyer, he could see Sam leading Freya and Morgan away. "We haven't finished talking to him."

McIntosh's expression remained impassive. "If you're not arresting him, you've no grounds to detain him any further."

Mo exhaled slowly through his nose. He hated it when the flashy suits turned up with their rule books and unflinching certainty. A good lawyer knew that a voluntary attendance could turn into a compulsory one so smoothly you wouldn't even notice the seam. A bad one would just focus on the 'voluntary' part. "He's free to leave if he wants," he said. "For now."

McIntosh nodded, a smirk tugging at the corner of his mouth. He turned and gestured towards Alistair, who was standing next to the waiting area bench.

As Alistair reached the door, Astrid's voice rang out. "Hey!"

Everyone turned. She was stood where Alistair had been, eyes narrowed.

"If you called that brief of yours, he can bloody well act for me too."

Alistair hesitated, his hand hovering over the door handle. He frowned, then gave a slow nod. "Fine."

McIntosh turned to Mo, one eyebrow raised.

Mo suppressed a groan. "Fine. We're letting her go, too." *So the two of them can compare stories.* Not that he was sure they'd even want to speak to each other, after what he'd witnessed.

Astrid breezed past him. "Thank you, Detective."

"I'll be wanting to speak to all of you again," Mo replied, his voice flat.

Astrid looked back with a shrug. "Of course." Then she was gone.

The headache building at the base of Mo's skull intensified. He turned away, catching sight of Stuart coming out from behind the reception desk. Sam had disappeared into an office and Petra was hovering outside the door, no doubt watching Astrid and Alistair.

"Wendy's on her way," Stuart said. "She's bringing a SOCO colleague to help process the knife. They'll do a full search of the site after."

Mo nodded, leaning on the desk. "I'm going to need more resources if we're locking that campsite down. No one's getting in or out, not a chance."

"Agreed," Stuart said. "Have you... have you spoken to the boss?"

Not yet. And he'd been hoping to handle this case alone. "I will." Mo pinched the top of his nose. "We need to get it right. Can't have anyone trampling over evidence."

It had been two days since Erik's death. Chances were,

that had already happened. But if the knife had been planted in Morgan's tent, that would only have happened this morning. Any earlier, and they'd have found it themselves....

Petra appeared beside them, frowning. "You OK?"

"Fine." Mo pushed back irritation. "You've been watching them all. Anything stick out to you?"

Petra placed her hands on the back of a chair. "Plenty odd," she said. "That lot could write a textbook on dysfunctional behaviour, but as for anything suspicious? Not yet, no."

Mo nodded. "Keep your eyes open. I need you on point for anything that might connect back to Erik."

"I'd appreciate proper images of the knife," Petra added. "If there's a link to the writing that Stuart found..."

"Of course." Mo drummed his fingers on the reception desk. "Morgan had the knife in their tent. That alone gives us grounds to arrest them."

"Makes sense," Stuart said. "What about Freya?"

"She's got no direct link to the weapon," Mo said. "We can't force her to stay."

"We can ask her to, though," said Stuart. "Provide us with background information."

"We can." Mo leaned over the desk and beckoned for Sam. "Where is Freya Haldane?"

"Interview room. I've put your other one in the holding cell."

"Thanks." He turned to the DC. "Stuart, can you handle the arrest? I want to speak to Freya before she gets wind of the fact that people are walking out of here."

He pushed himself up and followed Sam, ignoring the stiffness in his back.

The room was small, with a single window high in the wall. Freya was huddled in a chair she'd pulled to the corner, her pale face streaked with tears. She flinched when Mo opened the door, shrinking back as if bracing for a blow.

Mo kept his voice calm. "Freya. I've got a few more questions to ask, and then you can go home."

She shook her head, her shoulders trembling. "I can't."

"Please," he said. "I just want to know more about the other members of the—"

She was shaking her head. "Not that. I can't go."

He frowned. "I've got no grounds to hold you here."

"You don't understand." Her words came in a ragged gasp. She buried her face in her hands, sobbing again.

Mo watched her. Sure, she was emotional, but he was worried he might not get her alone again. Did Sam have a female colleague he could bring in?

When her sobs had quietened to shaky breaths, he crouched down, bringing himself level with her. "Freya, you said you couldn't go. Tell me why."

She lifted her head, her gaze meeting his. For the first time, her eyes were hard. "Because I killed him."

Mo blinked. "What?"

Freya straightened, the tears now falling silently. "I killed Erik."

The room spun for a split second. Mo opened his mouth to reply, but she cut him off.

"He abused me. Coercive control, you call it. Controlled my every move. I couldn't face it anymore. So... So I killed him."

He stared at her. *What?*

She stood, her movements shaky but deliberate. "Do it properly, Detective."

Mo stood as well, too stunned to speak.

Freya held out her hands, wrists upwards. "You heard me. Arrest me."

CHAPTER TWENTY-NINE

Mo PUSHED OPEN the door of the station, letting the heavy metallic groan and the faint scent of sweat follow him out into the crisp air. He wasn't sure why he'd thought stepping outside might clear his head, but staying in the unfamiliar station felt too much at the moment. He stuffed his hands into his pockets, scanning the quiet road that passed the station and the school opposite it and headed off somewhere into the hills.

Petra sat on a step right outside the door, her arms crossed tightly over her coat. In front of her were two police cars; one belonging to Sam, and the other to his colleague Vera, who Mo hadn't met yet. He wondered how shift patterns worked here, and if the two of them spent much time together.

Petra didn't look cold, exactly, but there was a stiffness about her, like she was trying not to feel much of anything. Her eyes were fixed ahead, on two people standing a few paces apart on the opposite side of the road. One, a man, stood beside the sign for the high school, while the other was further away, standing beyond the low wall that formed the school's boundary. A far cry from the schools he'd visited in Birmingham, with their high fencing and security gates.

Astrid and Alistair. He couldn't catch what they were saying, but their voices carried in sharp, clipped bursts as they threw words back and forth. Astrid's arms moved in sharp gestures; Alistair didn't say much, just stood there staring along the road towards Brodick. Then, suddenly, two taxis arrived and pulled up in front of the pair. First Astrid got into one, slamming the door with force, and then Alistair, who barely looked back before stepping inside his ride.

As the taxis disappeared into the late afternoon haze, both heading back towards Brodick and presumably on to Lochranza, Mo rubbed the back of his neck and turned toward Petra. "What do you make of them?"

Petra didn't answer. She'd been staring across the road while all this happened, unmoving. She blinked, almost absent-mindedly.

"Petra?" Mo tried again. "What do you make of that?"

She flinched, then shook her head. "Sorry. What?"

"Are you alright?" He frowned, stepping closer. "I asked what you make of Astrid and Alistair."

Petra sighed, leaning back against the step. "I've got no idea with this lot. It's like trying to untangle barbed wire."

Mo rocked back on his heels but didn't sit. The ground was cold and damp, and he wondered what it had done to the hem of Petra's coat. The tension in his shoulders hadn't gone anywhere, and if he remained standing he could at least attempt to shrug it out. He pulled in a long breath.

"You won't believe what just happened," he said.

She didn't look at him. In fact, she didn't do much of anything.

"I said" – he leaned slightly forward – "you won't believe what just happened."

"I heard." Her voice was flat. She turned her head towards him. "What happened?"

"Freya," he said, crouching to bring himself closer to her. "She asked me to arrest her."

Petra said nothing. Mo peered at her from the side, worried.

"Petra?" He watched as she wrinkled her nose in response to her name. "Are you—"

"Sorry, I'm fine," she said. She stood up, not meeting his gaze. "Did you say Freya asked you to arrest her?"

"I did. She told me she killed her brother."

"And did you?"

"No."

Her brow creased. "But she confessed."

"I don't believe her."

Petra brought her hands out of her pockets to pat down her coat. "I'm no lawyer, but even I know that if you don't think she was coerced into confessing, and she was brought in lawfully—"

"She's scared," Mo said. "She's scared, Petra. Of one of them."

Her eyes narrowed, the way they did when her mind was working. "Alistair or Astrid?"

"Either. Both. I'm not sure."

"What about Morgan?" she said, cocking her head. "They're the one with the knife."

"You've watched them," Mo shot back. "D'you think Morgan could be the killer?"

Petra's mouth tightened. She tilted her head, then said,

"Maybe." She turned to face him. "Look. Can Sam give me a lift back to Lochranza? I need to crack on with my report."

Mo hesitated for a moment before nodding. He glanced back into the station, then turned back, looking fully at the psychologist.

"Are you sure you're alright, Petra?"

She didn't answer. Her thumb hovered over her phone screen, her face illuminated faintly by its light. It was late afternoon, and almost dark now. She wasn't typing, though, wasn't doing anything more than staring.

"Petra," he repeated. "Are you alright?"

Her head snapped up, her features morphing into an insincere smile. "I'm fine. Don't worry about me, Mo." She gestured toward the station. "Just get me that lift, so I can do my job."

CHAPTER THIRTY

Mo stepped into the makeshift incident room and let the door shut behind him, taking in the faint smell of beer and old wood. The whiteboard's surface was littered with photos, scribbled notes, and thin red lines connecting one name to another. Wendy had added a photo of the knife, dead centre, its jagged blade gleaming under the harsh strip lighting.

He sighed and sat heavily on one of the benches that lined the space, trying to imagine what it would be like to socialise in here. His back ached from the drive back from Lamlash with Stuart. There was something about these island roads, winding and uneven, that drained the energy out of him.

Petra appeared through the door at the back of the space, her long hair loose for once, her laptop tucked under her arm. She must've come straight from her room. Wendy, already seated, had her coat wrapped around her, the cold still seeping off her. She noticed him looking.

"Don't say it," she muttered.

"Haven't said anything yet."

The door creaked open, and the community centre manager and sometime barmaid Fiona poked her head through, her hands covered in flour. "You lot be wanting a drink?"

Stuart was right behind Mo; he nodded, rubbing his hands together. "Hot chocolate with a splash of brandy if you've got it."

"I'll have a lager," Wendy said, slumping deeper into her chair.

"Coffee for me," Petra added, setting her laptop down on the table. Mo raised an eyebrow, and she gave him a faint smile.

"I've got my report to finish for Jade. Need to stay up late."

"And you'll let me see it first?"

"Course."

She seemed steadier now. No sign of the pale, detached version of herself he'd seen sitting on that step outside the station. And she'd changed into jeans and a thick shirt. She looked nothing like the Petra he was used to: skirt suit, high heels, hair piled on top of her head. The casual look took ten years off her.

"What about you, Mo?" Wendy asked.

He hesitated, then glanced at Stuart. "Hot chocolate with brandy sounds good."

"Right. Back in five," Fiona said, retreating.

Mo's gaze flicked to the photo Wendy had pinned up. The knife. The serrated edge made his stomach twist, though he wouldn't have admitted it. He'd seen plenty of those in Birmingham, some in Glasgow too. And most of the time, the hands behind those knives belonged to people far too young to be involved in that kind of thing.

Maybe the hand they were looking for really was Morgan's...

When Fiona returned, he rose and took the tray from her, not wanting her looking too closely at the board.

"You don't trust her?" Petra asked as she left.

"It's not that." He set the tray on the table, sliding each drink to its rightful recipient. He took a testing sip, and then a longer one before continuing, the warmth of the brandy hitting his stomach instantly. "No one should have to look at this sort of stuff."

Wendy set down her pint and leaned forward, elbow on the table. "No one except us."

Mo gave her a grimace in acknowledgement. "Right," he said, straightening in his seat. "Updates. Wendy?"

She wiped her mouth and nodded toward the knife photo. "Did a bit of digging. It's not old, not ritualistic. You can buy it online from any number of dodgy sites. Or at some of these obscure new-age events. I've seen them at those markets before."

Stuart raised an eyebrow. "Thought new-age types were all about peace and love."

Wendy snorted. "Some of them are just as bad as anyone else. Selling you incense in one hand and a lethal weapon in the other."

"Do we know if it's the weapon?" Mo asked.

"Still unsure," Wendy replied. "We'll need to send it off, see if it matches the wounds. I'll arrange for someone to come collect it tomorrow morning."

"Good." Mo shifted his attention to Stuart. "What about Morgan?"

Stuart rubbed the back of his neck, frowning. "Tried to interview them earlier, but they were a wreck. Proper panic attack. Kept saying they didn't know anything about the knife. Couldn't even get a formal statement. No responsible adult available."

"Who can we get?" Petra asked.

"Not Astrid, that's for sure," Mo said. He paused, thinking. "I'll ask Sam to find someone local, see if we can get it sorted by tomorrow."

Stuart looked doubtful. "Think we'll find anyone who actually gives a damn? Someone sympathetic?"

Wendy waved a hand dismissively. "Sympathy doesn't come into it. You just need someone to sign the paperwork."

Mo didn't quite agree. But that was a conversation for another day. He turned to Petra. "What've you got so far?"

She leaned back, tapping her fingertips – long and red, so at least some of the usual Petra was still present – against the lid of her laptop. "Been piecing together the dynamics of the group. It's even more dysfunctional than I'd suspected. Astrid runs the show. She's got the others under her thumb, but Alistair controls her."

"Bullies her," Mo said.

"Exactly. But what's strange is he doesn't seem to care about controlling the others. He's laser-focused on Astrid, which... well, it doesn't fit. It's not how I'd expect someone like him to behave in a group dynamic like this."

"Is he a suspect, in your opinion?"

"No." Petra shook her head firmly. "Though I wouldn't trust him in general."

Stuart leaned forward, a glint in his eye. "What if Astrid was having it off with Erik? You think Alistair might fly off the handle then?"

Petra didn't even blink. "No evidence of that. And Alistair's psychology doesn't fit the profile of a man who'd kill another man over jealousy." She paused, as if choosing her words carefully. "If he were going to kill anyone, it'd be Astrid."

Mo's head snapped up. "You're saying he might kill her?"

"Only in that any abusive man might kill the woman he's abusing, under certain circumstances. But no, I've got no reason to think he'll do it imminently."

Wendy flinched at Petra's words, a barely perceptible wince that she tried to hide behind another sip of her lager.

Mo nodded. For now, there weren't any answers, but they were closing in. And somewhere on this beautiful, desolate island, was the truth.

The room was quiet except for the hum of the overhead light. Mo leaned forward, resting his elbows on the table. He looked up at the photo of the knife again, then at the web of connections spidering across the whiteboard.

"So what kind of person does this?" he asked.

Petra pressed her lips together in thought. "Not someone acting out of belief," she said. "At least, not the sort of belief this group preaches. The way Erik's body was arranged, it's off. It's trying too hard to look ritualistic."

Stuart frowned. "Didn't you say this lot go in for all that spiritual nonsense?"

"They do," Petra said, nodding. "But it's not accurate. The symbols are misplaced, contradicting their own beliefs."

"I thought there was a theory that the more accurate it was, the more likely it was to be faked," Mo said.

"To a point," Petra agreed. "But we've passed that point. And it doesn't line up with what Morgan wrote in those notebooks." She turned her laptop. "Astrid's calendar backs that up, too. She keeps records of their rituals. No mention of anything that matches the specifics of Erik's staging. Someone's faking it."

"Why?" Wendy asked, crossing her arms.

"All manner of reasons," Petra replied. "Maybe to throw suspicion around. If you ask me, whoever did this knew enough to make it look convincing at a glance, but not enough to fool anyone actually paying attention."

"So you think it's Freya or Morgan?" Stuart leaned back. "Always the quiet ones, eh?"

"Not necessarily." Petra kept her gaze on the laptop. "Could just as easily be Astrid or Alistair, framing the other to take the fall. They've both got motives." She looked at Mo. "What about Freya's confession? What did she say?"

He rubbed the bridge of his nose. "She's claiming she did it. Says Erik was abusive, controlled her, she did it to be free of him." He sighed. "It doesn't sit right. She didn't have detail – none of the specific things she'd know if she'd been there. It's..." He paused, searching for the right word. "Ambiguous. I reckon she's hiding something, but it's not murder."

"Then why would she confess?" Wendy asked with a frown.

"Maybe she's scared," Petra suggested. "Could be she wants to deflect attention from someone else. Protect them."

"Or," Stuart cut in, "she actually did it and she's just dreadful at covering her tracks."

Mo shook his head. "Nah. I don't buy it. We'll let her sleep on it in the cell tonight. Given time, people start questioning their own lies. Tomorrow morning, we'll sit her down and see what's actually in her head."

Petra nodded, seemingly satisfied. She glanced down at her phone, the glow of the screen illuminating her face.

Mo raised an eyebrow. "Everything alright?"

She met his gaze for just a moment before shoving the phone back into her pocket. "It's fine."

"Good." He ran his hand over his face, feeling the rough scratch of stubble. "Right," he said, straightening. "It's late. And you lot need a break."

Wendy sat up slightly. "What, call it a night already? I've got hours before I can sleep."

"Either stick around here, set the world to rights over another pint, or go grab some sleep. But don't stay glued to this." He gestured at the board. "It's not good for you."

"What about you?" Stuart asked, watching him.

"I'm going for a walk," Mo said.

Petra frowned. "You don't think that's risky? Someone out there could be watching."

He thought of Freya, the last time he'd been out there, sitting alone at the edge of the loch. "Maybe they are. Don't worry, I know what I'm doing."

CHAPTER THIRTY-ONE

THE FAINT HUM of the traffic on the M73, just under a mile away, filled the silence in Jade's office. It was late, Patty long gone home to her recalcitrant husband and the book she was currently reading – *Game of Thrones*, she was experimenting with a new genre. Only Jade's desk lamp was lit, pooling in a golden circle on the scuffed surface of her desk.

Jade leaned back, rubbing her temples. The notes on the case spread in front of her and Petra's report was open on her screen.

She'd left Mo alone, expected him to run this thing by himself. And today things had kicked off at the campsite, and it looked like the team was confused about who they should and shouldn't be arresting.

She was distracted, she knew it. Not by the symptoms this time, but the thought of it. Multiple sclerosis. Would the words become familiar? Or would she always shudder when they passed through her mind? She glanced at the coffee cup by her elbow. Cold, of course.

A soft knock at the door broke the stillness. She jolted, then cleared her throat.

"Hello?" No one came here at this time of night. No one came here ever. Except...

The door creaked open, and Fraser stepped inside, holding up a brown paper bag in one hand and a pack of Tunnocks in the other. Rory's favourite. Hers, too, although she didn't like to admit it.

"You've not eaten," he said, scanning the room with a faint smile. His tie was loose, his shirt sleeves rolled up to his elbows. He looked knackered but calm. And – her stomach jolted at the thought of it – sexy.

"I'm fine," she said, though her stomach growled the second the smell of fried noodles hit her.

"Don't lie to me, Jade," he said with a smile. He dropped the bag onto the desk and sat on the edge of the chair across from her. "You're as bad as my sister was when she was studying for her medical degree. Worked right through dinner, then ate beans on toast at eleven."

"Sounds efficient," she quipped, but reached for the bag all the same. "I didn't know you had a sister."

He shrugged. "We don't see much of each other. Too busy."

She rummaged through the bag. "You really didn't have to."

"I did," he said, leaning back in the chair, watching her with that steady gaze of his. "It's Szechuan noodles, your favourite. I think." He gave an exaggerated shrug. "I hope."

"It is." She pulled out a carton and started to eat, suddenly aware of how hungry she was. Then she slowed, not wanting to make a mess of her blouse. He watched, his eyes sparkling.

I've got something to tell you...

Not yet.

She shifted, reaching for her water bottle. Her left hand trembled as she grabbed it, the tremor too faint for Fraser to clock but enough to make her want to cry. She set the bottle down and switched to her right hand.

Fraser didn't seem to notice.

Thank God.

"Long day, then?" he asked as he opened his own container of food.

"Every day's long," she said and rotated her shoulders, trying to ease the tension in her back. "Especially when none of this makes sense. No one saw anything. We've got a potential weapon, but it was found in the tent of the most unlikely suspect. And that bloody commune Erik was living in..."

Fraser picked up his fork. "Takes all sorts to make a world, Jade. You know that."

"I do," she said, stabbing at the noodles with her chopsticks. "Still annoying, though."

"Welcome to policing," he said with a dry chuckle that she echoed.

They ate in silence, Jade worrying that the burden was on her to speak, but unable to find anything to say. She didn't have the energy to talk about the case, which kept sliding out of her mind every time she tried to focus on it.

At last Fraser broke the silence.

"How long's it been since you took a proper break?"

She glanced up with a frown. "I'm fine, Fraser. Seriously."

"I didn't say you weren't."

"You didn't have to." She sighed. "I appreciate what you're doing, but I don't need looking after."

"I'm not looking after you," he said as he put his container down. "I'm just... I don't know. Worried. Is it us? Are you regretting this?"

"No!" she exclaimed. "No. Not at all. I'm... happy that we're..." She gestured between them with the chopsticks, not yet ready to put it into words. "It's not what I was expecting, but... Can I tell you something?"

He nodded, his gaze intent on her face.

"A couple of days ago I watched birds flying over Loch Lomond, and it didn't make me cry." She looked down into her food, embarrassed. "It's the first time in a while."

He reached over and put a hand on her knee. "That's good. But you don't have to forget Dan just because you and I are together. He was a good man. A good husband. Great dad," he added with a grin. "I don't expect you to obliterate your past."

She frowned. "That's not what I meant. There's no danger of me forgetting Dan, don't worry about that. Every time I look at Rory, his dad's there in his face. But what I meant was that the grief is getting easier. You've helped."

He squeezed her knee. "Good. I'm glad."

She looked up at him. Was he really this good a man? Or would this last for a few months and then it'd be back to focusing on work, and their relationship relegated to something secondary?

"I haven't told Rory yet, you know. About us."

He nodded. "Of course not. You have to wait until the time is right."

Which might be never. Especially if he reacted the way she thought he might to her news.

She said nothing, but nodded.

He smiled, but his eyes didn't quite follow. His gaze

lingered on her, steady and searching. She felt her heart pick up pace, her face growing warm and damp.

"I mean it," he said, his voice lower. "You've been pushing yourself too hard. I get it – you want to do all you can despite not being on site. But Mo knows what he's doing." He raised an eyebrow. "There's every chance he'll get promotion, within the next year."

She gasped. Was that it? Did Fraser know? Was he planning for her successor already?

"But..." she began.

He smiled. "Don't worry. I have no plans to give him your job. He's shown interest in moving closer to where his wife works. I'm sure there'll be something for him."

She stared at him. Without Mo, possibly without her, too, the CCU would cease to exist. Fraser was the only senior officer who supported them.

She couldn't do that to Stuart and Patty. Petra... Petra would find her own way. But she'd miss the woman.

"I'm fine," she said, but the words felt hollow even to her.

Fraser tilted his head. "You're stubborn, you know that?"

"One of my better qualities."

"Sometimes, yes." He leaned in and kissed her forehead. She tensed.

He felt it, and moved back. "Sorry," he said. "Not in the office, eh?"

Jade swallowed. A lifeline. "No. Let's keep things separate. Yes?"

He pulled back his hand and stood up. "You're right. Let's. Now, am I going to start feeding you pieces of this chocolate bar, or are you going to kick me out of here?"

She checked the clock on her screen. "I have to go home to Rory in ten minutes."

"Of course. I'll see you very soon, yes? Hopefully spend some proper time together."

"Of course."

He bent to grab her hand and give her a light kiss, but fumbled it and ended up kissing her sleeve. The two of them laughed.

"I love you, Jade," he said. "And I'll do whatever you need me to, to be with you."

CHAPTER THIRTY-TWO

Mo walked along the shoreline, his boots crunching on mixed sand and shingle. A light breeze carried the faint scent of salt and seaweed, mingling with the earthy tang from the dunes behind him. Ahead, he could just about make out the silhouette of Lochranza Castle against the blue-black of the sky beyond.

He paused, hands in his jacket pockets, and let his eyes roam over the horizon. Waves lapped against the shore in a steady rhythm, their sound a soothing counterpoint to the stress of the day.

Scotland had felt alien when he'd first arrived. Too cold, too weird, too cut off. He missed the thrum of the Birmingham traffic, the bustle of crowds, even the distant roar of planes overhead. In Scotland, he'd felt lost. But tonight, Mo found himself leaning into the stillness, drinking it in.

It was as if, by passing through the relative sedateness of Scotland and out the other side to this tranquillity, he'd found somewhere he could feel at ease.

He took a deep breath, closing his eyes. Overhead, he

could hear birds – no idea what they were, but he could learn. He knew that behind him on the rocks were seals. *Seals!* His girls would be ecstatic.

He pulled out his phone and stared at it. At times like this, he liked to talk to Zo. His old boss, DI Zoe Finch.

He scrolled until he found her name, then paused.

Zoe was in Cumbria, investigating a corrupt business-man. And solving a few murders along the way. She was happy, or seemed to be, with her partner Carl, a PSD officer. She missed her son Nicholas, at the University of Stirling and in touch with Mo more than his mum these days.

He couldn't imagine what it would be like when Isla and Fiona left home. He hoped they wouldn't go too far.

He tapped on her name, fingers trembling a little from the chill. It rang out. But before it could connect, Mo quickly cancelled the call.

Should he be doing this, reaching into the past to seek comfort from his chats with Zoe? Or should he focus on the here and now? He scanned the shoreline. The here and now was pretty damned beautiful.

He tapped *open contact*, found the entry for Catriona. He selected the message field and typed.

It's beautiful here.

He pictured her reading it. Would she smile? Would she get it? Would she let him bring her here, when the case was done?

The case. He shook his head and turned back towards the community centre, pushing it from his mind. He'd think about that tomorrow. For now, he needed sleep. It was only nine pm, but the fresh air and busy day had left him exhausted.

I'll just walk up to the ferry terminal and back again.

He wandered along the beach, avoiding piles of seaweed and eventually retreating to the road when he realised his shoes were getting wet. The road was empty, no sign of traffic. He walked along the line in the centre.

Imagine doing this, in Brum. He grinned and threw his arms out wide as he walked.

His phone buzzed in his pocket. Mo frowned, debating whether to pull it out and ruin the moment.

It buzzed again. With a sigh, he retrieved it and looked down at the message from his wife.

I'm glad. :)

He smiled. She got it. He would bring her up here, her and the girls. And then maybe...

Well, he'd come to that when he came to it. For now, there was a case to solve.

CHAPTER THIRTY-THREE

Mo's FACE filled Jade's screen as she adjusted her laptop for the umpteenth time. His brow was creased, and the bags under his eyes looked deeper than usual. She wondered what the beds were like in the rooms above the pub-cum-community centre they were also using as an incident room.

"Right, boss," he said. "I've sent over the pictures Wendy took at the scene. You should have them now."

Jade squinted at her monitor, leaning closer. "The resolution's awful, Mo. Can you sharpen it up? Everything's blurry." She tapped at her mouse, zooming in on a grainy image of the boat where Erik Haldane had been found.

"I've already bumped it as much as it'll go." Mo sounded tired. Or was she projecting? "We're in the middle of nowhere here. The upload speeds are prehistoric."

"Or my eyesight's giving out," Jade muttered under her breath. "OK," she said. "What about the campsite? Anything yet?"

"Wendy's headed over there. She's only got one other SOCO with her, it's slow going."

Jade sighed, pinching the bridge of her nose. "Right. I think you and Stuart should head over there too. Interview Alistair and Astrid before they bugger off on the next ferry."

Stuart's face appeared just behind Mo's. "Agreed, boss."

Mo frowned. "They won't agree to talk."

Jade was having none of that. "Caution them. A lethal weapon was found on a site they're managing, unofficially, at least. If nothing else, Astrid was acting in loco parentis for the person whose tent the knife was in. The two of them could be culpable. Make it clear to them that this is serious, without doing anything to tempt Alistair to get his lawyer out again. Not yet."

"If we caution him..."

She sighed. "I know. And if he does want a lawyer present, then that's fine. He's less likely to tell us anything useful, but it's not like we're not used to that. Good luck, both of you."

"Thanks," Mo said, tipping his forehead in mock salute.

"And I've already asked Petra to observe. I want a read on their dynamic."

Mo, still staring into the camera, nodded. "It's that relationship of theirs we need to crack," he said. "There's something more going on between them. Petra thinks they're both capable of planning something like this, unlike Freya and Morgan."

"Petra's assessment also means nothing conclusive," Jade reminded him, switching screens to the psychology report. Petra's analysis had been sharp as always, but it left plenty of room for doubt. And none of it would help them secure a conviction. "And from what you tell me, Astrid's slippery as hell. If we don't corner her properly, she'll worm her way out."

"She won't slip past me," Mo said. "I'll keep pushing till something gives."

Jade studied her screen. The frustration written on Mo's face mirrored her own. "Good. But pace yourself. You look like you're running on fumes."

"As if you don't, boss," he shot back, with the faintest of smiles.

"Touché." She rubbed her temple, blinking to bring Mo back into focus. "What about Morgan? Have we spoken to CPS yet about the weapons charge?"

"Not yet. I'm waiting on the go-ahead," Mo admitted. "But there's no chance we'll get murder to stick with Morgan. Possession's solid, though. It might rattle Astrid when she hears about it."

"That's what I'm banking on," Jade said. "Why don't you speak to Morgan first, find out what you can from them about Astrid and Alistair? If Morgan's scared, they might be more likely to open up."

He nodded.

"Have you found a chaperone yet?"

Another nod. "The deputy head from the school across the road. We know we can trust him to be professional."

"Right," Jade continued, her headache bubbling. *Is this what it's going to be like, from now on?* "Let's get on with it. Check in with CPS. Find a gap in Astrid and Alistair's stories and tear it open. Mo, you're on the field interviews with Astrid and Alistair. Make them count. Petra's there for a reason – use her."

"Understood." Mo straightened in his chair. "We'll get results, boss."

CHAPTER THIRTY-FOUR

THE CAR ROLLED along the narrow winding roads leaving Lochranza behind, the bulk of Goat Fell looming ahead of them. Mo kept his hands firmly at ten and two, his eyes scanning the road, ready for a wandering deer or sheep. Petra was in the back seat, one leg crossed over the other, her stiletto tapping against the seat in front of her. Stuart sat in that seat, his arm propped up against the door, scrolling through his phone.

Mo yawned. What he hadn't told the boss on the video call was that he'd barely slept last night anyway, tossing and turning with fragments of Freya's confession and thoughts of Astrid and Morgan swirling in his head. He'd hoped his late night walk would clear his head. He'd been wrong.

Stuart's phone rang. "It's Wendy," he announced. "Wendy, what's the update?" He switched to speaker and Mo strained to hear. The signal was even worse here.

"The blood on the knife," Wendy's voice came, slightly distorted, "it's Erik Haldane's."

Mo drew in a breath.

Petra exhaled behind them. "A concrete lead for you, finally."

"Hang on," Mo said, his voice measured. "The knife was found in Morgan's tent. That doesn't mean Morgan's the killer. It just means the knife was there."

Petra grunted. "Exactly. It tells us they had the weapon in their possession, but not who wielded it."

"Have we got prints from it yet?" Mo asked, glancing at Stuart.

Stuart looked at the phone in his hand. "Wendy, any prints on the knife yet?"

There was a pause before Wendy's voice returned, muffled but clear enough. "Still waiting on results from the lab."

"Right, thanks." Stuart ended the call. "No prints yet, but let's be honest – pretty damning, isn't it? Knife in Morgan's tent. Erik's blood on it."

"It puts Morgan under a brighter light, but let's not jump to conclusions," Mo replied. "We need more. Motive, opportunity, and hard evidence."

"Well, motive's hardly a stretch," Stuart said. "Morgan's loyal to Astrid. Devoted, even. If Erik was a threat to Astrid, that alone could be enough."

Mo glanced at Petra through the rear-view mirror. "Thoughts?"

Petra gave a shrug and adjusted her hair. "It's possible. Morgan's insecurities run deep. They've aligned their entire sense of purpose and identity with Astrid's group. More specifically, with Astrid. If they thought Erik was undermining the cohesion of the group – or worse, Astrid herself – they might've decided he had to go. But it's all theory until we have something concrete. And I still don't think

Morgan is capable of a crime like the one we're dealing with here."

"So," Stuart said, turning in his seat to face Mo, "what's the play with Morgan? We bring that knife up and confront them with it?"

Mo considered. "Not yet. Not until we have more. Get those prints, delve into their relationship with Astrid and with Erik, and see if there's any history of threats or animosity. I want to know what goes through Morgan's head before I challenge them with evidence."

Petra leaned back in the seat, arms crossed. "A word of caution, though. Everything about that cult – their dynamics, their worldview – it's driven by Astrid's control and manipulation. Whatever we ask Morgan, we can't discount Astrid's influence. How much of what Morgan does or says truly comes from them?"

Mo mulled this over. Stuart shifted, clearly itching to push the matter further. Instead, he folded his arms and stared out the window, watching the grey sea pass by to the left.

"Until those prints come in, we keep our distance with Morgan," Mo said at last. "And we keep pressing Astrid. There's more going on with her and that group than any of them are letting on."

Stuart smirked. "Astrid doesn't scare you, does she, Sarge?"

"Not in the slightest. But that doesn't mean I'll underestimate her."

Petra let out a low chuckle. "With people like Astrid, you're either useful or expendable. And I'd wager she doesn't think we're all that useful."

Twenty minutes later – it didn't take long to get from one

end of this island to the other – Mo sat across from Morgan in the stark interrogation room, the fluorescent lights casting harsh shadows. Morgan's fingers twisted together in their lap, a picture of nervous energy. Petra perched on a chair to Mo's left, her stilettos tapping quietly against the floor. To Morgan's left sat the deputy head of the school across the road from the station, a large man in his fifties with a kindly smile who threw reassuring glances in Morgan's direction every few seconds.

"Let's talk about the dagger found in your tent, Morgan," Mo said, keeping his voice steady. "Can you explain how it got there?"

Morgan's gaze flicked up. "I don't know."

"Did you put it inside your sleeping bag?"

A shake of the head. "No."

"My colleague found it rolled up inside your sleeping bag, at the back of your tent. Can you explain that?"

"I never leave my bag rolled up. I put it in the stuff sack every morning. Keeps it clean."

"Can anyone else corroborate that?"

"Yes. Erik." Morgan's face fell. "Astrid. She supervises tent maintenance."

Jeez, this woman really does think she's the poor kid's mother. "Astrid?"

A nod.

Mo wrinkled his nose. "So is the knife familiar to you?" He pushed a photo across the table.

Morgan's gaze darted between Mo and Petra. "It's ceremonial. We use it in our rituals, for blessing and protection. Never for harm."

"We?" asked Mo.

A shrug. "Astrid. Sometimes Alistair. But..." Morgan's eyes widened. "Sorry. I'm not saying any more."

Petra sighed. Mo tried to hide his frustration. The young person in front of him was more interested in protecting Astrid than themselves, it seemed.

"We found Erik's blood on it," he said.

Morgan's face drained of colour. "That's impossible. It can't..." They stopped, swallowing hard. "It wasn't me. Erik was my friend."

Petra passed Mo a note: *friendship*.

Mo leaned forward. "Was he? Or was he becoming a problem? Questioning Astrid, threatening the group's stability?"

"No!" Morgan's voice cracked. "I mean, yes, he had questions, but that's normal. We all question sometimes."

Mo watched Morgan's hands, gripping the edge of the table. "Tell me about your relationship with Astrid."

"She saved me." Morgan's voice softened. "When my family rejected me for who I am, Astrid showed me acceptance. She helped me find my true self."

"And if someone threatened that acceptance?" Mo pressed. "If Erik's doubts were putting everything at risk?"

Morgan's eyes filled with tears. "I didn't kill him. I couldn't. And Astrid's a woman of peace. She loves us all. She could never... Please, you have to believe me."

Petra shifted in her chair. Mo continued. "Morgan, help us understand. What was happening in the camp, the night Erik died?"

"I was with Astrid in her tent, talking. Astrid had asked me to focus on purification rituals. At sunset, we performed a thanksgiving ritual. I didn't see Erik at all that night."

Mo noted how Morgan's shoulders tensed at the mention

of purification. "These purification rituals – what do they involve?"

"Just meditation, cleansing with herbs. Nothing violent." Morgan wiped their eyes. "I would never hurt anyone. That's not what we're about."

"So did you see Astrid at all that night?"

Morgan's head shot up. "No. But—"

"Or Alistair?"

A shrug. "No. I never see him. Astrid was with Freya. That's what she told you. She—"

Mo stood up. "Thanks, Morgan. We'll tell you if we need to speak to you again."

CHAPTER THIRTY-FIVE

JADE SAT at her desk in the CCU offices, the only sound the tap of Patty's fingers on her keyboard. Patty kept glancing over at Jade with a worried look that was starting to get irritating.

I can look after myself.

Patty had worked with Jade for years, in Glasgow CID before Jade had recruited her to the CCU. Despite Jade overtaking Patty in rank twelve years earlier, the other woman had always treated her in a way that was almost maternal.

Most of the time, it was touching. When Dan had died, it had been the only thing that kept her coming into work. But today, it wasn't what she wanted.

Jade put down the glasses she'd picked up in a pound shop in the hope they might help her see the screen better, and massaged the bridge of her nose. The cheap specs left dents in her skin; she had to get to an optician.

But was it worth it? Would her eyesight just deteriorate further by the time she'd got used to wearing glasses?

She was pulled out of her thoughts by her phone ringing. She picked it up with relief.

She leaned back in her chair. "DI Tanner."

A clipped male voice came over the line. "Rohan Joshi, forensics. I've got preliminary observations on the dagger Wendy Douglas sent over."

Jade straightened. Wendy's colleague clearly wasn't one for niceties. But today, she didn't need niceties. "Go on, then."

"The blood on the blade is Erik Haldane's. That checks out," Rohan began. There was a pause, just long enough to make her sit up further. "But the blood pattern suggests it didn't end up there as part of an attack."

"I'm sorry. What do you mean?"

"That blood was placed on the blade. It's... it's been smeared. Dolloped, if you will. By someone who clearly has no idea what they're doing."

"Smeared?"

"Am I not making sense?"

No, you're not. "Sorry, Rohan was it?"

"Rohan Joshi. Forensics Technician. I've been—"

"Yes, I know what you've been analysing. So how are you suggesting the blood found its way onto the knife, if it didn't get there during his murder?"

"As I just said, it was placed there."

She sniffed. Across the desks, Patty had stopped typing. "Maybe the killer tried to clean the blade, but was interrupted."

"The pattern isn't consistent with that. If that blade had been used to kill Mr Haldane, there would be tiny particles of blood between the serrations, along with fragments of skin and flesh."

She nodded. "And there aren't."

"Nothing. All the human material is on the side of the blade. Some on the hilt. Mr Haldane's blood is on this knife, but it didn't get there during an act of violence. And the blade is sharp. No abrasions, no snags. It's never been used."

Jade let that sink in. Her brow knitted. "Are you saying the dagger wasn't the murder weapon?"

"That's what the evidence shows."

She restrained her frustration and scribbled notes on a pad. "What about fingerprints?"

"Two sets," Rohan replied. "One set belongs to the victim. The other is incomplete – smudged, partial. But it doesn't match any prints on file. Whoever it is, they're not in the system."

Jade felt a familiar tension building in her chest. "No match. Great." Her pen hovered over the page. "Any idea how recent the prints are?"

"Difficult to determine. The smudging suggests the knife's been handled recently, but exactly when or by whom, I can't say."

"What about gloves? Could it—"

"I can't confirm anything beyond what I've told you, DI Tanner," Rohan cut in, his tone sharp. "We deal in facts, not suppositions."

She exhaled slowly, resisting the urge to snap. "Right. Anything else?"

"I'll contact you when I have more from the physical examination of the blade. At this point, all you've got is incomplete data."

"Brilliant," she muttered. "Thanks." But he'd already hung up.

Jade stared at her phone for a moment, then tossed it

down on the desk. She rubbed her temples, biting back a surge of frustration. They had so much evidence, yet it just seemed to lead them further into the fog. A knife with Erik's blood, but no proof it killed him. Two sets of prints, but one of those matches was dead, and the other unknown.

"Damn it," she whispered. She looked at Patty. "Did you catch that?"

Patty nodded. "What now?"

"We continue getting background on the members of the group. I want to cover all bases."

"Mo and Stuart are heading to the campsite this morning."

Shit. "You're right." Jade grabbed her phone.

"What about Liddy Drummond?" Patty asked.

Jade frowned, listening to Mo's number ringing out. "What about her?"

"How tight is her alibi?"

Jade put her hand over the phone. "She left the island days before Erik died."

"She could have returned."

Jade stared at Patty. The DC was right. Leaving and then returning without anyone knowing would be one way to hide the crime.

She nodded. "Check ferry passengers, between Liddy claiming she left the island and when she came in to see me."

"Right."

Mo's number was still ringing out. She tried Stuart; no answer. She went back to Mo's.

His voicemail clicked in.

"This is DS Mo Uddin. Please leave a message."

She ended the call before the beep, her anxiety ramping up a notch. Mo usually answered. She told herself he might be in an interview or somewhere with no signal. But her stomach churned all the same. If Astrid or Alistair were behind Erik's death, there was no telling what they were capable of. And now they had evidence that didn't fit cleanly into anyone's story.

Jade hit redial. Still voicemail.

"Mo," she said, aware her voice shook. "It's Jade. Call me back. Soon."

CHAPTER THIRTY-SIX

THE CAMPSITE WAS a patchwork of damp grass and soggy ground, the kind that never quite dried out no matter the season. Petra picked her way towards the tents, her boots sinking into the soft earth. A cold fire pit sat at the centre, smouldering quietly.

Astrid Thorsen was waiting for them, standing in the doorway of her yurt like the lady of the manor welcoming them to her country pile. Arms crossed, chin tilted high, she was doing her best to look like she was in charge.

"Detective Sergeant," Astrid greeted Mo, who walked slightly ahead of Petra and Stuart. "I assume you're here to disrupt us further. Shall we begin, or is there some other way we're to be persecuted today?"

Mo met her gaze but said nothing. Petra glanced at Stuart, who was scanning the other tents. Morgan was still at the police station, but there was no sign of Alistair or Freya.

The flap of one of the smaller tents unzipped, and Alistair emerged. He squinted at his wife and then at Mo. His greying hair was mussed, his fleece top wrinkled, and his trousers had muddy patches on the knees.

He stood up, smoothing down his fleece. "I'll not be answering any questions without my solicitor present." He ran a hand through his hair. Petra suppressed a smirk.

Mo turned to him. "Where's your lawyer then, Professor?"

"He's on his way," Alistair's voice was stiff. "And I suggest that until he arrives, you refrain from harassing me. It's unbecoming."

Astrid stepped towards him. "This wasn't part of the plan," she muttered.

Alistair's jaw shifted, but he didn't meet his wife's gaze. Petra narrowed her eyes. Mo was watching her, waiting for her assessment.

It'll all go in my report.

Astrid sniffed. "Bastard," she said, loud enough for all of them to hear, before turning her attention on Mo. "You might as well come in, then."

Without waiting for a reply, she disappeared into her yurt, the heavy fabric falling shut behind her.

Petra shot a glance at Mo. "Charming, isn't she?"

"She's not boring." Mo took a few steps towards the yurt, but stopped halfway. "Stuart."

The DC straightened. "Sarge?"

"You stay here. Keep an eye on Professor MacLeod in case he decides his legs work faster than his mouth."

Stuart looked from Mo to Alistair and then to Petra. Petra said nothing.

"Yes, Sarge." Stuart sniffed and turned to face MacLeod's tent, his boots squelching in the mud. MacLeod had disappeared inside.

Mo raised an eyebrow, gesturing for Petra to follow him. She nodded and followed.

Inside, the yurt was warmer than she'd expected, the air heavy with essential oils and incense. In her professional assessment, it bloody reeked.

Astrid was already in her armchair, a woollen throw over her knees. Her hands rested lightly on it, though Petra noted tension in her fingertips.

"What do you want this time?" Astrid asked.

Petra watched Mo scanning the yurt. She took the low cushion she'd had yesterday, inwardly cursing the effect it would have on her back, and followed his gaze. Nothing of note had changed: there were bottles of essential oils, books, clothes on a metal rack to one side. Astrid followed his gaze but said nothing.

"You act like we're inconveniencing you, Ms Thorsen," Mo said. "But someone's dead. And your... colleagues seem unable or unwilling to answer our questions."

Astrid inhaled, placing one hand on top of the other. "I've already told you, the Circle has nothing to hide."

Except a murder, Petra thought.

Mo stepped forward, his eyes narrowing. "Freya told us that Erik had doubts about you and your teachings. Did he want to leave?"

Astrid looked up at him. "People come and go from the Circle all the time. Erik was no different. The tragic nature of his death doesn't change the fact that I had no role in it."

"Did you get much chance to observe Erik and Freya's relationship?" Mo asked.

Astrid frowned. "Of course."

"Were they close?"

"Very. He was protective of her."

"Controlling?"

She held one finger tightly between the thumb and fore-finger of the other hand. "I wouldn't..."

She looked between Mo and Petra. Realisation?

"On the other hand," she continued. "He was... he did dominate her. Freya is a sweet soul, one who trusts all those she meets. Erik, of course, she trusted above all others."

"Did you witness any conflict between them?"

Astrid watched Mo's face for a moment. Petra knew what she was up to. Working out what Freya had told them. Guessing, correctly perhaps, that Freya claimed he'd controlled her.

She gave a long, slow nod. "I heard arguments. In Freya's tent, late at night. Raised voices." A smile. "I'm sorry, I didn't hear the details."

Mo opened his mouth to speak, but Astrid got there first. She put a hand to her chest in mock surprise.

"Are you suggesting Freya killed her brother? Is that why she hasn't returned to the camp?"

Mo folded his arms. He cocked his head, then clearly decided to ignore the question.

You're learning, pal.

"You spoke about unity last time we met," he said. "About how Erik was no different from anyone else in the Circle. But others say he pulled away. His actions didn't exactly scream unity by the end, did they?"

Astrid's fingers traced the edge of a rune-carved pendant she wore. "Spiritual growth isn't always comfortable, Detective. He struggled, yes. But he wasn't pulling away. He was recalibrating."

Mo raised an eyebrow. Petra resisted the urge to scoff.

"So nothing he did upset you? When he started questioning the rituals, for example?" Mo asked.

Astrid didn't waver. "Erik and I had deep discussions. He was troubled, no doubt because of the grief he carried. At times, his questioning felt disrespectful to the group's work—"

"Work?" Mo interrupted. "You mean your rituals? Your performances dressed up as ancient Norse practices?"

Petra leaned back, watching Astrid's expression harden. The woman pursed her lips and blinked.

"The Circle draws on traditions that you, Detective, couldn't hope to comprehend, with your rigid metrics of law and order," she said.

Mo stayed silent, forcing Astrid to speak again.

"Erik unsettled some," she continued. "Freya most of all. She adored him. His doubts hurt her. But nothing he said threatened us as a collective. It made us... reflect."

"Freya looked up to Erik, then," Mo said, and Astrid nodded. Petra heard a buzz from Mo's pocket – his phone? – which he ignored. "She also said you counselled Erik directly," he continued. "Care to share what you advised him?"

Astrid paused, her hand still on the pendant. "I listened more than I advised. Support, Detective. That's what the Circle stands for. Not coercion." Her jaw was clenched, her voice tight.

"And yet – this support network of yours didn't stop Erik from dying," Mo said.

"I am not a miracle worker," Astrid said. "Nor am I responsible for the actions of others."

"That so?" Mo tilted his head. His phone buzzed again. His fingers flickered at his side, but he didn't reach for his pocket. "What about Morgan, then? We know you'd been speaking to them quite a bit, particularly in the days leading up to Erik's death. Care to explain why?"

Astrid straightened her back, her hand returning to her lap. "Morgan has been a loyal follower since they arrived. A guiding voice in the Circle when others have faltered."

Mo nodded. "Did Morgan attempt to rid Erik of his doubts, then?"

"Morgan did nothing that might have caused Erik distress. If you're trying to pin this tragedy on one of my Circle, you'll need far better evidence than hearsay and assumptions."

"So you're saying no one from the Circle could've been involved?"

"Absolutely." Astrid stood up. Petra, now feeling at a distinct disadvantage on the floor, stood too, taking pain to disguise how difficult that was.

"This was the act of an outsider," Astrid said. "A villager, perhaps. You've seen how they resent us being here. 'Outcasts,' one of them called us the other day at the harbour."

Mo narrowed his eyes. "But we have no evidence that the villagers regarded you with quite such a degree of hostility."

Astrid leaned forward. "I believe outsiders are far more dangerous than anyone you'll find here. Your suspicion is misplaced, Detective."

Mo glanced back at Petra. They weren't going to get anything useful here, and they both knew it.

CHAPTER THIRTY-SEVEN

JADE SAT AT HER DESK, the post-mortem report on her screen. Her phone lay just to the side, close enough to glance at every few seconds but far enough away that she wouldn't snatch it up prematurely. No missed calls. No messages. She exhaled sharply. The waiting was starting to get to her.

She looked back at the report. Erik Haldane's cause of death: a single, precise stab wound. The forensic pathologist had noted that his injuries were consistent with the blade of the dagger found in Morgan's sleeping bag. But then there was the kicker – the part that had her frowning into the dim glow of the desk lamp. The lack of tissue between the serrations. And the blood.

According to Rohan, Erik's blood hadn't been deposited during the attack. It was smeared onto the blade afterwards. But why? It made no sense.

She leaned back, sighing. Patty's voice brought her out of her thoughts.

"You look like you're trying to bore a hole through that

screen," Patty said, setting a mug of coffee down on the desk next to her.

The doctor had told her to limit her caffeine intake. But she was a DI; she needed coffee to function.

Jade tilted the screen towards her. "The blood on the dagger wasn't the result of the stabbing – it was added later. Planted, even."

Patty frowned. "So it wasn't used to kill him?"

"That's the thing. The wound matches. But there was no tissue between the serrations. Rohan said it had never been used. But if that *was* the knife, why clean it and then smear the blood back on? And if it wasn't, where's the real weapon?"

Patty folded her arms, her no-nonsense expression firmly in place. "Could there be another blade? Maybe one with an identical edge?"

Jade pinpointed the section of the report that detailed the serrations and carvings on the handle. She zoomed in on an image of the weapon. The notches on the blade were uneven, distinctive.

"If there's another one," she said, "it'd have to be an almost perfect match."

Patty reached for her own mug again. "What about the carvings?"

Jade squinted at the decorative markings on the photo of the handle – intertwined, almost knot-like. "There are no specific symbols or runes as far as I can tell. Nothing Norse, and nothing else, either. Just... abstract."

Patty sniffed. "Might be worth having another set of eyes on it."

Jade grunted. The last time they'd brought in an external

expert, it had been a Macbeth scholar who'd turned out to be the killer.

Her phone buzzed against the desk: Mo.

"Finally," she muttered, swiping to pick up. "Tell me you've had a breakthrough."

Mo's voice was calm. "Not exactly. I'm just as confused as you. We've just been with Astrid, but she's slippery. Nothing concrete. Same with Morgan."

Jade pinched the bridge of her nose. "That knife's a problem, Mo. If the blood was planted, then someone's trying to frame Morgan. This whole thing's starting to stink."

"Or," said Mo, "it's a red herring. To throw us off entirely."

Jade's shoulders slumped further. "Could be. But we haven't got much left to go on, have we? What about Freya?"

"She's scared," said Mo. "Terrified, actually. I reckon she thinks she might be next."

"Do you believe her confession?"

Mo inhaled. On the line, Jade could hear birdsong. It made her think of Dan, and then Fraser. She smiled.

"No," Mo said. "But I certainly believe she's scared. Whether it's guilt or someone really is after her, I can't say."

Jade considered. "Hold her for as long as we can without charging her. See what else she gives us. And keep her out of harm's way."

"What if she gives us nothing?"

She twisted her lips together. "We let her go. But not before I talk to Liddy again. She knows more than she's letting on, and if anyone's going to give us something close to the truth about what's happened at that camp, it's her."

"Let's hope so. Let me know what you get. I'll chase down anything else Freya lets slip."

Jade ended the call and slouched back in her chair, staring at the image of the knife still zoomed on her screen. The ornate carvings almost seemed to shift under the light, inviting interpretation, but offering none. Someone had gone through a lot of trouble to use it – or make it seem as though it had been used.

She thought of Erik, his bloodied body in that rowing boat, and shut the laptop. There were too many theories swirling in her head, and her brain felt like it was full of fog. She rubbed her eyes, wishing all this was easier.

CHAPTER THIRTY-EIGHT

Mo ENDED the call with the DI, got out of his car and scanned the campsite for Alistair MacLeod. The professor stood near a sleek silver Mercedes, in quiet conversation with a tall, broad-shouldered man in a sharp suit. Charles McIntosh, the lawyer. Alistair was bouncing on the balls of his feet, arms crossed tightly across his chest. The lawyer placed a firm hand on Alistair's shoulder, leaning in with a few measured words before catching sight of Mo.

Mo picked up his pace, making a beeline for the pair. "Professor MacLeod," he called out.

Alistair fixed Mo with a thin-lipped smile. "Ah, DS Uddin. Good timing. I was just explaining to my solicitor here that I'm happy to cooperate. Naturally, though, we'll need appropriate conditions for any further discussion."

Mo frowned. "Conditions?"

McIntosh stepped forward, all professional polish. "My client has no intention of speaking with you in that tent, DS Uddin. Frankly, it's unsuitable for a formal conversation, and I'm sure you'll agree we don't want anything to risk procedural integrity. I've arranged for us to use a private room in the village hall instead."

Mo's pulse ticked up. "The village hall," he repeated. McIntosh couldn't mean the community centre; they were using that for their incident room.

"It's just that way." The lawyer opened the car door for Alistair with a flourish. Alistair ducked inside while his lawyer's eyes lingered on Mo, a faint smirk on his lips. He rounded the bonnet and slid into the driver's seat. The engine growled low as the car nudged onto the gravel track.

"Like hell," Mo muttered.

He turned back towards the yurt. "Stuart!" he shouted. "Petra! Both of you – get to the car, *now!*"

Petra emerged from the yurt. Stuart had been by one of the smaller tents, talking to Wendy. "What's going on?"

"We need to move!" Mo snapped, already jogging to his car.

Petra was with him surprisingly quickly. "What's he done now?" Her hair was still intact despite the rush.

"Off to the village hall with his brief," Mo hissed. "Wherever that is."

Stuart arrived, looking vaguely sheepish. "He'd better not be going for the ferry," he grumbled, yanking the passenger door open as Petra got into the back.

Mo started the engine. *Let's hope not.*

They bumped along the gravel track, driving much too fast for the surface. Stuart tapped on the dashboard while Petra sat unnervingly still, her sharp gaze fixed out the window.

"We're all going to end up with blood pressure issues, you know," she muttered.

Mo ignored her and turned sharply to the right as they hit the main road. The Mercedes had gone off that way.

Lochranza was barely half a mile from the campsite, but it felt like far more. The sleek Mercedes was nowhere in sight, but Mo had noted the buildings and thought he knew where they might be heading.

The castle was visible on the right as he spotted the car. It was off to the left, parked outside a low white building. Mo yanked on the steering wheel to take the turn and park beside it.

Inside the village hall, an elderly woman stood in the hallway, clutching an oversized keyring. She did a double-take as Mo and the others entered with impatience and cold air streaming off them.

"You with Mr McIntosh?" she asked warily.

"That's right," Mo said, pulling out his ID. "Which room?"

She pointed, looking puzzled and a little scared. "Back corridor. Room Two. He told me he'd be bringing the police, all sorted ahead of time."

Mo wondered how embedded Alistair's solicitor was in the life of this island. "Thank you. Please, which way was it again?"

She opened a door, letting them into the corridor. "Second door on the left."

Mo marched down the hall, Petra and Stuart trailing behind. Most of the rooms were empty, frosted glass affording glimpses of mismatched chairs and abandoned noticeboards. Mo pushed open a door marked 'Room Two' to reveal a simple, square space with a large wooden table and four folding chairs.

Empty. The professor and his solicitous lawyer were yet to make their grand entrance.

Mo let out a breath and turned to Stuart. "Where the hell are they?"

A shrug. "Beats me, Sarge. What did he say?"

Petra turned back along the corridor. "They're here."

So they'd got to the building before them, reserved a room, and left them to arrive alone. Some kind of power play? Or were they simply conferring in advance?

And what should he read into it, if anything?

"OK," he said. "Time to see what Alistair MacLeod has to say for himself."

Mo took a seat by the window and stared at the table, the laminated surface scratched and dented from years of use. He folded his arms, deliberately making himself look broader as he watched Alistair settle into the chair opposite. The professor's knee bounced under the table, his fingers fidgeting with his jacket cuffs. Beside him, Charles McIntosh sat like a statue – calm, aloof, his grey suit immaculate.

Petra perched on a chair in the corner, sighing as she crossed one leg over the other. She looked bored, but Mo knew she wasn't. Her sharp eyes missed nothing.

Stuart was to Mo's right, fumbling with a recording app on his phone. The DC's shirt was patched with sweat. His usual confident demeanour had been replaced with a quiet determination.

Mo leaned forward, resting his forearms on the table. "Right then, Professor," he said, voice even. "We'll skip the small talk, shall we?"

Alistair smirked. "How charming, Sergeant. Straight to the point."

"Let's talk about Erik Haldane."

The smirk disappeared. Alistair folded his arms, mirroring Mo's posture. "What, specifically? You'll need to be more precise."

"What was his role in your group?" Mo asked.

Alistair glanced at McIntosh, who gave a faint nod. "He was a member. Enthusiastic, mostly. Passionate about the cause. A... sensitive soul, I'd say."

Petra snorted softly from her corner. Alistair's gaze flicked towards her, irritation flashing across his face.

"Sensitive," Mo repeated. "And yet, we've heard from others that he was having doubts about your 'cause.' That he didn't agree with some of the things Astrid believed in."

Alistair's face hardened. "Is that so? Well, I suppose people can read into things whatever they like. Erik cared deeply about what Astrid was doing. Perhaps his emotions got the better of him at times, but that's hardly unusual in an intense setting, is it?"

Mo leaned in. "Intense? Is that how you'd describe your group's rituals? Intense enough to end with Erik dead in a boat at the castle?"

McIntosh broke in. "DS Uddin, unless you're accusing my client of something specific, I'd advise steering clear of inflammatory statements like that."

Mo took a breath. *Don't let him rattle you.* "Let's refocus," he said, looking at Alistair. "Did Erik have conflicts with anyone? Astrid, for example?"

Alistair shrugged, shifting in his chair. "Astrid? Hardly. If anything, Erik was fiercely loyal to her. You've spoken to Morgan, haven't you? Erik spent most of his time trying to keep everything calm and harmonious during... difficult moments."

"Difficult moments like what?"

"Personal matters," Alistair said dismissively. "Nothing relevant to your investigation. You'd be better off asking Astrid herself."

Mo caught Petra rolling her eyes out of the corner of his eye. He decided to push harder. "We're hearing about tensions within the group, Professor. Erik questioning Astrid's leadership, people feeling uneasy about the rituals she was pushing for. Are you saying none of that rings true?"

Alistair's shoulders stiffened. "If someone was unhappy, they should have brought it up directly."

"Maybe they tried, and Astrid wouldn't listen."

"Nonsense," Alistair snapped. "Astrid's far more patient than most would be in her position. Erik didn't have a problem with her leadership."

"What about Freya, then?" Mo asked. "Were there any issues between them?"

Alistair hesitated. "Well," he began, his voice lighter, "Let's just say there's more to that story than you might think."

Stuart, who'd remained silent so far, furrowed his brow. "What's that supposed to mean?"

Alistair tilted his head, his tone turning conversational. "Simply that their relationship was complex. More so than your little tick-box questions might reveal."

"Stop skirting, Professor," Mo said. "If you've got something to say, just say it."

Alistair shrugged, almost too casually. "Fine. If you must know, I think you're looking in the wrong direction. I believe Erik and Astrid were... involved. Romantically."

Mo froze. Even Stuart's hands stilled over his phone as Petra straightened in her seat, her expression unreadable.

"Is that a fact," Mo said flatly.

Alistair smirked again. "Call it an observation from someone with eyes."

"Observation," Mo repeated.

"That's right."

"Any evidence to back this observation?"

Another shrug. "Do I need evidence to notice chemistry, Sergeant?" His tone was mockingly polite. "Things were... intimate between them. I'm simply providing context."

"Context," Petra muttered.

Mo ignored the comment, staring at Alistair. "So you've got nothing solid. No proof. Just a story to throw everyone off."

"Believe what you want," Alistair replied. He shifted uneasily.

Mo leaned back, allowing the silence to settle. He glanced at Petra. She gave him the faintest shrug: *he's full of it*.

"Thanks for clearing that up," Mo said dryly. He looked at McIntosh. "Suppose you'll be wanting a word with your client after all this. We might have more questions later."

McIntosh gave an almost imperceptible nod, but Alistair's scowl said it all. Mo stood, gesturing for Stuart to cut the recorder. Petra's gaze lingered on Alistair as she got to her feet.

Outside, Mo turned to Stuart. "This lot are going to run us in circles before we get close to the truth."

Stuart nodded. "You're right, Sarge. But I reckon there's more he's hiding."

Petra brushed non-existent dust from her sleeve. "Oh, he's hiding alright. But the question is, is Freya in the kind of danger she thinks she is, or are this lot just full of hot air?"

CHAPTER THIRTY-NINE

THE GLASGOW RAIN pelted against the car's windscreen, the wipers struggling to keep up as Jade gripped the wheel tighter. Easterhouse wasn't far from the office, but the wet-weather traffic turned a ten-minute drive into double that. Beside her, Patty scrolled through her mobile, her lips pressed into a firm line.

Jade broke the silence, her voice low but tense. "So. She might not be in, but I wanted to try. She hasn't returned any of my calls."

Patty nodded. "I just tried again. No answer."

Jade sighed. Turning up at Liddy Drummond's house like this was a long shot, but at least they didn't have far to go.

Patty sniffed. "If she knows anything helpful, she'll talk. She called you first, didn't she? That's got to mean something."

Jade knew Liddy might clam up. Victims or witnesses – or however you classified someone like Liddy Drummond – were unreliable at best when it came to dealing with cults or fringe groups. Fear, pride, or some warped sense of loyalty could make them retreat. Jade tapped her thumb against the steering wheel as they passed a row of modern semis on the right.

"It's the one on the end," she said.

Patty peered out at the small front garden. Liddy's house was neat, the neighbour's not so much: a wheelie bin lay on its side, rubbish spilling out.

"Cheerful," the DC said.

Jade pulled into a space along the road and stepped out into the rain. Patty followed, her coat pulled tight as they approached the grey front door. Jade rang the bell then knocked for good measure.

It took a full minute before the door opened a crack. Liddy Drummond wore mismatched tracksuit bottoms and an oversized hoodie, her hair tied up in a loose bun.

"What do you want?" she asked, her voice sharp but edged with fatigue.

"Liddy, we need to talk," Jade said. "It's about the Circle."

Liddy glanced past them into the street. "You... you didn't call ahead."

"I've been calling all day. Can we come in? It won't take long."

Liddy hesitated before stepping back and motioning them inside. The house smelled faintly of damp washing. An overloaded clothes horse stood in the corner of the living room, next to a worn sofa draped in a blanket. Liddy walked over to a half-empty coffee table, swept aside some mugs, and sat on the edge of the sofa.

Jade sat down across from her. Patty took an uncomfortable-looking armchair.

"What's this about?" Liddy asked. "I already told you everything I know." She glanced towards the window.

Not scared, surely?

"The cult," Jade replied. "We need to know more about Astrid. And Alistair."

Liddy barked out a laugh. "Calling it a 'cult' now?"

Jade kept her tone neutral. "Call it whatever you want, the Circle is at the centre of everything that's happened. And we both know it."

Liddy shook her head. "I told you what Astrid was capable of. And about Erik."

"We've been looking into them," Jade said. "But some of what you've said isn't adding up. For instance, you mentioned a ritual with a goat."

Liddy's eyes brightened. "Have you followed up on that?"

"There's no evidence of the Circle procuring a goat. None," Jade said. "But there have been mentions of... rituals. What kind of rituals are we talking about, Liddy?"

Liddy exhaled sharply. "She's dangerous, you know. You need to shut them down. Her business, this whole thing – it's all just a front. Astrid's using it to make money, same as she always has."

Liddy fumbled for a cigarette, lighting it despite the slight tremor in her hands. She blew smoke towards the ceiling, avoiding eye contact.

"Erik objected to something. What was it?"

Liddy leaned forward, letting ash crumble onto the floor. "He saw her for what she was. That's why he's dead. Do you get that? She killed him."

The sound of rain hammering on the windows filled the

silence. Jade rested her elbows on her knees and met Liddy's gaze.

"Do you have evidence? Anything solid to back that up?"

Liddy's nose twitched. "I don't."

"If we're to investigate this properly, we can't act on accusations alone. Not without evidence."

"Evidence?" Liddy spat the word. "Look, Astrid's clever. Do you think she'd let anything lead back to her? She's always a step ahead. Always."

Patty cleared her throat. "You know these people better than we do. If you've got something, now's the time to share it."

"It's not that simple," Liddy muttered. She scratched at the side of her neck, her knee jiggling nervously. "Everything they do is wrapped up in nonsense. Runes, chants, 'sacred' texts. It's enough to confuse anyone."

"You came to us for help," Jade said. "We need more from you. Who else might have pushed things too far?"

Liddy stared at the cigarette as it burned low. "You're focused on Astrid, and maybe that's my fault, but Alistair's just as bad. Worse, maybe. He feeds her ideas. Makes them sound academic."

"Explain that," Jade said.

"You think she came up with all this on her own?" Liddy answered, her voice hard. "No. Alistair's the one with the brains. She's just the face. They make a perfect pair. But if..."

Jade tilted her head. "What?"

"If you're serious about stopping them," Liddy muttered, "you'll have to act soon. Before they do something worse." She stubbed out the cigarette. "But you won't, will you? Because there's no 'evidence.' Just like you said."

Jade eyed the younger woman. "What about Morgan? Were you close to them?"

Liddy's frown deepened. "Nobody's really 'close' with anyone in that group – not properly. Astrid doesn't allow it."

"What does that mean?" Patty asked.

Liddy gave her a look. "Morgan's being used, like all of them. But Astrid's got her claws in deep. She's manipulative – knows exactly how to play on someone's insecurities. And Morgan? They've got plenty."

"How was Astrid taking advantage of them?" Jade asked.

Liddy reached for another cigarette but seemed to think better of it. "Morgan's vulnerable. You don't need to be a psychologist to see that. They were desperate for acceptance, for a place to belong, and Astrid gave them that. Or made them think she did. She's got them convinced they're some kind of chosen disciple. They'll do anything for her."

Jade straightened in her seat. "Anything – including committing a crime?"

Liddy shrugged. "It wouldn't surprise me. Astrid wraps people around her little finger. Makes them think her approval's the only thing that matters. Morgan worships her."

"But?" Jade pressed.

"But Morgan didn't kill Erik."

Jade exchanged a glance with Patty. "Why not?"

Liddy stubbed out her cigarette and leaned back against the sofa, crossing her arms. "Erik died on Monday night, right?"

Jade nodded slowly. "He did. Why do you ask?"

"Because Morgan was on a Zoom call with me on Monday night."

Jade felt herself stiffen. "Zoom?"

Liddy nodded. "They didn't want to be overheard, so they went somewhere away from the camp. They were rattled – something had happened. They didn't say much, but we were on that call from six until just before seven."

Jade leaned forward, her mind already piecing together the implications. "Morgan told our officers they were at the camp with Astrid. Apparently, they performed a ritual at sunset."

Liddy shrugged. "They lied then. They were talking to me."

"That's only an hour of the evening," Jade said. "They could've been with Astrid before or after that."

"They weren't," Liddy replied. "They wanted to get as far away from the others as possible. They told me they caught a bus to Brodick."

Jade frowned, processing this new information. "Brodick? Are you sure?"

"You can look it up if you don't believe me," Liddy said, a defensive edge creeping into her voice. "Check the bus schedules – sunset was, what, around sixish? They were talking to me at that time. Not with Astrid."

Jade glanced at Patty, who leaned back in her chair, her expression thoughtful. If Morgan wasn't at the camp, where did that leave their alibi – or Astrid's?

"You're certain about the time?" Jade asked, her tone sharper. "No chance you've got it wrong?"

"Certain." Liddy's jaw tightened. "Morgan was in Brodick that night. You can check the CCTV, the timetables, whatever you need. I'm telling you, they weren't there."

CHAPTER FORTY

THE COMMUNITY CENTRE, with its makeshift incident room, was closer to the village hall than the campsite was. Petra didn't need Mo to tell her that even if they planned to speak to Astrid again, they needed to confer first. And it was getting dark. Without speaking, he turned left out of the village hall and made for the centre of the village, the castle staring out across the loch to their right.

Mo's phone buzzed from its holder on the dashboard, and he glanced at it before accepting the call. "Boss," he said, flicking it onto speaker. "What's the latest?"

Petra leaned forward between the seats to listen in.

"Patty and I have been with Liddy," Jade began. "She's saying Morgan wasn't with Astrid when they claim to have been. She reckons Morgan was on a Zoom call with her at the time Erik was killed."

Mo glanced across at Stuart. "Can she prove it?"

"We can access her account details. And Patty's already checked bus timetables, along with the time of sunset. If she's telling the truth, there's no way that Morgan and Astrid did some sunset ritual together that night, let alone talked until midnight."

Petra leaned further forward to make herself heard. "If Morgan lied about their alibi, they might be covering for Astrid."

"Not for themself?" asked Jade.

"I'm increasingly coming to the view that Morgan is an innocent victim in all this."

Mo gave a slow nod. "We've just been talking to Alistair MacLeod. He's alleging that Astrid and Erik were having an affair. I think he's trying to throw her under the bus."

These people, Petra thought. They certainly hated each other.

Mo was looking at the phone. "Can you let us know when you've confirmed from the Zoom account?"

"Of course. And talk to me if you're planning on interviewing Astrid. If we need to caution her, I want to know." Jade ended the call.

Petra whistled. "That's going to stir the pot."

"Stirring's what we need," Mo said. "This whole case is like digging through quicksand."

The car pulled into the small parking area outside the community centre and Mo jumped out. Petra lingered, one foot on the tarmac, checking an incoming text as Mo and Stuart headed inside.

Shit. She raised her hand to stall them as her phone buzzed again.

"I've got a call to deal with. You go on," she said, turning to head for the shelter of a bus stop opposite.

"You're sure?" Mo asked.

She nodded, already waiting for the call to connect.

As the two men headed inside, the call connected. It was Aila, her ex. She felt goosebumps prickle her skin as Aila's voice came over the line.

"Petra. How are you?"

Formal, then. "I'm fine. Is everything OK?" She hadn't heard from Aila for months, not since Aila had told her they couldn't be together if Petra didn't face up to her demons.

"Fine. Well, I'm fine. You... Well, you need to know something."

Petra felt a lump form in her throat. "What?"

"I... I went to your flat today. I left some books behind. I know it's been a while, but... sorry I didn't say anything sooner."

Petra didn't remember seeing any books she didn't recognise. But then, Petra had a lot of books. "I'm not there," she said. "I'm away on a job."

"Isle of Arran. Yeah, I know. Look..."

Petra waited.

"Aila, what's up?"

"I spoke to your neighbours, those guys downstairs."

"OK." Petra couldn't see what this had to do with anything.

"They've been trying to contact you, apparently. Your flat was broken into."

"What?" Petra glanced up at the community centre, pushing the phone closer to her ear. "What did you say?"

"Sorry, Petra. I know this isn't great, when you're away... but they've trashed the place. I know you're having decorating work done. And..."

Petra was getting worried now. "What is it, Aila? Can you just tell me?"

"Sorry. Yeah. Look, they took the paint that was out, waiting to be used I guess. And they wrote on your wall."

Petra felt her blood run cold. "What did they write?"

"It's..."

"What did they write, Aila?"

"I'm sorry Petra. But they wrote *KILLER*."

CHAPTER FORTY-ONE

Inside the community centre, Wendy was pacing across the makeshift incident room, wringing her hands like she was auditioning for a part in *Macbeth*. She looked at Mo and Stuart as they entered, her eyes wide with eagerness.

"You're going to want to see this," she blurted, motioning them towards the table. Set before her was a laptop, its screen displaying paused footage. "It came in anonymously to Crimestoppers late last night. We've only just had it forwarded."

Mo stepped closer, Stuart tight on his heels. "What are we looking at?"

"Video footage," Wendy explained. There was a tremor of excitement in her voice. "Captured early in the morning, along the beach between the castle and the ferry terminal. It's meant to be seals – it's mostly seals – but... well, have a look."

She pressed play.

The grainy video came to life, its timestamp blinking: 7:24 on Tuesday morning. Waves mirrored the overcast sky, and in the foreground, seals lolled on the shore. But as the camera panned, catching the silhouette of Lochranza Castle in the distance, a figure appeared – just barely visible at first.

"Pause it." Mo leaned closer.

Wendy froze the frame.

The figure wore something long and flowing – a dress, it seemed, shifting in the breeze. The distance made it impossible to see the face, but the person moved with purpose, bending down to conceal something among the rocks.

They watched in silence.

"Shit," Stuart muttered.

Mo swallowed. "Play it again."

Wendy rewound the footage and hit play, slower this time. As the figure disappeared from view, Mo frowned.

"That timestamp..." he said. "Early in the morning, some time after Erik was killed. But it's not clear enough for an ID."

"I thought the same," Wendy admitted. "But it's a woman, or at least someone wearing a dress."

"Can you blow it up?"

Wendy froze on the clearest frame and magnified the shot. It was impossible to see the face, but the shape was feminine – a clear waist, long dark hair.

The door behind them creaked, making Mo jump. Petra walked in, shoving her phone into her pocket. She looked haunted.

"What's happened?" she asked.

Mo gave her a look. "Come and see."

She moved in. Wendy played the footage again.

"Shit," Petra muttered.

"You recognise something?" Mo asked.

Petra tapped the screen with her manicured nail, her expression grim. "That dress. I saw it. In Astrid's yurt."

The dress was long and flowing, with a swirly pattern and a wide, tied belt. It didn't look like the kind of thing you'd pick up on the high street.

Mo straightened. "You're sure?"

"As sure as I am about anything in this bloody case." Petra folded her arms. "It was hanging on the far side of the yurt, near the candles. Distinctive pattern – Norse symbols stitched into the hem."

Wendy looked uneasily between them. "We need to figure out what they were hiding, too."

Mo nodded slowly. "Rewind it again. See if we can pinpoint the exact location."

Wendy played the footage again, her finger hovering over the pause button. As they neared the moment where the figure bent down near the rocks, Mo pointed. "There. Slow it."

Wendy paused, frame by frame, until the woman's hands vanished beneath a cluster of large rocks near some bushes.

"That's where we start," Mo said. "Stuart?"

"On it." Stuart's chair scraped back loudly as he shot to his feet, already grabbing his coat before Mo could say more. He was out the door in seconds.

Wendy perched on the edge of the desk, rubbing at her temple. "The footage came in anonymously. No names, no number, just dropped in the system."

Mo leaned against the back of a chair. "Whoever sent it wanted us to see this, though."

"They might be scared," Petra said. "Astrid's not exactly the forgiving type."

"Or," Wendy suggested, "they're just trying to stay out of whatever this is."

Mo wasn't so sure. "Either way, we need to find out why they filmed this – and whether there's more."

He sat in the chair, his mind racing. "Play it for me again."

Wendy handed over the phone, pressing play as she did so.

Mo watched again. The figure was vague, shaded. But the shape... it was a woman. A tall woman.

Like...

The door slammed open.

"Sarge!" Stuart burst in, holding up an evidence bag. His breathing came fast and his face was flushed.

Inside the bag was a torn sarong, dark patches staining its thin fabric. "Found it right where the video showed."

Mo took it from him carefully, his throat tightening at the sight of the blotches. Blood. Too much blood. A glance back at the screen lingered on the shadowed figure in the dress.

"Well," Petra murmured, "that changes things."

Mo turned to Wendy, his heart racing. "Get it to the lab. Now."

CHAPTER FORTY-TWO

BACK AT THE CCU OFFICE, Jade blinked to focus on the papers in front of her. Notes from Liddy's interview, Erik's post-mortem results, and a half-finished cup of tea littered her desk.

She didn't need to look up to know Patty hadn't left. The DC was standing by the door, coat on, hat pulled firmly down on her head. But she was watching Jade. Jade was avoiding her eye, but she knew when she was being stared at.

She looked down at her hands. *Stay still.*

"You're overdoing it again," said Patty.

Jade resisted a sigh. "I'm fine."

"You're not fine, boss." Patty took a step forward. "I saw your hand shaking earlier. And don't tell me it's the coffee. You always drink coffee."

"Patty—"

"Look, this isn't a courtesy check-in. You *need* to see someone. A doctor. Not just for your sake, but for Rory's. You're driving yourself into the ground."

Jade bristled. She was Patty's boss, but the years had brought familiarity. Only Patty could tell it like it was.

"I've already told you I'm fine. Can we just get back to the case? Erik Haldane? Ritual sacrifice, maybe? Those things?"

"Not until we sort this out," Patty fired back. She pushed the door shut and walked back, perching on the chair opposite Jade's desk. Her tone softened as she leaned forward. "Whatever's up, it's bigger than just being tired. What is it? Is it serious?"

Jade glared down at her papers, wishing for an escape route. *I'm not ready*. "I've got everything under control. I don't need a bloody intervention."

Patty pulled in a breath. "And I don't need to be a detective to know you're hiding something. You're my boss, I can't tell you what to do. But I'm worried about you."

"No. You can't." Jade looked up, instantly feeling guilty. Patty wasn't Stuart, or even Mo. Patty had been there when Dan had died. She'd covered for Jade, helped her juggle her commitments so she could still be a mum for Rory while continuing to earn a living.

"You're scaring me, boss. I've worked under plenty of bosses who've burned themselves out. I'm not letting you go down the same road."

Shoving the papers aside, Jade finally looked Patty in the eye. She stared at the DC for a moment, weighing up her options.

I haven't even told Fraser.

"I've already been to a doctor," she said.

Patty blinked, waiting for more.

"I've got an... early diagnosis," Jade continued, her voice faltering. She hesitated. "They're calling it the early stages of MS. Multiple sclerosis, if you want the full name."

Patty's expression turned to shock, then softened quickly to quiet acceptance. It wasn't pity, though. Patty didn't do pity. She hadn't when Jade was widowed, and she wouldn't now.

The DC cocked her head. "And you didn't tell me because..."

"I don't want people looking at me like I'm broken... or like I'm about to drop the ball on a case."

Patty leaned back. "But not telling *anyone*? That'll only make it harder."

"The high-ups would ship me off to some desk job faster than you can say 'reasonable adjustments.' I'm not done with the CCU. I can handle it... I just need to figure this out on my terms."

Patty studied Jade's face. Jade tried to imagine how Fraser would look at her, when she told him.

"Right now, it's manageable," Jade added. "Some days are better than others, but it's not... it's not something I can't work through."

Patty crossed her arms. "So what happens when it *isn't* manageable anymore? What if it flares up at the worst possible time? Like when you're chasing some lunatic through the woods or trying to stop Stuart throttling a suspect?"

Jade grunted a laugh. "If that happens, I'll say something. I'm not an idiot, Patty. But you've got to let me decide what I can handle."

Patty gave a slow nod. "Alright. It's your life. But if I catch you putting your health at risk or hiding something again..."

Jade smiled. "You'll stage another intervention?"

"You bet your arse I will." Patty's lips twitched into a smile, quickly replaced by sternness. "For what it's worth, Jade, I can see you're scared. And that's fine. That's normal. But this isn't the sort of thing you deal with on your own."

Jade leaned back, her hand drifting toward her mug: *conversation over*. "I'm used to dealing with stuff on my own."

"And that's the problem," Patty muttered. "You need to lean on me, like you have before. And..." She stood up, pulling her hat down again. "And you need to tell the super."

CHAPTER FORTY-THREE

THE PUB WAS BUSTLING, the hum of conversation mingling with the clinking of glasses and the occasional burst of laughter. Mo knew that the villagers were looking across at them repeatedly, but he'd decided to ignore it.

He took a long sip of his ginger beer, his attention flickering between Stuart, grinning at one of his own jokes, and Petra, who seemed to be somewhere else entirely. She hadn't touched her wine. Her hands stayed clasped around the thin stem of the glass, fingers tense.

Stuart didn't seem to notice. "That sarong nails her, doesn't it? Blood on it, near the scene – it's hers, isn't it? Astrid's got to be our killer."

Mo frowned. "Keep your voice down."

"Sorry, sarge. But I'm right, yes?"

Mo placed his glass down. "The lab hasn't confirmed anything yet. We've got to be methodical."

Stuart huffed but didn't argue. Instead, he drained his drink and shook his empty glass. "Right, I'm off to the loo. Another round after?"

Mo gave a nod, watching as Stuart navigated a path between the tables towards the toilets. Once the DC had gone, Mo turned to Petra. Her gaze was fixed on a knot in the worn table, her expression distant.

"Petra." He kept his voice low. "You alright?"

She blinked and let out a breath. "What?"

"You seem... distracted. Has something happened? You took a call, earlier."

Her lips pressed into a thin line, then parted. She hesitated. Mo waited. Finally, she leaned back in her chair and wrinkled up her nose. "My flat's been broken into."

Mo straightened up in his seat. "You're joking. When?"

"Got the call earlier today. Aila – my ex – she went in to get some of her stuff. Should have got her key off her, but I guess it's a good job I didn't. She rang me about it." Her voice was hollow.

"Was she there when it happened?"

"No." Petra shook her head. "She went in after and found the place turned upside down. The police reckon... well, the police don't reckon much. Aila's secured the place, but..." Her fingers tightened on her glass.

"But what?"

Petra glanced up at him. "It's not a coincidence, Mo. It can't be. There's been... incidents lately. Notes through the door. Messages online. And now this. They... they left a message, if you can call it that. Someone's targeting me."

Mo felt an urge to put a hand over hers. "Petra, you've got to go home. Sort this out. No question."

Her shoulders stiffened. "I don't want to leave you lot in the lurch. You're stretched as it is."

"Rubbish. You've already given us your initial report,

haven't you? We're at the stage where we're working through the video evidence and forensics. We can manage while you deal with this."

She looked at him, trying to gauge whether he meant it. Eventually, she gave a brief nod. "I'll work on collating my thoughts on the journey. Try to send something comprehensive by the end of tomorrow. I've been thinking about Morgan and Astrid. About why Morgan might've given Astrid that fake alibi."

Mo leaned forward. "That'd be appreciated. But seriously, get on that ferry first thing."

"When I spoke to Aila, she said the place is safe now, but... I hate the idea of them coming back." Petra pushed her glass away with a grunt.

"Then get back fast. We can cope. Tomorrow, yes?"

She shrugged. "I've got to run it by Jade, but I'd like to catch the early crossing tomorrow. In and out. One night there. Two, at most." She paused. "I need to talk to the builders. Call off the work."

"You can't face finishing it?"

Her lips twisted into a half-smile. "I've lost my enthusiasm for it."

He held her gaze for a silent moment. He'd never seen her vulnerable like this. And she'd never mentioned someone targeting her.

Did the DI know about this?

Before he could ask anything more, Stuart reappeared, shrugging his way back into his seat. "What'd I miss?"

Petra gave Mo a warning look and plastered on a faint smile. "Not much. Just discussing decorating disasters."

"Decorating? What for?"

Petra raised her glass, feigning a toast. "Because I'm bloody terrible at it." She gave Mo a warning look: *this conversation didn't happen.*

CHAPTER FORTY-FOUR

Freya sat cross-legged in the centre of her tent, staring at her phone. She didn't like being back here, wished they'd let her stay at the police station. She screwed up her face as she read the message again.

Ask Alistair about the knife.

Liddy's text offered no explanation, no follow-up. That was typical of her: cryptic. Freya typed a response.

What knife?

She hit send and waited. The seconds ticked by on her charity shop watch. No reply.

What knife? Did Liddy mean the one they'd found in Morgan's tent? Or some other knife? How could Liddy know anything about it?

The low hum of an engine broke through her thoughts. A car. The police? Or someone else?

She grabbed her jumper from under the sleeping bag and pulled it over her head. Her feet were bare against the damp ground as she scrambled to the tent flap. Unzipping it halfway, she peered into the darkness.

A set of headlights cut through the damp night, behind them the shape of a Mercedes rolling into the campsite. Not the police. Alistair, and his fancy solicitor.

She pressed her palm to the cold canvas of the tent to steady herself and forced her breathing to slow.

The car door opened, and Alistair climbed out. He looked older in the dark, his woollen coat crumpled like he'd thrown it on in a hurry. He glanced across the campsite, then made his way towards Astrid's yurt at the far end.

Freya shoved her phone into her pocket and stepped out of her tent. The night air jabbed at her skin. She quickened her pace.

"Alistair."

He turned, frowning until recognition softened his features. "Freya." He sounded tired. "Are you alright? I'm so sorry about Erik." He stepped closer, putting out an arm then withdrawing it. "How are you holding up?"

Freya blinked. The last person she expected false sympathy from was Alistair. She pushed back the lump in her throat. "I need to ask you something."

He tilted his head. "Of course. Anything."

"The knife," she said. "The one that killed Erik... what do you know about it?"

The frown was back. "What're you talking about?"

"The knife, Alistair." She stepped forward. "Where did it come from?"

He gave a short, humourless laugh. "How the bloody hell am I supposed to know? I'm an academic, Freya, not a bloody bladesmith."

Freya stared at him. "It must've been part of a ritual. One of the artefacts, maybe."

He shook his head. "You're grasping at straws." He

smiled. "Goodnight, Freya," he said, turning away. A breeze caught his coat as he made for Astrid's yurt. The door flapped open, swallowing him up before she could get another word in.

Freya stood there, suddenly aware of how cold her feet were. The campsite was alive with nighttime sounds – the rustle of wind through the trees, the distant thrum of waves against the shore. She grabbed her phone and stared at Liddy's number.

Ask Alistair about the knife.

She'd asked. She'd just got a denial. She didn't even know why she'd asked. She opened the text thread again and typed.

I spoke to him. He wouldn't tell me anything. What do I do?

Her finger hovered over the send button.

She had no one to tell her what to do – not Erik, not anyone. She was alone. Liddy didn't care about her. She had her own agenda, and Freya wasn't entirely sure what that was.

She deleted the message and hurried back to her tent, wishing she'd never ventured outside.

CHAPTER FORTY-FIVE

NEWTON ROAD WAS a peaceful stretch of tarmac that gave way to packed dirt as DS Mo Uddin walked further along the track. He passed the *No cars beyond this point* sign, level with the last house, and pushed out a long, slow breath.

The air was cool, faintly salty from the sea to his left, and alive with the rustling of grass blown by the breeze. With every footstep, the muffled sounds of Lochranza – the occasional hum of a boat motor, a distant dog bark – were replaced by near-silence, just the wind and the rhythm of his boots.

He reached a curve in the track and stopped. To his right, the water stretched out, glinting where shafts of sunlight broke through grey clouds. Beyond, the mainland rose up with its dark outlines of cliffs and forested hills, barely visible where they faded into the horizon. Behind him, rugged, heather-dappled moorland fell and rose in gentle undulations, the starkness of Goat Fell just visible beyond. No houses, no people. Just a sheep chewing on scrub grass, its head turning to glance at him.

Mo shoved his hands in his coat pockets as he gazed across the loch. His breath slowed to match the lapping of the water on the rocks below. The peace of it made him feel strangely emotional. Like he was connected to something bigger than himself.

The headache that had been pricking at him since this case had begun was finally easing, and his chest felt full of clean air. All the stress of the ongoing investigation into Erik Haldane's death, the frayed tempers of the team, the knife, the sarong, Freya's confession – all of it retreated to the back of his mind. It had been years since he'd felt anything close to this. Not in Birmingham, not in Stirling.

Back home – his real home, the West Midlands – had been different. Noise and crowds were normal, constant. In Stirling, he and Cat had aimed for a quieter life, but even that had felt unsettled. It wasn't like this – this stillness.

Mo turned to scan the horizon. The mainland seemed impossibly close, like he could just grab one of those rowing boats he'd spotted on the way along the path and be across there in moments. But he didn't want to. That was the point.

He thought of Catriona. They'd video called last night and she'd been tired, but pleased that he was enjoying Arran, if not the case. This walk had been her idea.

Did she know?

He wondered what she'd make of this. Stirling was fine. The girls were adapting, and Catriona was glad to be closer to her parents. But it was neither one thing, nor the other.

This, whatever it was, felt more real than Stirling. Out here, he felt rooted.

He thought of his daughters – Isla's drawings taped to the fridge, Fiona learning about Scottish history. Maybe they'd like it out here too. Not Arran specifically, but something like it. Something quieter. Somewhere he wouldn't have to force himself to breathe every time he stepped through his front door.

But he barely had time to see them now, with his workload and his commute. How hard would it be to commute from a place like this? And Arran wasn't a paradise. Erik had died here. There was death here, and lies, and confusion.

Would a place like this be calm, or would he end up getting dragged into everyone's business?

Mo knelt to pick up a smooth, flattish stone from the edge of the track. He stood and skimmed it over the water, smiling as it bounced three times.

What about Cat? Could she live in a place like this? Could she find work?

Only one way to find out. He had to talk to her, if he wasn't going to lose his mind. But first, he had to get back to the case.

CHAPTER FORTY-SIX

THE SCENT of coffee and the dull hum of conversation filled the makeshift incident room. Mo sat near the window, legs stretched out, a steaming cup of tea balanced on the windowsill. A well-worn OS map of the Isle of Arran was spread across the table in front of him. Beside it, his laptop was open, the screen filled with the latest notes from the case. His early morning walk had cleared his head, but the case still hung over him like a cloud.

Petra appeared from the back door to the bedrooms, her heels clicking on the linoleum floor. As ever, she cut a striking figure, in her tailored navy skirt suit, her black stiletto heels making her appear taller than her barely five-foot height warranted. Her towering updo was immaculate, but there were dark circles under her eyes. She had a long day ahead.

"Been out walking?" she remarked with raised eyebrows, taking in Mo's muddy boots and the map.

"It helps to clear the mind," Mo said. "And this coffee is finishing the job."

She smiled. "You like it here. You're holding yourself differently."

He shrugged. "I do." He wasn't sure if he was ready to say anything more on the subject.

Petra grabbed a mug of coffee and two slices of toast and perched on the edge of a chair, perusing the incident board. "But after some exercise and a dose of caffeine, are you any clearer about the Celestial Circle?"

"Not as clear as I'd like," Mo admitted. "Hoping today'll give us something solid."

The door swung open again, and Stuart entered, already clutching a bacon roll in one hand and his phone in the other. His hair gave him the look of someone who'd rolled out of bed fifteen minutes ago.

"Morning, all," Stuart mumbled through a mouthful of bacon, dropping into a chair across the room. "Anything juicy to kick us off?"

Before Mo could reply, Wendy arrived holding an envelope. "Morning," she announced briskly. "The lab results from Glasgow came through first thing." She placed the envelope on the table.

Petra leaned over the table. "Analysis of the sarong? Or the knife? Tell me we're finally going to see something concrete."

Wendy pulled out a sheet of paper and handed it to Petra, her smile tight. "The blood on the sarong is Erik's. And on the knife. We're trying to find fibres from the sarong on the knife. Haven't got any yet."

It was a start. And if they did find those fibres, it might point to the sarong being used to smear blood onto the knife in order to frame Morgan.

But Mo still wanted to know... why?

He yawned. "OK. Let's review where we're at."

They gathered around the board, people alternately sipping coffee, munching breakfast, and yawning. Mo chewed the inside of his cheek, the ease the morning walk had brought him already beginning to wear off. Beside him, Petra worked through a theory.

"So," she said, "Erik Haldane, conflicted cult member, ends up dead. Knife in Morgan's tent, blood consistent with Erik's wound. Convenient alibi from Astrid. Alibi that it turns out is a lie."

Mo nodded. "Morgan's devoted to Astrid. If they discover that Astrid used that sarong to smear blood on the knife then planted it in their tent, will that loyalty stand? Can we push them enough to get a statement?"

Petra shook her head. "They've drunk the Astrid kool-aid, I reckon. I suggest we look to Freya."

Stuart looked up. "Local police released her last night. No reason to hold her any longer."

"How was she when they let her go?"

"Asking if they could hang onto her for longer, according to Sam." Stuart sniffed. "D'you think she's really in danger?"

"We need to know more about Erik and his doubts about the group, his arguments with Astrid," Mo said. "Was Freya part of that? If she was, that might explain her fear."

"Unless it's something else altogether," suggested Wendy.

"Like what?" Mo asked.

Wendy shrugged. "No idea. I'm just a SOCO."

He smiled at her. There were so few of them here, they needed all the brains they could get.

And the biggest brain was about to get on a ferry back to the mainland.

He nodded. "Petra's going to need to take a brief trip back to Glasgow on business. I'll be driving her to the ferry terminal after this. And then, I think we need to have another chat with Freya."

"I'll go to the campsite," Stuart said. "Make sure she doesn't go anywhere."

"Thanks. I know she's not a suspect, but we don't want any of them leaving the island. She'll probably be glad of your protection. Petra, any thoughts?"

The psychologist shook her head. "I'm working on some theories about Astrid framing Morgan, and why she might want to. It seems more logical to frame Freya. Easier to establish a motive, with her being related to Erik."

"Maybe Morgan could be relied on not to tell us they'd been framed," Stuart suggested.

Petra wrinkled her nose. "It's an option. I'll do some more thinking on the train, send over my updated report."

She looked at Mo, who nodded. "Thanks," he said. "It's time we headed off."

In the car, he stared out at the sea and the sky, wondering what Erik would have seen before he died. The post-mortem had shown no evidence of drugs in his system, so he would have died in pain.

Poor man.

Petra was chewing on a fingernail, gazing out at the sky.

"You look deep in thought," he said.

"I keep coming back to motive. Who in this so-called 'Circle' or outside of it benefits from Erik's death?" She tapped a fingernail on the dashboard. "Erik wasn't just some random sacrificial victim. Or a goat."

Mo shook his head. "Could be Astrid, but Morgan might have acted on her behalf."

"I thought we were working on the assumption that Morgan was set up."

Mo nodded. "It's likely. Especially with Astrid supposedly hiding that blood-soaked sarong."

"You need to establish whether that was used to put the blood on the knife."

Mo nodded. "And if that knife isn't the murder weapon, what is?"

"Any chance it was? Astrid could have cleaned it after using it, then put blood on it?"

"Why would she do that? It makes no sense." He scratched his chin. "Very little about this makes sense."

"Liddy Drummond reckons Astrid's dangerous," Petra said. "To my mind, she's controlling and potentially volatile. I've watched how she reacts to Alistair's behaviour around her. It puts her on edge, makes her jumpy. She's used to being a leader. Having followers. If one of those followers were to challenge her, she might snap."

Mo glanced at her. They were entering Brodick now, the ferry terminal just visible up ahead. "That's your hypothesis?"

Petra wrinkled her nose. "I'm not sure yet. I'm going to give it some thought on the train. It's not as if I won't have plenty of time."

"Good luck. I'm sure you'll get things sorted."

"I hope you're right," Petra replied, her voice thin.

Petra stepped out of the car at the terminal, narrowing her gaze at the ferry pulling into dock. "Thank you for the lift," she managed. "We'll get there, I'm sure of it."

He raised an eyebrow. "I'm glad someone is."

CHAPTER FORTY-SEVEN

THE TRAIN JOLTED as it pulled out of Ardrossan Harbour, the Isle of Arran only vaguely visible in the distance. Petra watched the sea retreat from view. The train, with its rhythmic movement, seemed as restless as she felt. She pulled her laptop closer, willing herself to focus on work, and not the growing dread of her impending return to Glasgow.

Her flat would still be a state. She hadn't had time – or courage – to make arrangements to deal with the mess since the break-in.

KILLER. She wasn't a killer. Someone else was, but not her. But there were those who would always blame her.

And she knew who they were.

Question was, did she have the heart to report them to the police? After everything they'd suffered?

The very thought of unlocking her door and finding her home violated caused a tightness in her chest she couldn't shake. Would it smell? Would it be impossible to paint over?

"Get a grip, McBride," she muttered under her breath,

then glanced between the three other passengers in her carriage.

The Ayrshire countryside sped past in blurred greens and browns. Bare trees clumped together on windswept hills. Low stone walls twisted through paddocks where sheep meandered. All serene. Oblivious to the fate of Erik Haldane, or the complications Petra had unearthed within the Celestial Circle. A different world.

She opened a new document, lips pressing together in thought. She needed to start the case summary. Her fingers began moving, nails clacking against the keys.

Subject: Summary Report: Investigation into the Murder of Erik Haldane, Internal Dynamics of the Celestial Circle Retreat:

The Celestial Circle Retreat functions with a layered hierarchy defined by its alignment to Norse mythology, led by Astrid Thorsen. Thorsen's role within the group is that of a spiritual authority figure, though evidence from interviews suggests her influence is rooted in psychological manipulation rather than earned respect or loyalty.

Among the members, Morgan Douglas holds a position as Thorsen's most devoted follower. Douglas displays a fervent desire for validation and appears to operate more as an extension of Thorsen's will than an individual within the group. Their blind devotion to Thorsen calls into question the extent to which Douglas might execute instructions with questionable ethical or even legal parameters.

Petra paused, fingers hovering over the keys. The conversations she'd listened to with group members prodded at her memory. Could she believe any of them? She could only trust what she observed.

She frowned and picked up where she'd left off.

Relationship Tensions and Conflicts of Interest:

Preliminary investigations suggest friction between Erik Haldane, Astrid Thorsen, and perhaps other members of the Celestial Circle. Notably, Erik's concerns over emerging trends toward extremism – and Astrid's tightening control over group practices – left him vulnerable. His status within the group came into question before his death, largely owing to rumours he'd considered leaving the Circle.

Freya Haldane (Erik's sister) exhibits a dual role in the investigation. Her connection to Erik and emotional instability following his death make her both a potential source of insight and a complicating factor. The extent to which Freya was aligned with Erik's apparent dissent before his murder remains unclear. Freya's recent confession to Erik's killing is questionable. Present results from psychological interviews indicate significant gaps in both consistency and motive.

Petra leaned back in her seat, staring out the window. Rain smudged the countryside into streaks. She rubbed at her temples. Morgan and Freya. One with damning evidence in their tent, the other making what Petra still believed to be a false confession. Both victims, in her opinion.

Her focus returned to the screen.

The Nature of Erik Haldane's Death:

Erik Haldane's murder bears allusions to ritualistic execution as perceived within Norse mythology. His body was discovered within the ruins of Lochranza Castle, placed in a small rowing boat resembling traditional Viking burial practice. The significance of the location, combined with the personalised symbolism noted in the group's rituals, indicates a motive extending beyond mere violence.

Physical evidence complicates this narrative. The knife

recovered from Morgan Douglas's tent contains traces of Erik's blood, yet their prints aren't on it. And the blood appears to have been added post-mortem. The recently discovered sarong bearing Erik's blood raises new questions that require attention regarding Astrid Thorsen's wardrobe and surroundings.

The sound of her nails hitting the keys felt too loud. The man directly opposite gave Petra a pointed glance before looking away again. She ignored him. The words on the screen blurred slightly. She adjusted her glasses, letting out a sigh. She'd barely slept last night, images of her flat with the word *KILLER* daubed in pink paint dancing through the darkness in front of her eyes.

Ritualistic elements, yes. But for these people, killing wasn't just about dramatic placements and tributes. And people didn't just snap into that sort of mindset overnight. Something here went beyond the narrative of ancient gods and sacrifices. It was personal.

Suspect Profile: Astrid Thorsen

As spiritual leader, Astrid Thorsen maintains control over the Circle with an uneasy confidence. Initial profiling of Astrid suggests narcissistic tendencies. She demonstrates adeptness in reframing questions as irrelevant or trivial in interviews, evading questions surrounding Erik's death. There is reason to believe she might benefit from Erik Haldane's death, as he was challenging her authority.

Thorsen's ambiguous presentation during the most recent confrontation indicates ongoing concealment of information. The possibility of coercing Morgan Douglas into complicity remains.

A body had been found, but Astrid hadn't panicked. At least not outwardly. Beneath the surface? Petra wasn't sure.

She frowned; her assessment felt lacking. Erik's death wasn't just about his rebellion, it was personal. Targeted.

And what about Astrid's husband?

Suspect Profile: Professor Alistair MacLeod

MacLeod presents as an academic whose involvement with the Circle appears driven by intellectual curiosity rather than spiritual conviction. However, his relationship with Astrid Thorsen suggests deeper emotional investment than initially apparent.

The deterioration of his marriage to Astrid presents a possible trigger point. Evidence suggests Erik may have been romantically involved with Astrid, providing a motive for MacLeod.

Petra paused, considering the professor's behaviour during questioning. His carefully constructed responses hadn't quite masked his body language.

She added:

MacLeod demonstrates classic displacement behaviour when discussing Erik's death, redirecting the focus of discussion. This suggests either guilty knowledge or loyalty to the actual killer, even in the face of violence.

She typed and erased another sentence about potential suspects twice, realising just how empty the keys sounded in a train carriage filled with sleeping strangers. At last, she sighed and shut the laptop with a careful clack.

The lights of Glasgow came into view through the window. The train changed tone, deepening until the engine's noise dulled into a crawl. Petra saw the platforms appear, commuters shuffling under the glow of the station canopy.

The train slowed further. Her stomach sank further.

Stepping down onto the platform, Petra felt a wave of

dread. The break-in at her flat – the graffiti – came rushing back. Her legs stiffened and every footstep felt heavy.

Glasgow Queen Street buzzed – but it didn't feel like home. Not anymore, if it ever had. *Not while you're being hounded.*

Brushing the thoughts aside, Petra made for the taxi rank. She needed to get this over with, so she could return to the case. And she needed to decide what to do with her flat.

CHAPTER FORTY-EIGHT

JADE LEANED back in her chair, rubbing the bridge of her nose. The CCU offices smelled faintly of stale coffee mixed with printer ink, a scent she didn't recall noticing before. Patty sat opposite, her chin propped on her hand, scrolling through Astrid Thorsen's social media.

"This woman's a piece of work," Patty muttered, squinting at the screen. "Everything's curated – like she's running a lifestyle brand instead of a cult."

Jade looked up. "Anything useful?"

"Well, she loves a photoshoot. Look at this." Patty turned the laptop to show Jade an image of Astrid on a windswept cliff, the Firth of Clyde stretching behind her. She was wearing a patterned dress, sheer enough to ripple dramatically in the breeze. Jade could see why people might fall for her. Charisma radiated from the woman, her dark hair flowing in the wind as she gazed somewhere just beyond the camera.

"That could be the dress on the footage." Jade tapped the screen. "Keep looking – see if there's any sign of that sarong."

Patty sighed and turned the laptop back. "This whole case makes me want to chuck my computer into the Clyde. Everyone's following her like she's enlightened or something, but it's all manipulation. Smoke and mirrors."

"That's her strength, though," said Jade. "She plays to people's weaknesses and masks it as empowerment. And now Erik's dead and we've still got no clue who killed him."

Patty gave her a quick glance. "You're not blaming yourself for that, are you?"

Jade said nothing. She forced her attention back to the photos in the inbox instead. The knife from Morgan's tent, stained with Erik's blood, dominated. The pieces were aligning. Or were they?

The trill of her mobile cut into the silence. She snatched it up. "Mo."

Mo's voice was calm. "Uniform have just done another drive past the campsite. Nothing new, but I've got Wendy's latest results. Blood's consistent – Erik's on both the knife and the sarong. But that's as far as we're getting for now."

"Tampered or genuinely used?" Jade asked.

"Knife looks staged," Mo replied. "No tissue between the serrations, no spatter indicating movement. Sarong's got nothing but smears. My gut says it's been wiped."

Jade held her breath for a moment. "Right. So either Morgan's being framed, or someone's messing with evidence to throw us entirely."

"Exactly." Mo paused, then added, "We're at the point where Astrid needs formal questioning. I spoke to Petra earlier, and I think it's time."

"You reckon she's got something to hide?"

"Without doubt," Mo said. "But I'm not sure what yet.

Look... if we interview her under caution, it's less aggressive. Stir things up, finally get her off that podium."

Jade nodded to herself. "I agree. But not an arrest – not yet. We need to clear up the knife's real origins before the CPS gets a chance to chuck this out. See if it's the weapon or if there's another one. Which I can't believe there would be. Think she'll come in willingly?"

Mo grunted a thin laugh. "She'll enjoy the chance to spin her side of things."

"Then do it," Jade replied. "Be polite but firm. Keep it calm, and use Petra, yeah? Astrid'll underestimate her, and that's when Petra works best."

"Petra's had to go home. Her fla—"

"Of course. Well, take Stuart. When will Petra be back?"

"Tomorrow, she says. But it's a Sunday, so—"

"OK. Well, you don't need Petra for this. Get a recording. And try and pin Astrid down on facts, not just rhetoric."

Mo nodded. "Astrid's confident – too confident. She knows we're circling, but she doesn't seem worried."

"She should be," Jade muttered. "Call me afterwards, yeah?"

"Of course."

Jade put the phone down and looked back at Patty, who was watching her with that all-seeing protective gaze.

"You're wishing you were there, doing the interviews."

Jade smiled. "You know me so well. But there's no way I could have taken the time away from Rory to stay on Arran. And Mo's doing a good job."

"He is. Doesn't mean you can't wish you were there."

This was true, in part. But what Jade really wished was that Patty would stop second-guessing her, and focus on her job. "What about the social media?"

"Nothing definitive yet. I'll keep trawling."

"Try some other platforms. Groups she'll have been in. Celestial stuff."

Patty scoffed. "If I have to read any more of this shite, I think I'll stick myself in a wee boat with a dagger in me."

Jade raised an eyebrow. *Not funny*. But she knew how Patty felt. "Focus on that sarong, Patty. Pinning that down gets us closer to the truth."

Patty sniffed. "Fine. But I'm keeping a close eye on you – don't think you're off the hook." She returned to her screen, mumbling as she resumed scrolling.

Jade moved to the window, staring out at the drizzle.

Astrid Thorsen. Charisma and control made her slippery, but Mo was right – confidence could become a weakness.

"Yes."

Jade turned to see Patty staring into her screen, fist clenched.

She looked up, her eyes dancing. "Got the sodding sarong. July post – Astrid on a beach somewhere, arms out like she's welcoming the next bloody season of sacrifice."

"Good," Jade said. "Send it to Mo. Let's see her talk her way out of this one."

CHAPTER FORTY-NINE

PETRA PUSHED OPEN the door to her flat with her shoulder, trying to ignore the dread in the pit of her stomach. The hinges gave their familiar whine, but the sound didn't comfort her the way it used to.

She stepped into the narrow hallway, dumped her bags and walked into the living room.

There it was. *KILLER,* daubed in dripping letters across the lounge wall in what looked like pink emulsion paint.

Petra froze. Her breathing slowed, her body rigid. She stared at it, barely daring to breathe.

They'd got in here, then. They'd been following her for years, standing outside her flat and watching her.

But breaking in? Doing *this*?

After what felt like hours, she forced herself to move. She edged towards the wall, heart pounding in her ears, and leaned over to look at something she'd spotted on the floor. A white envelope, with her name scrawled on the front.

Her hand shook as she picked it up. The paint fumes

jabbed at her nostrils. The rest of the tin had been upended, dumped on the carpet. Her Aunt Lydia's carpet, ruined.

Petra swallowed and opened the envelope. Inside was a single sheet of paper. Large, neat handwriting: *His blood is on your hands*.

She dropped the letter onto the floor. She wanted to act, to do *something* – but what? Call Jade? No.

And she understood how they felt. That was the worst of it.

But now they'd gone too far. She'd never spoken to the police before, but Aila had made the call, and she couldn't duck out of it.

She closed her eyes and breathed a prayer. *Sorry*. She wasn't sure who she was apologising to, but she had regrets, alright.

Aila. She pulled out her phone, staring at her ex's name for a moment. She needed to know more about the break-in. That was the only reason she was calling, wasn't it?

"Hey, it's Aila. Leave a message."

Shit. Petra ended the call with no message, and stared at the wall again.

She couldn't go back to Arran. She had an appointment at the police station in the morning, and she'd miss the last ferry anyway.

Did she really have to spend the night here?

Her aunt's mirror still hung above the mantel. Petra's face looked pale and tired. She needed make-up before she dared see Aila. Or the police.

She turned towards the kitchen. Wine would help. Then she spotted it.

On the windowsill, a footprint. Clear as day, and

surrounded by a dusting of powder. So the police had sent in the SOCOs.

A footprint wasn't much. It was fingerprints they needed. And besides, she knew whose footprint it was.

She still wasn't sure if she wanted to inform on them. An elderly couple, whose son had died. It had been Petra's testimony that had freed the young man who'd killed him. Without her, the murderer would have been safely behind bars.

She'd thought he was recovered. That he wasn't a danger. She'd been wrong.

She swallowed. I can't stay here.

Petra turned towards the front door and picked up her overnight bag. She'd find a hotel, hang the cost.

And whether she ever set foot inside this flat again, remained to be seen.

CHAPTER FIFTY

THE YURT SMELLED of incense and mustiness, like the back of one of those shops that sold tie-dye T-shirts and astrological jewellery. Shadows from the dim lamps flickered along the canvas walls. Mo stood just inside the threshold, waiting while his eyes adjusted. Stuart was already inside, his mobile out, ready to record.

Astrid gestured for them to come further inside. She'd brought in two low chairs, seemingly ready for more visitors, and taken the wing-backed chair herself. Mo and Stuart sat, both a centimetre or so lower than her.

You won't intimidate us like that, Mo thought.

She looked at them with the patience of someone humouring children. Her calm should have felt stiff, but it was infuriatingly real – the sort of calm born of years of lording it over others.

"Recording is on." Stuart raised his phone and gave it a tap.

Astrid didn't flinch. "I've nothing to hide," she said, her tone flat.

Outside, the campsite had been alive with tension. Freya had emerged from the entrance to her tent as they arrived and stayed there, halfway out of the zipped opening, as they entered the yurt. Morgan was in their tent, a torch inside illuminating their silhouette. Alistair had been nowhere.

Mo licked his lips. *Don't rush it.*

"You were the last person to see Erik alive, Astrid," he said.

"Says who?"

Mo eyed her. Stuart held up his phone, ready to press play, and Mo grimaced then nodded.

"We have video footage of you," Mo said. "On the beach, hiding something in the rocks. We found the object you hid. A sarong, one that's draped around your shoulders in a number of social media posts."

She scoffed. "Do you know how many of those things they sell at festivals and retreats?"

"OK," said Mo. "In the video, you're wearing a dress." He pointed, hiding his glee that the dress had been hanging up when they'd entered. "That dress."

She didn't even turn to look at it. "Again, ten a penny. Can you see my face?" She beckoned impatiently. "Give it to me."

Mo nodded and Stuart handed the phone over. Astrid watched the full video then shrugged.

"I make no secret of where I walk. The loch and the shore are sacred places. You're trying to frame ritual and reverence as guilt." She gave a small shrug. "It speaks more about you than me."

Mo's patience was wearing thin. "You've got a history of manipulation and control and, according to what we've been told, Erik challenged that. Maybe wanted to leave. What was it, Astrid? Was his dissent bad for your image? Did it threaten your influence over the others?"

Her gaze slid to the corner, where an altar crafted of carved wood and animal skulls sat. "I guide the Circle. That's what they expect from me. If Erik had doubts, they wouldn't have been enough to warrant his death. Don't insult me or his intelligence."

Mo folded his arms. He made a gesture at Stuart, who reached into his bag and pulled out an evidence bag.

Mo took it from him and held it up, careful to make sure it caught the light. "Whose sarong is this, Astrid?"

She squinted at it. "That's the one you think belongs to me. Could be anyone's."

"Can you tell us where yours is right now, in that case?"

She barely blinked. "I donated it to a member of the Circle. A devotee who enjoined in a previous retreat."

Yeah, right. "Who is this devotee? Can they back your story up?"

"Of course. Xavier Williams. I can give you his phone number."

Mo looked at her. This Xavier would be another person under her spell, ready to say anything she asked.

It was pointless.

"Listen, Detective," she said. "Erik was... bad news. He was weak. He couldn't handle the kind of energy we channel. I counselled him, supported his grief, gave him the tools to heal. He didn't listen. He didn't *want* to listen."

Mo waited.

"But that doesn't mean I killed him." Her gaze went to the doorway. "Maybe his sister was frustrated, angry that he was about to leave us all. Maybe she felt abandoned."

The fabric was yanked to one side and Freya burst in.

"He wasn't leaving, you bitch! He saw right through you, and you killed him for it!"

Stuart was on his feet, ready to restrain Freya. Mo forced himself to remain seated.

"Freya," he said. "We'll speak to you when we're finished here, please. This is an interview under caution."

Her nostrils flared. "She killed Erik. I know she did."

Astrid's face was calm, her lips twitching in a smile. "I'm so sorry for your loss, Freya."

Freya raised her arms over her head, but Stuart was on her. He grabbed her wrists before she could attack.

"Sarge." Stuart had taken something from Freya's hands. It was an object, long and twisted.

He held it out, almost dropping it in his surprise.

Mo peered in to examine it. He looked at the object and then up at Freya.

A knife?

CHAPTER FIFTY-ONE

Mo's EYES fixed on the knife in Stuart's hand. The handle was decorative, twisted with intricate carvings designed to resemble branches from a tree. It was almost beautiful. Almost.

The serrated blade looked familiar. Like the one found in Morgan's tent.

Another one?

Freya struggled in Stuart's grasp. He held her upper arms, pulling her back from the group leader.

"You can't keep hiding, Astrid!" Her voice was high-pitched, cracking on the words. "I know what you did!"

Astrid stood still, her eyes wide and her arms trembling. Had her composure finally cracked?

She smiled.

"Are you quite finished, Freya?" Astrid tilted her head, her voice calm, her head held high. Mo almost felt sorry for Freya. *You never could handle pressure, could you? Always so... emotional.*

Mo gritted his teeth and moved towards Freya, who was still wriggling in Stuart's grip.

"Where is this from?" he asked as he slid the knife into an evidence bag he'd pulled from his jacket pocket. "Was it in your tent?"

The tents had been searched. They'd have found a knife.

She shook her head. "It's hers."

Mo chewed his lip. How could it be Astrid's when it hadn't been in her tent?

He sighed. "Freya Haldane, I'm arresting you for assault. You do not have to say anything, but it may harm your defence if you do not mention when questioned something which you later rely on in court."

Astrid's smile twisted into a grin. Mo resisted the urge to find another pair of cuffs for her.

He shared a look with Stuart. Neither of them thought Freya was the killer. Petra's profile didn't point to it, Freya's behaviour didn't point to it.

But if this knife...

He shook his head. "Let's get her in the car, Stuart. And that knife needs forensic analysis."

CHAPTER FIFTY-TWO

Mo STOLE a glance at Freya in the rear-view mirror. Hair plastered to her pale face, she looked hollow, but there was something else about her now – something heavier than the anger she had displayed earlier in Astrid's yurt. It was fear. Pure, numbing fear.

"We'll get you legal representation," Mo said, breaking the silence. She'd need someone competent, after the chaos of the last few days. "Unless you have a lawyer you want to call?"

She shook her head, her gaze out of the window towards the darkness of the sea to their left.

He nodded. "It'll be sorted."

Stuart, sitting in the back beside Freya, threw Mo a questioning glance in the mirror. He ignored it.

Truth was, he was confused. And he was wondering if he was qualified to lead this investigation, which seemed to be what he was doing.

Freya's earlier confession to killing Erik had been hanging over him since they'd released her. At the time, it had felt like the right decision. She'd been scared, and it had seemed obvious that custody was just her way of escaping.

But now... Now he wasn't so sure.

He tightened his grip on the wheel, turning inland at Lamlash and steering them into the tiny station car park.

They pulled up next to Sam Henderson's patrol car. The PC was waiting near the doors, arms crossed against the drizzle, his bulky frame hunched slightly.

Mo opened the car door, waving Sam over. "We'll need you to help take Freya through."

"She giving you much trouble?" Sam asked, keeping his voice low.

"Not yet." Mo glanced back at her. She was still as stone, although her shoulders quivered. An odd mix – like she could either break down entirely, or lash out without warning.

Stuart stepped out first, opening the back door and walking round to the other side of the car. "Alright, Miss Haldane. Out you get."

Freya didn't move. Then she let out a sharp breath and slid out, looking at Mo like she was waiting for a clue on what to do next.

"It's alright," he said. "Let's get inside."

She followed, her movements jerky, flanked by Sam and Stuart. Inside the small station, the fluorescent lights reflected off the walls and made Mo blink.

Stuart disappeared to sort the paperwork. Sam hovered by the desk, waiting for instructions.

"Get her processed and into a holding cell," Mo said, quieter now. "And let her know about representation. Have you got a local duty solicitor?"

"Hana Sato. She's young but good. I'll give her a call."

"Thanks."

Sam gave a curt nod and gestured for Freya to follow him. She hesitated, gaze flicking to Mo then back to Sam. Her feet dragged across the floor.

Mo waited until she'd disappeared round the far corner of the hallway, then leaned back on the nearest desk, letting out a slow breath. Stuart returned, a file in hand.

"I still think we've got the wrong one," he said. "It's Astrid. It has to be. Freya's scared of her."

Mo rubbed at his temple. They didn't make arrests on hunches, but when Freya's anger at Astrid had shifted to fear at the campsite, he'd clocked it. She wasn't scared of the police. She was scared of what Astrid would do. Or, worse – what Astrid had already done.

"Not the time, Stuart," he muttered.

Stuart grimaced. "Astrid's playing us, I'm telling you."

Mo kept his expression neutral. "Let's stick to the facts. We do this properly. No theory-spinning." *That's Petra's job*.

Stuart gave a reluctant nod and tilted his head toward Freya's cell. "She's terrified of Astrid. Can't just ignore that."

Mo crossed to the window overlooking the parking area. The mist had cleared slightly and he could see the school opposite.

"I think we've got a tangled mess to sort," he said at last. "Fact is, Freya confessed. And then she attacked another member of the Circle. That confession might not hold water, but it's more than we've got on anyone else right now."

"Yeah. But—"

"I'm not ignoring anything." Mo straightened, turning toward Stuart. "We let her go once, and we'll have to answer for it if we were wrong. So from here on out, we don't cut her – or anyone else – any slack. OK?"

Stuart gave a reluctant nod.

"Good." Mo picked up the file and slipped it under his arm. "In the morning we'll get to work on those forensic results from Glasgow. Let's see if Wendy's turned anything up about the blood on that knife."

"Should we go back to the campsite? Check things have calmed down?"

Mo closed his eyes. Stuart had a point. But when they'd left, Astrid and Morgan had disappeared to their separate tents. And there was no sign of Alistair.

He'd better not have left Arran...

"No. Let's get some sleep. Petra will be back tomorrow, and we'll have a lawyer so we can interview Freya."

"Sarge." Stuart headed towards the door.

"But," Mo said, yawning. He was exhausted. "Can you drive this time?"

CHAPTER FIFTY-THREE

PETRA PERCHED on the edge of the unforgiving bed in her budget hotel room, flicking through the case files on Erik Haldane. The stained wallpaper and faded floral curtains weren't doing anything to lift her mood. She exhaled sharply and rested the laptop on the thin duvet.

She couldn't stay in the flat tonight; that much was clear. *KILLER*. The word hung in her mind, heavy and unforgiving. Staying there would've been reckless.

Instead, she was here, in a third-rate room that smelled faintly of mildew, picking through the puzzle of Erik's death.

She opened the report she'd begun on the train, the sound of her fingers on the keys making her feel calmer. She needed to get more on the members of the Circle, though. Had to understand their history.

She went straight to Google, typing in the first name on her mental list: *Astrid Thorsen.*

The woman's online footprint was more advert than biography. Promotional videos for the Celestial Circle. Blog posts dripping with vague spiritual mumbo-jumbo. Phrases like "unlocking celestial power" and "ancient wisdom rooted in the earth" accompanied by sepia-toned photos of Astrid herself, windswept and statuesque, standing near stone circles or by the shoreline.

The woman wasn't stupid. Charisma and confidence oozed through Astrid's digital persona. It was an image which would tick all the boxes for the right client.

Petra opened another tab and typed in *Morgan Douglas*.

Once she'd ruled out all the other people with the same name, she was left with slim pickings. There was a locked Instagram account titled @Living_With_The_Ancients and nothing else. No Facebook, no TikTok, nothing. For the most part, Morgan had managed to keep their life private, which was either impressive or unsettling. Petra stared at the grey profile icon on the Instagram page before switching to another tab and searching for *Freya Haldane*.

This time, it wasn't as sterile. Freya's account was filled with personal snapshots from the Isle of Arran: mist-shrouded hills, seals basking on rocks, lochs mirroring slate skies. Her face appeared now and then, candid or posed, often with Erik smiling next to her. The sight of his smiling face brought sadness even to Petra's hardened mind.

She scrolled through the photos, repeatedly returning to one taken just over a week ago of Freya and Erik arm-in-arm near Machrie Moor. Freya was beaming, her freckled skin glowing in the twilight, while Erik's face carried the weight of sadness – his head tilted just a little, the smile not quite reaching his eyes.

Was this when he'd argued with Astrid? Did he know he'd be leaving the Circle? Did he know he was in danger?

Petra stood and paced the room, the worn carpet scratchy against her bare feet. She closed her eyes and stopped, trying to push memories of the word on her living room wall from her mind.

Focus.

She sat down again and typed in *Professor Alistair MacLeod*. There was plenty this time: dry academic articles and conference notes along with an old bio from the University of Aberdeen. Petra skimmed past most of the dull academia, zeroing in on a paper he'd authored years earlier.

"Blades of Belief: Ritual Knives in Norse Practice."

She felt her breath catch.

An image of a knife accompanied the abstract. The blade was longer and thinner than the one found in Morgan's tent.

But what caught Petra's eye was the handle: gnarled and twisted, carved to resemble branches of a tree. It was beautiful, if it hadn't been a weapon.

She reached again into the papers, retrieving photos of the knife bagged at the campsite. There was no tree-like design on the handle of Morgan's weapon. This blade in Alistair's paper was different. But was it important?

She dug through more of Alistair's online breadcrumbs until she landed on a student-generated profile from his tenure at Aberdeen. One image jumped off the screen. A display case, depicting a series of ceremonial Viking implements. Front and centre was the knife from the academic paper.

Petra rubbed her temple. Three years ago, MacLeod had left Aberdeen. No explanation given. Just gone. Paid off to leave without a fuss, she imagined; she'd spent enough time in academia to know how it worked. And now knives from his research kept worming their way into her brain.

She made a note to ask Mo in the morning – assuming she'd sleep tonight. Exhaustion was tugging at her.

Picking up her phone, she set an alarm. Her eyes lingered a moment on her inbox. Should she send off a quick message to one of her ex-colleagues in Dundee or Aberdeen? Maybe they'd have heard rumours about MacLeod?

She sighed and powered it off instead. It could wait. She had the meeting with the police to deal with, and in the meantime she needed to forget about that, and sleep.

CHAPTER FIFTY-FOUR

Mo leaned back, the phone pressed to his ear, the cold stone of the steps up to the community centre no doubt ruining his trousers. He'd needed air, space to think. And Arran had that in spades.

It had been a while since he'd last spoken to his old boss DI Zoe Finch, but her no-nonsense tone felt like slipping back into an old, comfortable pair of shoes.

"This Erik Haldane case you've got sounds like a mess," Zoe said, her Brummie accent fading with the time she'd spent in Cumbria. "You lot are chasing cults now, are you?"

"It's not a cult, not exactly," Mo replied, his voice low enough to avoid anyone who might be passing. "At least, that's what they keep saying. But there's something... off about the group. Too much silence and too many secrets."

"Silence usually means guilt, or fear. Which one is it?"

"Maybe both." Mo rubbed his forehead, wishing the headache that was fermenting in there would back off a little. "Astrid, the leader – she's polished, her words are careful, and she deflects like a pro. But dig a little, and you start to feel the veneer cracking. Freya, Erik's sister, confessed to stabbing him, and attacked Astrid tonight. We've arrested her for assault. But something about it doesn't sit right. And then there's this knife... Sorry. Not knife. Knives. Plural."

"You sound knackered, Mo."

He let out a short laugh. "Is it that obvious?"

"I've known you long enough." Zoe's tone softened, the friend slipping through the professional. "This island, the group, they're doing your head in, yeah?"

Mo hesitated. "It's not just the case. It's the place itself. Arran's beautiful – wild, untouched in a way that pulls at you. But it's isolated, too. It's not like home. Hell, it's not even like Stirling."

Zoe was quiet for a moment. "Sounds a bit like Cumbria to me. Those lakes can tug at you, same as your lochs, I imagine. But they've got a way of closing in, too. The kind of place where you can feel invisible and under a microscope at the same time."

"Exactly. The locals have their lives, their habits. You come in as an outsider, and you're always an outsider."

"And your poor little Brummie brain's fighting against it, isn't it?" There was fondness in her voice, mixed with humour.

"I grew up in the city," Mo admitted. "Stirling was a change, but this? It's... disorienting."

"Best advice?" Zoe cut in. "Don't fight it. You'll wear yourself out before you've even solved your case."

He smiled. Somewhere out in the darkness, he heard a faint grunting sound. The deer he'd watched the other evening? "Easier said than done," he said.

"Tell me about it. I'm up to my neck in Myron Carter and his lot. Drug trafficking, intimidation, God knows what else. And you know what I'm doing tonight? Sitting in front of a whiteboard with connections that lead me nowhere." She sighed. "You'll get through it. You always do."

Mo leaned his head back, closing his eyes. Zoe's confidence in him was steadying. "It's just... This Erik thing isn't linear. Forensics say one thing, but the behaviour of everyone involved says something else. And Astrid – without hard evidence, she's untouchable. I hate it when it's like this."

"Then don't do anything just yet." Zoe's voice was firm, the no-nonsense detective back. "Don't let the frustration push you into shortcuts, Mo. Focus on what you've got, what you can prove. Right now, sounds to me like you've got red herrings all over the shop."

He nodded. "What about you? Any progress?"

"Myron's slippery, but not invincible. I have a feeling the trafficking's going to be his undoing. You can't just buy and sell people and expect them to keep quiet about it." Her voice was confident now. "The trick's not to let the big picture distract you. You might wanna try that."

"Sounds about right," he replied. "But I can't shake the feeling I'm missing something."

"You'll figure it out. You always do." Zoe paused. "But listen – you've got one advantage up there you've not had before."

"Oh?"

"You've got Jade," she said simply. "And from what you've told me over the years, she's good. Use that."

Mo sighed. "She's not even here."

"That's OK. You need someone co-ordinating back at base."

Mo considered. Was Jade co-ordinating things? Or had

she disappeared, if not in body, then in spirit? She hadn't seemed all that engaged with this case.

She'd have other cases on her workload. And he needed to prove he could cope. It would be fine.

"Yeah, you're right," he said, not wanting to be disloyal.

Zoe laughed. "I always try to be. Get some rest, Mo. And call me if you need to."

"I will. Thanks, Zo. And good luck with Carter."

"You too," she replied, and ended the call.

Mo put the phone in his lap, staring out into the darkness. The loch was out there, the mountains, the majesty of it all. It brought a tear to his eye.

And in the meantime, the case wasn't going to solve itself, but Zoe was right. Don't get distracted by the big picture. One step at a time. For now, that was enough.

CHAPTER FIFTY-FIVE

THE COMMUNITY CENTRE'S hall seemed emptier than it had done the day before, the echoes of their voices bouncing off the walls. Mo stood at the head of the table in the corner they'd taken to using, a cold mug of tea near his elbow.

Stuart stood by the whiteboard next to the bar, where a picture of the knife Freya had used to attack Astrid was pinned in the centre. His pen hovered in mid-air, unused, as he stared at it.

"That's ceremonial, isn't it?" Stuart said, half to himself. "The carvings on the handle? Symbolises something, surely?"

"I'd imagine," Mo agreed, running a hand along the stubble on his jawline. He hadn't shaved, hadn't had time. He'd struggled to sleep last night, too full of thoughts of Freya, and Astrid, and Erik. Not to mention the landscape outside his window. So he'd slept through his alarm and only just made it down here before the kitchen closed for breakfast.

"Wendy will have more," he said, "once the lab's taken a look."

Stuart turned. "D'you think it's the murder weapon?"

Mo's gaze moved past the map of the island taped to the wall, where pins marked Lochranza Castle and the Celestial Circle campsite.

"We can't jump there yet," he said finally. "Wendy said they'll need to compare the blade to the wound. No use speculating."

Wendy's face appeared on Mo's laptop screen; at last, enough signal to be able to see her. The boss was on the call too, watching in silence. Mo motioned towards the screen. "Wendy, you're on. What's the update?"

Wendy pushed her glasses up her nose, the grimy shelves of her office visible in the background. "I've been reviewing the post-mortem report again. Erik's wound... clean, slightly curved entry. If this new knife has that curve, we might have something."

Mo leaned over the table, staying close to the laptop. "And if it's a match? Does that mean Freya's the killer, or is it more complicated than that?"

The DI, small in her window of the call, leaned forward. "What does Petra think?"

"She's still in Glasgow, dealing with her..." Mo wasn't sure how much Wendy knew about Petra's break-in. "She's got a meeting this morning," he said. "Then she'll be on the ferry early afternoon."

"Good. And you're interviewing Freya after this?"

"We'll hang by the campsite en route, check things are calm there, and then head over to Lamlash." Mo was glad the roads on Arran were quiet; he seemed to be spending half his time on the road that circled the island. He wondered what the western side was like, further from the mainland. Beautiful, no doubt.

The boss nodded. "Good. Liddy Drummond's convinced Astrid's bad news, but we need more than that. Including Freya's account of why she attacked her."

Mo nodded and looked at Wendy onscreen. "Freya's prints will be on the knife, obviously. But I'd like to know if anyone else from the Circle has handled it, and importantly if it has Erik's blood on it."

"There's no obvious sign of blood," said Wendy. "But obvious isn't everything."

The DI leaned into the screen. She was squinting, alternately opening one eye and then the other. Mo wondered, not for the first time, if she was OK.

"Feel free to keep speculating," she said. "Keeps you busy." She tried for a light-hearted smile, but it fell flat.

Mo sighed. "Freya could've used the knife to kill her brother. They're family; emotions run deep. But..."

"She attacked Astrid with it," Stuart added. "We saw how angry she was. It didn't feel premeditated."

Mo shook his head. "Exactly. If she wasn't thinking it through when she lashed out at Astrid, what kind of state would she have been in if she'd used it on Erik? It doesn't fit."

Wendy cleared her throat. "I'll look at what I can and update you." Her screen went blank.

The DI tilted her head. "Everything OK there? You must be missing your family, Mo."

Mo felt a sudden pang of guilt. "Er, yes. It's fine, though. Part of the job. Hope things are OK back at base."

She grunted assent and shut down her screen. Mo closed his laptop and slid it further down the table.

Stuart crossed his arms. "So what now? Freya's already confessed once, though if you don't buy it..."

"Her confession's flimsy and we both know it," Mo said. "There's got to be more behind that outburst at Astrid. She's scared – but why, precisely? That's what we need to know."

Mo picked up his jacket from the back of a chair and took out his mobile to dial Sam.

"Sarge," said Sam, picking up on the first ring.

"Morning, Sam. Stuart and I are on our way over to interview Freya. Is her lawyer on her way?"

"She's already here waiting."

"Good. We'll be slightly delayed. I want to check the campsite first."

"You want me to head over there? Keep an eye on things?"

Mo considered. "I don't need you stationed there, but drive past every hour or so, yes? Just to check there's nothing kicking off."

With Freya out of the picture, he hoped that wouldn't happen. But what if Morgan changed their attitude to Astrid? And what had Alistair made of it all, when he'd returned last night?

He wished he had Petra here.

CHAPTER FIFTY-SIX

Petra wove her way through traffic to cross Dumbarton Road and approach the modern building that housed Glasgow's West End Police Station. The air was sharp, the kind of chill that made her regret her choice of strappy heels. Four inches tall and emerald green, they made her feel in control, but every step felt precarious on the steps leading up to the entrance.

She looked around, uneasy. Petra prided herself on being able to read places, people, situations, but here she felt exposed. It was too close to Aunt Lydia's flat.

She wasn't even thinking of it as *her* flat anymore.

She adjusted her coat, tugged at her bag's strap, and squared her shoulders before pushing open the glass doors.

Waiting by the reception desk was a woman, talking to a young man behind the desk. She was solid, in her late forties or early fifties, her short-cropped hair highlighting sharp cheekbones. She looked up as Petra approached, with a flicker of appraisal. Petra took note of the station's greyness: grey walls, grey carpet, even the desk was grey.

"You must be Dr McBride," the woman said, her voice brisk but not unfriendly.

Petra nodded. "Guilty as charged. You're DC Vance?"

A nod. "Shirley. Meeting room's this way." Shirley picked up a notebook as she stood, motioning for Petra to follow.

Petra's heels tapped, uncomfortably loud on the floor as they walked. Shirley didn't bother with polite small talk, not that Petra minded. Silence suited her just fine for now. Still, the bland, windowless walls had begun to close in on her by the time they reached a small room at the far end of the corridor: less a meeting room, more a repurposed storage cupboard with a table squeezed in.

There was no coffee machine, no biscuits. No effort to make the place welcoming. This wasn't a station set up for friendly chats.

Shirley opened the door wide and gestured for Petra to enter first.

"Right," the DC said, sitting across the table. She tapped on her notebook with a biro, her eyes steady on Petra. "You reported a break-in while you were away." She checked her notes and frowned. "Consulting for the CCU on the Isle of Arran. Nice work." She looked up. "Want to tell me what happened?"

Petra leaned back in the chair – it wobbled slightly at the movement – and slipped on her professional mask.

"My ex, Aila, she went to my flat while I was away," she began, keeping her voice flat. "She needed to pick up her stuff. Anyway, she found that someone had broken in. They forced the lock, painted the word 'KILLER' on my living room wall, and left a note implying..." She swallowed. "Well, more or less the same sentiment. They also left a footprint on the windowsill."

Shirley's biro hovered above the notebook. "That's in the Scene of Crime report. So they think you're responsible for someone's death?"

"My involvement in a case, yes. This isn't the first time I've been targeted by someone who lacks... perspective."

"I see." Shirley's brow twitched a little. "And you reckon it's connected to one of your forensic cases?"

"That would be the logical assumption," Petra replied. "Given I've been under scrutiny before regarding the release of a particular offender. And given the contents of the letter."

"You've had security problems at the flat before?" Shirley asked, her gaze sharp.

Petra shrugged. *You can do this.* "Minor disturbances. People hanging around, sending letters. Nothing that crossed into criminal damage or trespass until now." Petra straightened her back and crossed one leg over the other, careful to keep her voice stable. "This is... new."

"Well, they've gone to some effort. Sounds personal." Shirley scribbled a few notes, then paused. "Do you know who's behind it?"

Petra hesitated. Shirley tilted her head.

"I don't," Petra answered, choosing her words with care. "Not with certainty."

Shirley didn't press her but nodded slowly as she made another note. Petra hated withholding the full truth – it wasn't a good practice – but... Well, she could sympathise. His parents had been through enough. If it *was* them, did she really want a criminal record for the pair of them on her conscience, along with everything else?

"Alright," Shirley said. "We'll speak to your neighbours, see if anyone spotted anything unusual. You'll need to keep us informed if you receive any more threats."

"Of course," Petra said, although she knew she couldn't stomach sticking around Glasgow long enough for follow-ups.

"We've already dusted for prints. Aila allowed access."

Petra nodded. "That was with my consent."

"I should think so. We'll run checks against our database, but..."

Petra nodded. She very much doubted they'd find a match.

Shirley stood up. "I'll keep you posted, obviously. Let me walk you back out."

As they retraced their steps along the corridor, Shirley glanced at Petra. "You staying in Glasgow a while, or heading back out to Arran?"

Petra forced a tight smile. "Arran."

Shirley didn't seem surprised by the answer. She pushed the main doors open for Petra, who gave her a nod as she made her way down the steps. *Damn these heels.*

Looking up at the leaden skyline, she felt a twinge of dread. Shirley Vance was right: this felt personal. Too personal.

She pulled out her phone: the next train to Ardrossan was in half an hour. Catching it that soon would be a push, but not impossible. She'd need to send an update to Mo when she was on the ferry. Let him know she was coming back.

She hailed a taxi and slid inside, tossing her bag on the seat beside her. "Queen Street Station."

As the cab pulled away, her eyes wandered across the

tired buildings and crowded streets of Glasgow. The city, and memories of her aunt, had always filled her with nostalgia. But now, it just amplified her unease. She shouldn't feel so glad to escape.

But could she ever face coming back?

CHAPTER FIFTY-SEVEN

Sam parked his patrol car just outside the thin tree line that separated the road from the campsite. The gravel crunched under his boots as he stepped out, the smell of last night's rain still lingering. He squinted into the overcast morning light. A fire pit smouldered, wispy smoke curling into the air, but the place felt eerily quiet despite the scattered tents.

Astrid Thorsen stood near her yurt with her hands on her hips. Her burgundy shawl was neat and simple, her posture composed. She was talking to Morgan Douglas, although "talking" might have been overstating it. There was a gulf of space between them, and the tension hanging in the air thick was enough to choke on. Morgan's expression was muted, and their gaze flicked to the ground every few seconds. Astrid, meanwhile, stayed still, almost regal, like a queen observing a restless subject.

Sam scratched the back of his neck. No sign of Professor MacLeod. Last he'd heard, MacLeod had been nearly as difficult as Astrid, ducking questions and digging his academic heels in. Not seeing him meant something, Sam was certain, but he wasn't sure exactly what.

He approached, soles pressing into the soft earth of the campsite. Neither Astrid nor Morgan acknowledged him.

"Morning," Sam called.

Astrid offered a dismissive smile. "Constable."

Morgan glanced at Sam, hesitated, then mumbled, "Morning," before returning their gaze to the ground. They adjusted the cuffs of their thick knitted jumper, fingers twitching.

"Is Professor MacLeod around?" Sam asked, his tone casual.

Astrid tilted her head, her stare steady. "Alistair went off to clear his head earlier. Sometimes he... prefers solitude."

"Right." Sam nodded. MacLeod alone somewhere on this part of Arran? That didn't sit right. Not with everything that was going on.

He glanced back towards the road. The site was dotted with the odd camper – two women beside a pop-up tent stirring a pot on a gas hob, some indistinct figures near the parking area stretching after what looked like a morning workout. But no sign of Alistair MacLeod.

"Well," Sam said, clearing his throat, "you let me know if he turns up."

Astrid said nothing. Morgan's mouth opened slightly, but they closed it again at a look from Astrid.

Sam turned on his heel, pulling his phone from his pocket as he walked back to the car. He tapped Mo's number, pacing as it rang. Something wasn't right. It wasn't just MacLeod's absence. It was the way Astrid and Morgan barely looked at each other, the way they avoided physical proximity like repelling magnets. He'd been in this job long enough to recognise when something wasn't being said.

The line was engaged. Sam cursed under his breath, hitting redial but getting the same result. He gritted his teeth, stepping back to the car but keeping his gaze on the campsite. A movement caught his eye.

Morgan was pacing in a wide arc near the yurt, their hands balled into fists, shoulders tense. Astrid watched them, calm and unflinching. It almost looked like she was waiting – for what, he had no idea.

Sam tapped Mo's number again; still engaged. The DS was a busy man.

"Brilliant," Sam muttered, pocketing the mobile with a stiff jerk of his arm.

He'd go to the station, find Mo. He and Stuart would be busy interviewing Freya, but he wanted to update them when they were done.

He glanced back at the campsite. *Professor MacLeod, where are you?* And did Astrid and Morgan know more about that than they were letting on?

CHAPTER FIFTY-EIGHT

IN THE SMALL, spartan interview room, Freya Haldane sat stiffly across the table, her hands clenched into fists on her lap. Her eyes darted nervously between Mo and Stuart, before settling on her assigned solicitor, Hana Sato. The young woman, dressed sharply in a tailored navy suit, gave Freya a curt nod, her demeanour poised. She leaned back in her chair, one elbow resting casually on the armrest, but her gaze was firm.

"Let's go over this again, Freya," Mo began. His hands rested flat on the table, fingers spread. "Can you tell us how you came to be in possession of the knife?"

Freya's lips tightened, a flicker of defiance in her eyes. "It's not my knife," she muttered, her voice barely audible.

Hana placed a hand on her client's forearm, a subtle reminder. "You don't have to answer that." She turned her gaze on Mo. "But if the question is relevant to—"

"It's relevant," Stuart cut in, his voice firmer than Mo would've liked. He halted when Mo raised a hand, warning without words to let him handle it.

"Freya," Mo said, leaning forward and softening his voice. "You said it wasn't yours, fine. But you were holding it. How did you come by it?"

She exhaled, her shoulders trembling. "It was part of the rituals."

Stuart shot Mo an incredulous look but stayed silent this time. Mo stayed focused on Freya. "What sort of rituals?"

Freya shook her head, her pale brown hair falling around her face. "I can't..." She squeezed her eyes shut, frowning, her face twitching.

Hana leaned forward. "If answering the question causes my client undue distress, we'll need to stop."

"Ms Sato," Mo said, keeping his eyes on Freya, "your client's brother has been murdered. I believe she wants to help, or at least set the record straight. If that's true, these questions are necessary."

Freya opened her eyes, her gaze flitting briefly between him and the solicitor. "We don't own the instruments," she blurted. "None of us. They're part of the Circle."

"By 'we,' you mean everyone in the Circle uses them?" Mo asked, meeting her agitation with calm.

Freya gave a tight shrug. "Maybe Astrid. Or Alistair. I don't – none of us own anything like that. It's just... there."

Stuart scoffed, earning a glare from Hana. Mo ignored them both and pressed on. "Do you think it could be the knife that was used to kill your brother?"

Freya's head shot up, her eyes alight with fury and grief. "I didn't kill him."

Mo frowned. "But two days ago, you told us you did."

Her lips quivered. Fresh tears rolled down her cheeks. She shook her head. "I was lying," she sobbed. "I didn't... I couldn't... I didn't kill Erik. I'm sorry. I just said it because I didn't know what else to do..."

"That's enough," Hana said sharply. She turned to Mo, her expression set. "My client is clearly in distress, and this line of questioning isn't achieving anything constructive. Freya needs psychological support, not further inter-rogation."

Mo sighed, leaning back in his chair. He hated this part of the job. The human wreckage cases like this left in their wake, the balance of pressing for answers without crossing the line. "Alright," he said. "We'll stop here for now."

Stuart looked like he wanted to argue, but a sharp look from Mo kept him silent. Hana stood, her hand brushing Freya's shoulder as she motioned for her to rise. Freya looked at Mo, her tear-streaked face as full of fear as it was of desperation.

"I didn't kill him," she mumbled again, almost apologeti-cally. Hana guided her towards the door.

When they were alone, Stuart exhaled, throwing his pen onto his notebook. "She's lying."

"She's confused," Mo corrected. "And grieving. There's a difference."

"Doesn't mean she's not involved." Stuart crossed his arms. "C'mon, Sarge, she's all over the place. First, she says she did it, then she didn't? Flip-flopping like that doesn't look innocent to me."

Mo looked at him. "Let the facts guide us, Stuart. Not gut feelings." He rose, stretching out his back. "And until we've got more, that includes giving her the benefit of the doubt."

Stuart mumbled under his breath, but didn't argue. Mo

headed towards the door. "Compile the notes. We'll regroup before revisiting this."

He stepped into the corridor, where he could just make out Freya's retreating form, her shoulders hunched as Hana murmured quietly to her. Mo paused, frowning. The knife, the rituals, Erik's death – it all hovered maddeningly just out of their grasp.

He needed Petra back. And despite what he'd said to Zoe, he needed the DI firing on all cylinders.

CHAPTER FIFTY-NINE

FRASER STOOD in the doorway of the Complex Crimes Unit. Jade didn't notice the grim expression he was wearing until Patty nudged her arm.

"Super's here. Looks like bad news," Patty murmured, before turning back to her computer.

Jade glanced up, her stomach tightening when Fraser caught her eye. He motioned towards the meeting room with a tilt of his head, his face giving nothing away.

She stood, pushing her chair back. "I won't be long," she said to Patty.

Patty nodded. "Take as long as you need."

Patty would have worked out that Jade hadn't told Fraser about her MS. But had she guessed they were in a relationship?

Jade followed Fraser into the small, glass-walled meeting room. He shut the door behind them and faced her, arms crossed over his chest. The fluorescent light above cast sharp shadows on his features, deepening the lines etched into his face.

"Sit," he said softly.

She didn't. "What's going on? Has something happened with the case?"

His mouth opened, but no words came. He glanced at the floor, his fingers working at the cuffs of his sleeves. She stared at him, the knot in her gut growing tighter.

Whatever he was here to say, he was dragging it out.

"Fraser," she said more firmly. "Just tell me."

Her voice shook, dammit. She clenched her hands into fists. She wouldn't let nerves or fear beat her. Not here. Not in front of him.

Still, Fraser hesitated. And in that silence, something inside her broke. She swallowed thickly, the words out before she could stop them.

"I've got MS."

She put out a hand, feeling like the floor had suddenly stopped supporting her. She heard her own words echo faintly in her head. That was the first time she'd said it to anyone other than Patty. Not even her mum knew yet. Not even Rory.

Fraser's head lifted, his brows knitting in surprise, but no sound came from him. He took a step closer, then stopped, his hands dropping to his sides.

There. It was out. She pushed back her shoulders, ready for whatever came next.

"I—" Fraser started. He studied her face. His eyes softened, the worry changing into something deeper.

Her voice cracked when she said it again. "I've got MS, Fraser. Multiple sclerosis. Diagnosis isn't official, but the doc's certain. I'm waiting on another appointment to finalise it." She forced herself to breathe in through her nose and out through her mouth. Tears pricked her eyes, and she prayed none would fall.

"I'm sorry, Jade," he said softly. "I- I didn't know."

"Well, it's not something you just drop into conversation, is it?" She covered her face with her hands. "Sorry. I didn't mean that."

"Don't apologise," he said, his voice gentle. "This is... that's huge. Jade, it's bloody huge."

Before she knew what was happening, he'd closed the space between them and wrapped her up in his arms. For a moment she stiffened, out of habit, but then sank into it, her body trembling despite herself. She hadn't realised how badly she needed an anchor until now.

And then the tears came.

"Fraser..." she whispered. She clutched at his jacket, burying her face against his chest as silent sobs wracked her body.

"It's OK," he murmured. "You don't need to hold it all in, not with me."

She wasn't sure how long they stayed like that, but eventually the tears slowed, and her grip loosened. Her arms fell to her sides, and he stepped back, giving her space but staying close enough.

"I hate this. I hate that I've got to deal with it now. Rory's so young. What am I meant to do if..."

She couldn't finish that thought. Not here.

"You'll deal with it the same way you've dealt with everything else these last few years," Fraser said. "By facing it, one bloody day at a time. You're not alone in this, Jade."

She nodded, looking over his shoulder at the whiteboard covered in their sprawling flowcharts for Erik Haldane's case. *Distraction.*

"Thanks," she said, her voice steadier. "For... Just thanks."

"Anytime," he said.

She shook her head, brushing imaginary lint from the sleeve of her blouse. "What were you going to tell me, before I blurted all that out?"

Fraser's brows knitted together again, and his mouth tightened.

"Nothing," he said eventually.

Jade narrowed her eyes. "Fraser..."

He held up a hand. "Not now, Jade. Just – it's not urgent. It can wait."

He turned, pushing the meeting room door open and stepping out into the main office. She watched his retreating back as he strode past the empty desks and out towards the car park.

Out of the window beyond Patty's desk, she watched him lingering by his car, phone to his ear. He leaned on the bonnet, his head bowed. He looked weighed down.

Jade returned to her desk and sat heavily in her chair.

Patty peered at her. "What did Super want?"

Jade gazed at her computer screen.

"I'm not sure what I've done," she muttered, more to herself than to Patty.

Patty frowned. "That sounds ominous."

Jade didn't reply, her mind racing.

Turning her chair, she looked back at the car park. Fraser's car was still there, but he'd moved out of sight. For a moment, she wondered who was on the other end of that call, and whether it had anything to do with her.

CHAPTER SIXTY

PETRA STEPPED off the train at Ardrossan Harbour, heels clicking against the platform. She adjusted the strap of her handbag and glanced at her phone to see a message from Mo.

Freya's been arrested. Attacked Astrid. We've still got that earlier confession to the murder. But something's off. Need your input.

She shook her head. She didn't buy the confession either. Freya might've been rattled, maybe even unhinged, but murder? The motive wasn't clear, and neither was the method.

She tucked the phone away and scanned the ferry terminal. Cold gusts rolled in from the Firth of Clyde, tugging at the hem of her coat and carrying a distasteful mix of sea salt and diesel. It was quiet, save for the hum of the occasional lorry pulling up to the terminal. The ferry sat at the dock, an unmoving beast. A handful of passengers loitered by the waiting area.

Petra's gaze landed on a familiar face. She frowned.

What the hell are you doing here?

Professor Alistair MacLeod was at the wheel of a battered old Volvo, the window cracked just wide enough to allow the edge of a cigarette to protrude. He seemed lost in thought, staring through the windscreen as if the answers to the whole case might appear on the horizon.

Her stomach tightened. MacLeod wasn't supposed to leave the island. That had been made very clear. Steeling herself, she approached the car, her heels loud against the weathered pavement.

She rapped on the window. Alistair MacLeod startled and stubbed out the cigarette in a clumsy scramble.

"Professor MacLeod," she said, tilting her head. "You're far from where you're meant to be."

He wound the window down fully, raising his hands in mock surrender. "Dr McBride. The ever-watchful eyes of Police Scotland. What a surprise."

She didn't correct him: *not Police.* "DS Uddin said all members of the Circle were to remain available for questioning, on the island," she said. "Care to explain why you're here?"

Alistair leaned back in his seat with a half-smile. "You forensic types. Always so methodical. Tell me, do you ever question the rules?"

"Every other Tuesday," she said. "Now – explanation, Professor."

He tapped his fingers on the steering wheel, then flicked a glance to the passenger seat, where a crumpled rucksack sat. "Can we talk?"

"Of course we can talk," Petra replied. "But let's start with why you thought buggering off seemed like a brilliant idea."

Alistair opened the car door, stepped out, and gestured

back inside. "Not here. Too many ears. My car's warm enough, if that's alright with you? I assume we're both intending to be on the next ferry?"

Petra considered. Her instincts were buzzing. But she needed answers, and if Alistair MacLeod wanted to talk, she wasn't about to waste the opportunity.

"Fine," she said, stepping around to the passenger side. "But no funny business, Professor. I'm in no mood."

"Oh, perish the thought," he said, holding the door for her with an exaggerated flourish.

She slid into the seat, the smell of stale cigarettes and damp upholstery making her wrinkle her nose. Alistair took the driver's seat again, adjusting himself as though settling in for a long confession. Petra pulled the door shut behind her and waited.

"Well?" she prompted. "You've got my attention."

He exhaled through his nose, his fingers twitching on the steering wheel.

"Freya," he began. "She's not your killer."

"That's not news. Tell me something I don't know."

He turned to face her. "You're wasting time holding her. Look elsewhere."

"Like where?" Petra didn't have time for this. "Or should I say, like whom?"

Alistair studied her face. "Astrid. Or perhaps... someone Astrid's influenced."

Petra bit back the urge to groan. "Professor, forgive me, but Astrid Thorsen is the most predictable answer you could have given me. So predictable, in fact, that she's *not*. Too convenient. Too..." She waved a hand. "Obvious."

"That woman has more blood on her hands than you're willing to acknowledge," Alistair growled. "She preys on them. All of them. Erik. Freya. Morgan. Her influence is toxic."

"And yet, you were right there beside her, playing her little games. Weren't you?"

He sneered. "Because I believed in the rituals. The purpose of it all. Her methods –manipulative as they might be – sometimes worked."

"Worked?" Petra arched an eyebrow. "Worked how? Enlighten me."

He paused, as though hesitant to say any more. His fingers clenched the wheel tighter. "If you dig deep enough into belief, Dr McBride, you find truths you aren't prepared for. And some truths... some truths are too dangerous."

"How philosophical," Petra said. *What gobbledegook.* "But philosophy isn't going to cut it here, Professor. Did you see Astrid kill Erik? Do you *know* anything concrete, or are we wasting each other's time?"

He held her gaze. "I didn't *see* it. But I know she orchestrated it."

"Convenient."

"Call it what you like," he said. "But if you don't stop her, there'll be more bodies."

"Save the ominous warnings," she snapped. "You're telling me the woman orchestrated Erik Haldane's murder? Fine. Back it up. Tell me how she did it, and don't leave anything out."

Alistair scratched at his jaw. "It wasn't quick, if that's what you're asking. It wasn't even necessarily physical."

Petra stared at him. "You're losing me here."

"I didn't say she did it herself. I said she orchestrated it. And for now, that's all I'll say."

"For now?" Petra echoed, exasperated. "No, Professor.

That's not how this works. You've already tried to leave the island. Withholding information from me only makes you look worse."

"I've said enough," he said. "Believe me or don't, Dr McBride. Just don't turn your back on her."

His cryptic evasions had lit a fire under Petra's suspicions, but she bit back her retorts. Forcing him wouldn't work; he'd simply retreat further into academic arrogance.

"Right, well," she finally said, unclipping her seatbelt. "I'm sure your solicitor will enjoy hearing all about this little tendency of yours to withhold information, when the stakes are life and death."

Alistair shook his head. "I don't think so."

She resisted a laugh. "What are you on about?"

He flicked a button on his door and turned the key in the ignition. Before she had a chance to react, he'd pulled out of the queue and was turning around, the wheels screaming.

"What are you doing?" she gasped.

He gave her a look, eyes sparkling. "Not going back to the Isle of Arran, that's what."

Petra grabbed her door handle. He'd locked the doors.

Bastard.

She could release the catch on her own door, though. She did so, then realised they were driving away from the terminal, too fast for her to jump out.

What the hell?

"Let me out," she said, working hard to keep her voice level.

He laughed. "Not just yet. First we need to have a proper chat."

CHAPTER SIXTY-ONE

Mo PARKED up in the service vehicle area near the ferry terminal. The skies were grey, dark clouds racing over their heads. Beside him, Stuart fiddled with his phone, scrolling through the latest updates from the lab.

"Still nothing new on that sarong," Stuart muttered, shifting in his seat.

Mo glanced at him before looking back out at the rolling waves. "Wendy said it could take time. You can't rush this sort of thing."

"Feels like it's dragging, though. Freya's in custody, but everything feels... off. You reckon she's telling the truth?"

Mo didn't answer. He leaned forward, resting his forearms on the steering wheel, and watched the water. A ferry was just docking, the low hum of its engines drilling through the stillness.

"Something about all of this doesn't add up," he said. "But we're not about to decide it here, so let's leave it to the evidence, yes?"

Stuart gave a reluctant nod. Silence filled the car, punctuated only by the occasional buzz from Stuart's phone.

Mo turned to him. "You alright? You've been quieter than usual."

"Haven't been sleeping much, to be honest. Cases like this... And not to mention that bloody bed." Stuart tapped the phone screen repeatedly. "I dunno. I like a puzzle as much as the next man, but this one feels like I'm not seeing the pieces right."

"You're young, Stuart. You'll get used to cases feeling like this," Mo replied. "It's the messy ones where you learn the most."

Stuart looked unconvinced, but didn't argue.

The ferry's gangplank slammed down onto the terminal's platform with a metallic thud. Mo checked the time. Petra's ferry was scheduled to dock now; she'd texted from the train to let him know she'd catch this one, hoping for a lift.

"She'll be in one of those waves of passengers," Mo said, looking up at the glass-sided bridge that passengers were beginning to walk along. He switched off the engine and leaned back in his seat, relaxing slightly. "We'll wait here for her to find us."

Passengers began to emerge from the terminal building – a slow trickle at first, then more, bundled up in waterproof jackets and scarves against the island chill. Some wheeled suitcases over the concrete. Others carried rucksacks or clutched bags of shopping. Mo scanned the faces but couldn't see Petra.

"So what d'you make of her then – Dr McBride?" Stuart asked, breaking the silence.

Mo raised an eyebrow. "Petra?"

"Bit of a loose cannon, isn't she? Not exactly your usual

'hold your hand and give you a pat on the back' psychologist."

"She's good at what she does," Mo said after a pause. "Knows when to push people and when to step back. Might not work for everyone, but," he shrugged, "she gets results."

Truth was, he and Petra had rubbed each other up the wrong way, at the beginning. She'd understood him too quickly, and he didn't like it. She'd learned to back off, and he'd learned to accept the way she worked. Not to mention coming to the realisation that she knew what she was doing.

"You've spent more time with her than me," Stuart said. "She still seems a bit... intense."

"You should see me when I wake up in the morning," Mo joked. "Intense doesn't begin to cover it."

Stuart chuckled. "Fair enough. I'll give her a chance."

Mo's phone vibrated against the dashboard. He glanced down at the screen. Wendy.

"Take this as a sign," he murmured, unclipping the phone from the holder. He turned to Stuart, who was still scrolling. "Do us a favour, Stuart. Go and check the building for Petra. Maybe she's come out and somehow missed us. See if you can find her and bring her back here."

Stuart looked less than thrilled. "Right. Because wandering around ferry terminals in the rain clearly falls under 'other duties as assigned.'"

"It's good for you," Mo said as he answered the call. "Wendy, what've you got for me?"

Stuart left the car, sending cold air inside. Mo shivered.

"Lab's just come back with another result on the knife Freya used to attack Astrid," Wendy said.

Mo adjusted his seat, his free hand gripping the wheel. "Go on."

Wendy cleared her throat. "There's damage to the blade – the kind of damage you'd see if it'd hit something hard. Wood or bone, maybe. It's consistent with Erik's wounds."

"Right." Mo held his breath as he processed the words.

"But listen," Wendy added. "That doesn't mean it was the knife used in Erik's actual murder. It just makes it a possibility. We'd still have to reconstruct the injury to see if it's a match for *the* weapon."

"Still a far cry from wrapping this up in a bow, then?"

She sighed. "I know. I'm passing this to you first because I know you're wary of jumping to conclusions. Freya's confession complicates things further... doesn't gel, if you ask me."

"It doesn't gel because it doesn't make sense." Mo glanced out at the now-thinner stream of passengers exiting the ferry building. "But thanks, Wendy. I'll keep you updated once I run it by DI Tanner."

"Cheers, Mo. Take care."

The line went dead. Mo stared at the darkened screen in his hand, his thumb hovering for a moment over the DI's contact. He tapped it and brought the phone back to his ear.

It rang three times before going to voicemail. "Boss, it's Mo. I've just spoken to Wendy; the analysis on Freya's knife came back. Could be something. I'll fill you in when you've got a minute – call me."

He hung up, exhaling as the implications clicked into place. Freya's initial confession, then her retraction. The knife. Erik's murder. It was all wrong.

The passenger's side door flew open, caught by a gust as Stuart climbed back in, shaking his damp hair. "No sign of Petra. I checked everywhere – the shops, lounge, even further up into Brodick. Either she's taking her sweet time, or she wasn't on that ferry."

Mo frowned. "You sure she wasn't just blending into the crowd?"

"She's five foot nothing with an updo that makes her look like the bloody Queen. Fair to say she doesn't exactly blend in."

Despite himself, Mo smirked. "Fair point." His gut tightened.

He grabbed his phone and dialled Petra's number; no answer. He typed out a message: *At the ferry terminal, did you miss it? Let me know when to pick you up.*

He slammed his phone into the holder, frustrated. He didn't need this.

If Petra wasn't on the ferry, where the hell was she?

CHAPTER SIXTY-TWO

THE CAR ROARED along the M77, tyres swallowing up the miles towards Glasgow. Alistair MacLeod sat behind the wheel, his knuckles pale as he gripped the steering wheel. The countryside blurred by in a riot of deep green hills and slate-grey skies. Rain lashed the windscreen.

Petra sat stiffly in the passenger seat, glancing occasionally towards Alistair's rigid profile. Every instinct screamed at her to say something, but she forced herself to stay still.

Breathe. Think.

Her phone was gone, snatched from her hand and tossed out of the window as they were leaving Ardrossan. She'd leaned across the seats like she might leap out after it, but Alistair's foot on the accelerator had stalled that plan in its tracks. Now, she stared out of the window, trying to judge where they were.

But she didn't drive. Geography wasn't her strong suit, and Ayrshire's roads were unknown to her. All she knew was that she'd seen repeated signs for Glasgow. But who was to say they wouldn't turn off before they got there?

MacLeod was from Aberdeen, originally. That was hundreds of miles away.

All she could do was count landmarks, though half of them looked the same –another bloody hill, another sheep chewing on bracken, another road junction sweeping past under the clouded sky. A fork in the road that led... led where? She clenched her teeth in frustration.

"What are we doing, Alistair?" she asked, angry at the crack she could hear in her voice. "Where the bloody hell are we going?"

He didn't answer. His jaw tightened, the tendons in his neck standing out. His foot pressed harder on the pedal, the engine whining as the car picked up speed.

"Listen," she tried, her tone firmer. "You've dragged me out here under false pretences. You've taken my phone. Thrown it away, no less. This is kidnapping, you do realise that?"

The absurdity of the word hung heavy in the air. *Kidnapping*. It sounded like something out of a daft drama, not her actual life. Yet here she was, locked in a car with an academic who'd clearly lost the plot.

"Alistair," she said, sharper this time. "Whatever you're doing, it isn't going to end well for you. Talk to me. Tell me why you're doing this."

"Shut up," he muttered.

Her gut twisted. "Excuse me?"

"I said, shut up!" His hand slammed the dashboard, the noise jolting Petra. His eyes stayed glued to the road, his lips pressed together, but his voice was harsh. "You think you know everything, don't you? Crawling around on that campsite, poking and prodding at things you don't understand."

"Help me understand, then," she shot back. "You're an intelligent man, Alistair. Start acting like it. We can fix this."

His laugh was hard. "Fix this? Like I'm some wayward child who needs to be sent to the naughty step? Spare me your psychobabble."

Petra exhaled, flexing her fingers against the car door handle. But they were driving too fast, and she had nowhere she could run to anyway.

As the car thundered around yet another bend, she resumed studying the outside landscape, willing some detail to stick. A gnarled tree twisted like a grim sculpture, its branches stark and bare even in the early autumn drizzle. A distant farmhouse stood in the distance, smoke rising from its chimney.

She caught the sign for a junction just before they flashed past it. Wester Galston, wherever that was. She filed it away, desperate to note something concrete. *Keep talking, Petra.*

"Look, Alistair." She softened her voice, coaxing. She kept her eyes on the countryside, pretending she wasn't watching the strain on his face. "If this is about Astrid, you don't have to protect her. You and I both know she's dangerous."

His face flickered. Petra saw her chance.

"You think she gives a toss about you?" she said. "The way she uses people... Erik saw it too, didn't he?"

His hands tightened around the wheel so visibly she almost winced for him.

"He tried to leave," she continued, her tones still measured. "That's what Astrid couldn't stomach, right? Losing one of her precious disciples. But you're different. You're objective. You know she manipulates."

"Shut. Up." His voice was a growl, but there was a faint tremor running through it. Maybe she could talk him down. "You've got no idea what you're talking about," he snapped, his voice bristling now. "None. Do you think Erik was some bloody saint? He knew what he was getting into. We all do."

Maybe she couldn't.

"So you're admitting you know what happened to him?"

MacLeod's nostrils flared as his foot pushed harder on the accelerator. Petra cursed herself. Getting anything useful from Alistair felt like defusing a bomb with one hand behind her back.

The car sped up. Eighty miles per hour. Eighty-two. She forced her expression into neutrality.

"You weren't like this in your lectures, were you, Alistair?" she tried again, shifting tack. "Rational. Thoughtful. That's what Astrid must've liked about you. But she's twisted your ideals, hasn't she? Turned them into her own warped version of Norse mythology?"

She thought of the knife, those photos she'd looked at in her hotel room. She said nothing.

He shot out a hand, pushing into her chest with his palm. "Shut. Up. Just keep quiet. Or..."

He didn't finish the sentence. But she needed to listen to him. He had control, whether she liked it or not.

CHAPTER SIXTY-THREE

Mo LEANED against the table in the community centre, thumbing through his notes. Stuart was absorbed, twirling a pen between his fingers.

"Got the feeling we're running out of time," Stuart said, his eyes fixed on the timeline written on the whiteboard. "Too many threads overlapping, not enough ends to tie them all up."

"Focus on the details." Mo swallowed. "If we chase everything at once, we're going to miss something vital."

The door opened with a blast of cold air and Sam stepped in, his boots leaving muddy prints.

"Been back to the campsite," he said. "MacLeod's still not there. Morgan's saying he didn't come back last night."

"You spoke to them?" Stuart asked. Morgan wasn't one for words.

Sam shrugged. "Didn't get much out of 'em. Just that MacLeod left last night, hasn't come back."

Mo exchanged a glance with Stuart. "We specifically

told them..." He gritted his teeth and grabbed his coat. "Let's get over there. I want to know where he is."

"You sure?" Stuart asked.

It was fully dark now, and the community centre was warm. But Mo wasn't about to let that distract him.

"I am," he said. "Come on, both of you."

He yanked open the door, not caring about the cold. At last, he had a sense of purpose.

CHAPTER SIXTY-FOUR

THE SKY outside the CCU offices was dark when Jade shut down her computer. Staring at the screen had left her eyes sore. She rubbed her temples, the dull throb in her head refusing to shift.

"I'm not feeling too good, Patty," she said. "Going to take these case files home before the traffic gets too bad."

"No problem, boss."

Jade frowned at the sound of her mobile buzzing on the desk. She glanced at the screen: *Mo*. Of course.

"Tell me you've got good news," she said, cradling the phone between her ear and shoulder while she gathered up papers.

"Well, it depends on how you look at it," Mo replied. "MacLeod's gone."

Jade stilled. "What do you mean, 'gone'?"

"Sam's been keeping an eye on the campsite. He went there an hour ago, Morgan Douglas told him MacLeod left last night and hasn't been back since."

"Why the hell didn't they tell you earlier?"

"Beats me. We're on our way over there now. But... if he's on the mainland, we might need help."

"Sure." Jade rubbed around her eyes. There was a pain behind the left eye she didn't remember feeling before. "Call Patty. She can help you out."

"Er... OK. Everything alright over there?"

"Everything's fine. Just call Patty if you need us to involve Uniform. OK?"

"Of course."

Jade hung up, feeling bad. Mo was only doing his job, and he deserved an explanation from her.

But not yet. And not over the phone.

CHAPTER SIXTY-FIVE

THE DARKNESS FOLDED itself around MacLeod's car as it sped along the M8 past Glasgow. Petra considered waving and shouting, trying to get the attention of other drivers, but this was the motorway, in the dark. No one would see her, and even if they did, she'd be gone before they had time to react.

Past Glasgow and heading north, the headlights cut through the night, bouncing off the occasional reflective sign, but the rest was black and impenetrable. Petra sat stiffly in the passenger seat, gazing out at the faint flashes of country-side, her hands clamped together in her lap. She was starting to feel fear.

MacLeod hadn't spoken in almost an hour. His knuckles were wrapped tightly around the wheel, his focus locked on the road. He was either thinking ahead, or just hoping to avoid the inevitable.

She turned towards him, keeping her voice steady. "Alistair, I need to ask you something."

He grunted. "You can try."

"About the knife," she continued.

He turned sharply towards her with a frown. "What knife?"

Petra pursed her lips. "You know what knife."

He snorted, eyes snapping back to the road. His breathing had grown heavier.

"I did some research," she went on, keeping her tone neutral, like she was talking about the weather. "Pulled up a few research papers on ceremonial Viking pieces. You know, the kind you seem to have a particular interest in. There was a knife, one with a carved handle resembling entwined tree branches." She hesitated. "The police have it."

The car surged as MacLeod's foot pushed down on the accelerator, his earlier calm yielding to something less controlled. "How?"

"Freya Haldane used it to attack your wife."

He glanced at her, his eyes wild. "What?"

"Last night. When exactly did you leave the campsite?"

He hadn't been there. Had he been gone overnight?

"Freya used that knife to attack Astrid," she repeated. "We were there, we stopped her. Freya is now under arrest."

"Astrid?"

"She's fine," Petra said, noting the edge of worry in his voice. So he *did* still care about Astrid. "But," she continued, "I believe that knife was yours. Was it?"

"Fucking woman," he muttered. The car slowed and he indicated.

Petra held her breath. What now?

The car pulled off the road and into a lay-by. MacLeod stilled the engine. He sat for a moment, his hands resting on the wheel. His breathing was ragged, his shoulders hunched.

I've rattled him. Question was, had that been wise?

"You shouldn't have told me," he repeated, quieter now, almost resigned.

"Why not?" Petra asked, dead calm.

He gestured around them. "We're in the middle of nowhere, and I can tell by the way you've been trying to spot landmarks that you've got no idea about the roads."

He leaned towards her, his breath hot. She shrank back.

"And I," he said with a smile, "as I'm sure you've worked out by now, have a tendency for violence."

CHAPTER SIXTY-SIX

Mo stood at the edge of the campsite, Stuart and Sam behind him. Astrid stood by a campfire, her figure tall and rigid, her hair tied into plaits which caught the light. Morgan was a few steps away, head bowed, their shoulders hunched like a scolded child. Astrid's voice lashed out at them.

"Tell me, Morgan," she hissed, her voice sharp. "Why didn't you say anything? How long had you known Erik was planning to leave?"

Morgan stayed silent.

"Are you deaf? Or just disloyal?" Astrid's voice hardened. "Do you have any idea what he could have done — what he was prepared to destroy? He betrayed us, and you... you allowed it."

Mo stepped forward as Stuart cleared his throat.

"Sarge."

"Not now," Mo said. He approached the fire. "Astrid," he called out. "What exactly are you accusing Morgan of?"

Astrid turned to him, her expression venomous. "I don't answer to you, Sergeant."

"And yet," Mo said, planting his feet, "here I am, asking."

She pointed a finger at Morgan. "Loyalty and honesty are the lifeblood of our Circle. If someone fails to demonstrate those, they're a threat to all of us."

"Erik was hardly a threat," Mo shot back. "From what I've heard, he was trying to leave peacefully."

"Leave peacefully?" Astrid let out a harsh laugh. "He was planning to expose us!"

Morgan's head snapped up, their mouth opening, but no words followed.

"Expose you how?" Mo asked.

"You wouldn't understand." Astrid turned her attention back to Morgan, eyes narrowing. "Why didn't you tell me, Morgan? I trusted you."

Morgan dropped their gaze, their hands wringing and their silence painful.

"Where's Alistair?" Mo asked. He looked at the other tents around the site, but could see no sign of the professor.

Astrid's lips curled in disdain. "He went home."

"Sarge," said Stuart, a pace behind him. Mo waved a hand in dismissal.

"Home," Mo said to Astrid. "Where is home?"

She shrugged. "Wherever the wind takes him. He's had enough of me, that's for sure. Why, you want to talk to him?"

"Where has he gone, Astrid?"

She laughed. "You're asking the wrong person, Sergeant."

"Sarge."

Mo turned with a sigh. "What is it, Stuart?"

Stuart was holding his phone out. "Patty called. She's been onto CalMac ferries. Alistair MacLeod was booked onto the one arriving at Brodick at 13:55."

Mo's expression stiffened. A cold weight settled in his gut. "13:55?"

"That's the one," Stuart confirmed.

Mo swallowed. "That's the one Petra should have been on."

Mo pulled out his phone and dialled Petra's number. The line rang three times before a woman's voice answered – soft, tremulous. Not Petra.

"Hello?"

"Petra?"

"No, sorry pet. Is this her phone?"

Shit. "This is DS Mo Uddin, Police Scotland," Mo said, his voice tight. "I'm trying to reach Dr McBride. Are you using her phone?"

"I found this at Ardrossan, just lying there near the harbour. I was going to hand it in to the police."

Ardrossan. The phone had been dropped near the harbour.

Or...

Mo looked at Stuart. "It's Petra."

"I know, Sarge. I've been trying to—"

Mo grabbed the DC's arm. "No. I think MacLeod's got her."

CHAPTER SIXTY-SEVEN

Mo hurried to the car, thinking back to his conversation with the DI. *Call Patty*, she'd said. He dialled the DC's number.

"Patty, it's Mo. You've been speaking to Stuart, telling him abou—"

"Number plate for MacLeod's car's matched the ferry booking he used." Patty's tone was businesslike. "The system clocked him checking in on time, but he didn't get on the ferry. If he's got Petra, that's the vehicle they're in."

Mo glanced at Stuart, who looked agitated. "Right," he told Patty, "stay on the system, keep eyes on that plate if it turns up. Good work, Patty."

"What's the plan then, Sarge?" Stuart said. "We're not just staying put, are we?"

Mo rubbed the bridge of his nose. "The last ferry has long since left, and that wouldn't get us there in time to do anything useful. We have to sit tight, let the police on the mainland find her. Patty, we need to put out an ANPR alert, get Traffic to look for him on the main roads from Ardrossan."

"The ferry was due to leave about five hours ago," she said. "He could be in Glasgow by now, for all we know. Or past it."

Mo swallowed. *Petra, where are you?* "Put out that ANPR alert. Speak to traffic control for the motorway network, and the routes out of Ardrossan. Let's see if we can piece together a timeline."

"Already on it, Sarge." Patty hung up.

"Petra's in danger," Stuart said. "MacLeod's a nutter. God knows what he might do to her. How can we just... wait?"

Mo shook his head. "The best thing – the only thing – we can do is go back to the community centre. We can make ourselves useful from there."

Stuart got into the passenger seat, but he didn't look happy. "If we lose her..."

"We won't," Mo said, more to himself than anyone else.

Mo was about to start his car when there was a rap on the window. Astrid Thorsen was outside, as imperious as always.

"What's going on?" she asked when Mo opened the window.

"MacLeod's missing. So's our colleague, Dr McBride," he said bluntly. He watched her for a reaction.

She blinked. Her lips tightened into a fine line. Then, with the faintest shake of her head, she muttered, "Shit."

Mo straightened. "What is it, Astrid? Do you know something about Alistair you haven't bothered to mention?"

Astrid chewed her lip. She looked away from the car, towards the campfire, then back at him. "I might do."

Mo put a hand on the door handle, ready to jump out and grab her, force her to tell him what she knew.

"Sarge," muttered Stuart. "Don't."

Mo glanced at the DC. How had he known?

He took a breath. Long, ragged.

"Tell us, Astrid," he said. "You either tell us right now, or I take you to Lamlash to share a cell with Freya. What is Alistair capable of?"

"You really don't want to know," she replied.

CHAPTER SIXTY-EIGHT

Mo PUSHED the yurt flap aside with more force than necessary, his jaw tight as he stepped inside. The scent of incense hung thick in the air, mixing with the humidity of the canvas walls. Astrid had entered first and sat on her customary wing-backed chair. *That bloody chair.* Morgan stood behind her, subdued but watchful.

Stuart slipped through the flap after Mo, saying nothing, just standing silent by the open entrance.

Mo didn't waste time. "You claim to preach connection and healing, Astrid, yet a man is dead, another attacked, and fingers are pointing squarely at this so-called circle of yours. Care to explain how things have gone so thoroughly to hell under your watch?"

Astrid tilted her head, calm as a still loch. "An unfortunate string of coincidences, Detective Sergeant."

Mo snorted. "Coincidences. Right. Did Erik bleeding out in a Viking boat look like a 'coincidence' to you? Or Freya, wielding a knife, lunging at you? Because it doesn't to me."

He stepped closer. "Start talking, or I'll have to take you to the police station too and caution you."

Morgan stiffened behind Astrid, but kept their mouth shut.

Astrid sighed, shaking her head. "Freya didn't mean to attack me. She's confused... grieving."

"And the knife?"

Her gaze hardened. "Belonged to Alistair. He's the one who brought it here."

Morgan's lips parted in shock, their calm faltering for a second before they masked their reaction.

"And you're only *now* mentioning this?" Mo could hear his voice rising. He'd given up caring.

Astrid arched a brow. "You've been rather... excitable, Detective. I didn't think you'd take the revelation kindly."

"We both know you're hiding things, Astrid. What else are you going to 'reveal' when it's too late for us to act on it?"

She smiled, her gaze travelling into the distance. "If you must know, Erik and I were..." She paused. "... involved."

Mo blinked, caught off guard despite himself. "Involved," he repeated, voice flat. "Do elaborate, please."

She gave him a smug smile. "We cared for one another deeply. Erik understood me. Alistair... did not." She held his gaze. "Alistair knew about us. It bruised his pride."

Mo raised his arm suddenly, his hand stopping just shy of the canvas wall he'd nearly punched. Stuart stepped forward instinctively, a hand lingering near Mo's shoulder.

"You OK, Sarge?" Stuart's tone was hesitant.

Astrid's smile didn't waver. "Have I struck a nerve?"

Mo took two measured breaths, then leaned down so he was at eye level with Astrid.

"If my colleague ends up in a ditch – or worse – because of you playing coy..."

Astrid's expression shifted. Was that regret? "I would never wish harm on another, Sergeant. Mistakes have been made, yes, but I've told you everything I know now."

"Yeah, right," Stuart muttered from his position by the doorway.

Mo straightened but kept his gaze locked on Astrid. "You shrug off every chance to tell the truth, holding back as if this were a game. But you're not in control here." He gestured to Stuart. "Take Morgan out of here for a proper statement."

Morgan looked to Astrid, waiting for some unspoken permission. When none came, they followed Stuart without a word.

Alone now, Mo studied Astrid, wondering if he could drag more secrets from her. She gazed back at him, impassive.

He pushed out a breath and turned to leave the yurt.

Better to get out now, before he did something he regretted.

CHAPTER SIXTY-NINE

JADE GRIPPED the steering wheel as her car hugged the curve of the road, the loch a sinkhole of blackness to her right. The A82's route along Loch Lomond's western shore was as beautiful as it was treacherous, the road too fast and the streetlights too dim. It was where Dan had died, although that had been in the morning.

Still, she never enjoyed it. Maybe now, with Fraser a part of her life, she would move.

Did she dare do that to Rory? A new man, and a new home?

The road twisted, shadowed by trees on the left, their bulk outlined against a silver-sheened night sky. She couldn't decide whether the loch calmed or unsettled her, its vastness mirroring her swirling thoughts.

Her phone buzzed in the centre console, breaking the silence. She activated the hands-free.

"Mo," she said, her voice tight. *Call Patty*, she'd said.

"Boss." His tone was laced with an urgency that made her sit straighter. "There's something you need to know."

"Go on." She glanced at the clock. Rory would be getting ready for bed, snuggling down under his dinosaur-patterned duvet while her mum read him a story. And she'd hoped to spend time with him. *Damn Glasgow traffic*. Maybe she should move to the eastern side of the city. Maybe she should stop planning her future and listen to Mo.

She focused back on the road as he continued.

"It's Petra. She's missing."

Jade's stomach dipped. "What d'you mean, missing?"

"She was supposed to be back in Brodick," he said. "She didn't get on the ferry. We've got confirmation from the terminal. And before you ask, I've already checked her mobile. It was found at the harbour."

"Found?" Jade's grip on the wheel tightened as the road straightened out. "Where exactly?"

"On the roadside. I've put an alert out for Alistair MacLeod's car – he was supposed to be on the same ferry, and he checked in, but he didn't get on it either. We think he might have taken Petra."

"Fuck." MacLeod. Of course, it would be him. Jade drew in a deep breath, her mind racing. "And the rest of it? Have you found anything more about Erik?"

Mo sighed. "Astrid was having an affair with Erik." He let the words settle before continuing. "Apparently he'd been confronting her about what he saw as manipulation – wanted out of the Circle. Guess she had other ways of keeping control."

"So Astrid killed him?"

"That's not our current theory."

"And your current theory is...?"

"Alistair caught them together. He was jealous. Angry. The knife that was used to kill Erik... it belonged to him."

"Do you have any forensics linking him to it?"

"Not yet."

Shit. "You have to find him, Mo. If he's got Petra..."

"I know. He's our strongest suspect now. Alistair, not Astrid. But if she's willing to let us focus on him, it suits her just fine."

Jade eased her foot on the brake as the road dipped close to the loch. The headlights skimmed over the black ripple of water beside her. "The Circle members haven't told us everything," she muttered. "Not by a long shot. Astrid controls them, but Morgan – Morgan's the weak link. Question them."

"Without Astrid around?"

"Exactly." She nodded to herself. "Bring them in under caution. Lay it out – the knife, the affair, Erik's doubts. Let's see what cracks."

"You sure Morgan'll talk?"

Jade considered what she'd read in Petra's reports. "Astrid hides behind them because they're loyal, but if MacLeod and Astrid are both in the frame, loyalty might not matter as much." Her foot lifted off the brake as the road straightened again, home not far ahead.

"Alright," Mo said after a moment. "I'll take Morgan to the station for a formal interview."

"Good. Keep me updated." Jade's voice stayed steady as she approached the turning to her home. She slowed the car and flicked her indicator, her mind already on Rory.

"Boss," Mo added, breaking her thoughts again. "I hope you don't mind me calling you. I know you're on your way home."

"You did the right thing, Mo." She reached over to end the call. "You always do."

As she glanced back up, a flood of searing white obscured everything. Panic tightened her chest.

"Christ!" she screamed, her hands losing their grip on the wheel as the blinding glare consumed the windscreen.

CHAPTER SEVENTY

ALISTAIR'S FINGERS tapped against the steering wheel as the car idled in the lay-by. The road stretched ahead of them, desolate in the dark, the occasional passing headlights casting shadows across his face. Petra sat in the passenger seat, her pulse hammering at her temples, wishing she'd made a note of which road this was.

She could sense her mobile phone abandoned in a ditch somewhere miles back. And here... here was nowhere. Escape wasn't an option – at least not yet.

"All this... this mess – it's Erik's fault, not mine." Alistair's voice was low but agitated. "He couldn't keep away..."

Petra turned her head slightly, her movements slow and deliberate to avoid startling him. "What do you mean, Alistair? Keep away from what?"

He slammed a fist against the steering wheel, making her flinch. "Astrid! My fucking wife. But, no, he had to have what wasn't his to take."

Petra spoke gently. "Are you saying Erik had an affair with Astrid?"

"You think that's an affair?" He barked out a dry, humourless laugh. "No. It was a poison in the heart of the Circle, threatening everything we've worked for. I came back to the site, saw them together..." His voice broke. "It wasn't just betrayal. It was desecration."

His gaze was fixed ahead on the road's darkness. Petra slid a hand to the door handle. She braced herself, knowing she'd only get one shot.

"You killed him, didn't you, Alistair?" she asked, her voice barely a whisper.

He exhaled, as though relieved. "He was going to ruin everything. He was going to leave... Take others with him. Astrid would've let him do it, too. Always so soft when it came to him."

Petra tried to keep her breathing steady. "So, you decided he had to go."

"It wasn't a decision, Doctor. It was necessary. You wouldn't understand... None of you do. It wasn't about me. It was about the Circle."

"You didn't think Astrid would protect the Circle?"

Alistair's head snapped towards her, his face dark. "She brought him in. She let him..." He leaned back, fists clenched in his lap. "Foolish woman."

Petra barely heard his words. Her focus was on movement behind them – lights, faint but growing stronger. A car slowing as it approached the lay-by.

Alistair didn't notice. "You think this is about jealousy or pride, don't you? You have no idea what it costs to protect something sacred."

Petra felt the faint vibration as the approaching vehicle rumbled to a stop behind them. She could make out the shape of the driver, a light shining briefly across the interior. Then came the blessed whirl of blue lights.

She moved her hand to the lock, pressing the button with her thumb. The faint click was masked by the distant noise of a car door shutting behind them.

"What've you done?" Alistair's tone hardened.

But Petra was ready.

She shoved the door open and heaved herself out. "Over here! Police!" Her voice rang through the night.

She'd barely made it two steps when Alistair bolted out of the driver's side, shouting at her. But figures were running towards them – a uniformed officer, torchlight flashing across Alistair's panic-stricken face. Petra staggered towards them, her chest heaving.

"Petra McBride, CCU," she gasped out. "I work with DI Tanner."

The officer nodded, comprehension dawning. Alistair turned sharply, only to find another officer closing in around the front of the vehicle.

Petra sagged against the bonnet as Alistair's protests turned into venomous muttering. She allowed herself to breathe as another unmarked vehicle arrived. Backup – Mo, perhaps. She shut her eyes as the adrenaline began to subside.

CHAPTER SEVENTY-ONE

Mo, sitting in his stationary car on hands-free, heard the boss's scream. Her cry of "Christ!"

He felt his heart leap into his mouth. "Boss?"

"Mo—" Her voice was drowned out by a sudden screech and a muffled gasp. Then, silence.

Mo froze. "Boss? Jade!"

No answer.

He looked out of the car, his movements wild. Stuart had gone with Sam in the patrol car, Morgan in the back. Astrid was back in her yurt.

He was alone.

Mind reeling, Mo snatched the phone from the cradle, holding it to his ear. "Jade! Say something."

He waited. One minute, two, five. He repeated her name, over and over.

Where had she been? On her way home. The A82...

The A82. Where her husband had died, before they'd even met.

No.

"Jade," he said, his voice thin now. "Jade. Are you there? Are you OK?"

Fifteen minutes had passed. He sat in the car, unaware of the cold biting at him.

"Jade." He hardened his tone. "Speak to me now or—"

"Hello?" A voice, breathing heavily. Male.

Mo's heart jolted. "Who's this? Who's on this line?"

"My name's Freddie," came the reply. Calm. Too calm. "I'm a paramedic. Who are you?"

"I'm her friend. Her colleague. Is she...?" He blinked. What had just happened?

"You're going to have to hang up now so we can get on. We'll call you back, the number is in the memory."

Mo's chest constricted. "Hang up? No. I'm police – DS Mo Uddin. The owner of this phone is DI Jade Tanner, also police."

"I hear you," Freddie said, almost apologetic. "But you need to get off the line, pal. There's been an accident, and we need to work."

The line went dead.

CHAPTER SEVENTY-TWO

THE HOSPITAL CORRIDOR was too bright, the kind of sterile light that undercut any sense of warmth. It buzzed faintly, a noise Mo couldn't unhear once he noticed it. His footfalls, sharp against the gleaming linoleum, echoed as he strode toward the reception desk. The drive up from the Ardrossan ferry had been hell, the bends of the A737 sharp and unforgiving, the weight in his chest heavier with each mile.

It wasn't the drive he dreaded, though. It was what waited for him here.

Superintendent Murdo stood at the far end of the corridor, leaning against the wall, his arms hanging at his sides. The super had always seemed utterly composed, the picture of measured authority. But now, his face carried an unguarded rawness Mo had never seen before.

Mo approached, every muscle in his body tight with unease. "Sir," he began, his voice firmer than he felt. "What's the situation? How is she?"

The super looked at him with a thin smile. "She's going

to be OK. She lost some blood, and her leg's broken in two places. But she'll be OK."

Mo sank into the chair. *Jade*.

"What happened?" he said.

The super closed his eyes. "A car hit her, right outside her house."

"Where..."

A nod. "Where her husband died."

Mo swallowed. What were the chances?

The super took another step towards him and put a hand on his shoulder. "Thanks for coming."

"She's my boss."

A nod. "A good boss."

Mo pulled in a breath. The case was over, the boss would be OK. He needed to get home. He needed to see his family.

He stood up. "Tell her I was here, please? Tell her I'll be back to see her. Tomorrow."

The super frowned. "You're not hanging around?"

Mo eyed him. It was clear there was more than just professional concern in the man's eyes. Jade had someone to take care of her.

"I need..." he began. Tears pricked at his eyes. "I need to get home. To my wife. My girls."

CHAPTER SEVENTY-THREE

STUART LET OUT a low breath and shut the folder on his desk. Lamlash Police Station hummed with faint activity. Outside, the wind whipped up gusts, tree branches slapping against the windows.

Freya Haldane had been sitting quietly in the holding room for hours, her shoulders low like she'd been deflated. Her release papers were signed and ready, but no one had taught him how to handle this kind of suspect-then-not-suspect situation.

Time to take her home. If that campsite could be called home anymore.

As he stood to fetch her, his phone buzzed on the desk: Patty.

He missed Patty. He hadn't realised it until now.

"Patty? You at Cumberland Street yet?" Stuart pressed the phone to his ear, smiling despite himself.

"Just left." She sounded tired. "Arrested him without fuss. He's in custody. Alistair MacLeod's not as slippery as I thought."

"What about Petra? Last I heard, she was at the station with him. How's she doing?"

Patty hesitated. "I haven't seen her."

"What?"

"She didn't stick around." Patty's voice was flat. "She called a cab. Left the second they told her she could go."

Stuart frowned. "She's a witness. A consultant, but still a witness. That's not protocol, is it? She's got to give a full account."

"Look, don't worry about Petra," Patty snapped. "She's not going anywhere. She's not daft, and this isn't her first rodeo."

Stuart went quiet. The hum in the station seemed louder now. "Fair enough," he conceded. "And... the boss? Have you...?"

Patty cleared her throat, her voice carrying a sudden edge. "You don't want to ask that."

"But I am asking," Stuart pressed, stepping closer to the door. He needed to take Freya home. "How's the DI, Patty?"

"There's been an accident," Patty said, her voice tight. He could hear her trying to steady it.

"Sorry?"

The silence stretched again, longer this time. Patty spoke at last, her voice breaking. "The DI. A car hit hers as she was turning right... Oh, Stuart. It was..."

Stuart froze mid-breath. He could feel the hairs prickling on his arms. "Is she... is she OK?"

A sniff. "The sarge says she's going to be OK. But the spot where it happened. It's just..."

Stuart frowned. He hadn't known the DI when it had happened, but he'd heard about it. Her husband, Dan. Killed in an accident on the A82.

"Was it outside her house?" he asked, his voice low.

Another sniff. "It was. That bloody road."

"But she's going to be alright, yes?"

"She is. But she'd been doing so well. She'd even started seeing... And then there's the..."

"Then there's the what?"

Patty cleared her throat. "I can't talk about it, Stu. I'm sorry. Just get back here, yes? Once you've sorted the arrest and everything. I think things are about to change."

CHAPTER SEVENTY-FOUR

Mo SAT on the hard plastic chair in the hospital waiting room, his elbows on his knees, head bowed. His phone buzzed in his pocket, breaking the silence he'd been clutching to like a shield. He fished it out, staring at Catriona's name on the screen for a long moment before answering.

"Cat."

"Mo, what's happened?" Her voice was calm, steady, practical as ever, but laced with concern.

He swallowed hard. "The DI. Jade. She was in a car crash."

He heard an intake of breath. "Is she... is she alright?"

For a moment, he couldn't speak. He watched, motionless, as a tear dropped to his knee.

"Mo? Mo love? Is she alright? Are you alright? Where are you?"

He wiped his nose with the back of his hand. "She's OK. I haven't seen her. But the super... He told me..." He shook, his skin cold. "I'm at the hospital," he said.

The A82. So unfair.

"I'm so sorry, Mo," she replied. "Do you need me to come? What about her son? Rory, is it? Is he there?"

"He hasn't been told yet. The super... I guess the super will tell him, or her mum. Or Patty, maybe." Or was that his job? He was the DS, after all.

"The super? Fraser Murdo?"

"He and Jade. They're... I think they're... It was where her husband died, Cat. How's she supposed to cope with that?"

"From what you've told me, she sounds pretty tough. Rebuilding her life after he husband died. Looking after that little boy. Leading a brand new unit."

He gasped in a breath. "You're right. Look, Cat..."

"What? Mo, are you OK? Were you hurt, too?"

He took a shuddering breath. "No. I was on Arran. But... I can't do this anymore, Cat. This place, this job. It's too much. Life's too bloody short. I keep thinking... if something were to happen to me... to you. I'm miserable, Cat."

"Mo. Sweetheart. You're in shock. Don't let that dictate decisions you'll regret."

He tightened his grip on the phone. "It's not just that. It started before... before this. It's everything. Stirling, Glasgow. It's wearing me down, Cat. I think I've always known it wasn't for me, but Jade's accident... it's brought it into focus. I want something different for us. A simpler life, somewhere rural. Somewhere the girls can have fresh air and fields instead of traffic and endless grey concrete."

She sighed. "I get it, I do. But let's not jump into anything now, yeah? We've got a life here. My practice, the girls' schools... they're settled. You'd be uprooting a lot for a feeling that might pass once you've processed all this properly."

"It's not just a feeling," he muttered.

"Alright," she replied, calm. He knew how good she was as a GP. Her bedside manner. "Then let's talk about it. After you've taken a breath. After this case is... well, sorted isn't the right word, is it? But after there's some distance. OK?"

Mo pressed the heel of his palm to his forehead, leaning further forward in his chair.

"That's fair," he admitted eventually. "But you'll think about it too, yeah? About a different life for us?"

"I'll think about it," she said, her voice soft. "I promise, Mo."

CHAPTER SEVENTY-FIVE

FREYA STOOD on the edge of the harbour, the cold breeze off the water biting at her skin. Brodick was quiet this early, the occasional cry of a seagull the only sound breaking the stillness. In her hand, she clutched her brother's necklace – a simple, braided leather cord with a small pendant that bore runes she could never pronounce. Erik had worn it during every ritual, had claimed it kept him grounded. Now it was all she had left of him.

She stared across the water, wondering how she would feel about leaving this island. His funeral would take place in a week, at home in Denmark. The practicalities of getting his body back had been onerous but the police had helped.

Her phone buzzed in her pocket and she dug it out, glancing at the screen. Liddy. She pressed it to her ear, her voice stiff.

"Hi."

"Freya," Liddy's voice was soft. Too soft. "How're you holding up?"

Freya sniffed. "I don't know. I've barely slept."

"I guessed as much." Liddy paused. "Where are you now?"

"Brodick. Waiting for the ferry."

A pause.

"You're doing the right thing," Liddy said. "You know that, don't you?"

Freya's gaze flicked back to the water, her grip tightening on the necklace. "It doesn't feel like it. It feels like... like I'm abandoning him."

"You're not. Freya, he's gone. Leaving Arran won't change that. Staying there, trying to cling onto what he believed in when even he eventually stopped believing it... It'll destroy you."

Freya shook her head. Her voice wavered. "He trusted them, Liddy. He trusted Astrid."

"And look where it got him." The sharpness in Liddy's tone made Freya wince. "Astrid never cared about him. Or you, for that matter. All she's ever cared about is control."

Freya closed her eyes, the truth pressing down on her. She wanted to argue, to defend Astrid like she'd done so many times before. But Erik was dead, and Liddy wasn't wrong.

"You can come to mine," Liddy continued. "There's a spare room. I'll not bombard you with questions, I swear. But you shouldn't be alone."

Freya swallowed. "I don't know."

"Think about it," Liddy urged. "It's time to leave for good. You need to live your life, Freya. Not theirs."

Freya's fingers traced the pendant, cold and rough beneath her touch. She thought of Erik's face, the way his tired eyes had searched hers during their last real conversation. "Maybe it's time for us to go," he'd said. "Start over.

Far away from here." But he'd never got the chance to leave.

She looked down at the pendant again. She knew where he'd got it. Astrid had given it to him. A love token, or a symbol of control?

Either way, she didn't want to look at it.

She walked to the fence, looking over the harbour. She held out her hand and let it slip from her fingers. For a moment she almost grasped at it, but then she forced herself to let go.

Tears were pouring down her face. A family, watching the ferry dock, stared at her. She tried to smile back but all that came out was a sob.

"Liddy," she said into the phone, her voice trembling. "I'll come."

"Good," Liddy said, relief flooding her voice. "Text me once you're on the train. I'll come and get you."

CHAPTER SEVENTY-SIX

Mo sat at his desk in the CCU base, staring at his laptop screen. The cursor blinked at him as he reviewed his reports from the Isle of Arran. Erik Haldane, the ritualistic elements, Astrid's manipulation. And then, the boss...

He felt drained, both mentally and physically, but at least he could file this case away and move on. Glasgow roared outside the windows, but in here, there was only the tap of fingertips on keyboards and the low hum of the heating system.

The door to the DI's office opened, and the Superintendent Murdo stepped out.

"Mo," the super said, his voice low. "Got a moment?"

Mo pushed back from the desk, stretching his arms before heading over. "Sir," he said, stepping inside. "How have you been? Have you seen the boss?" The DI had disappeared after the accident, not calling in, not making contact. She'd had a couple of calls with Patty, but those had been focused on wrapping up the case, from what the DC had told him.

The super gave him a tight smile. "Holding up. Jade's staying with her mum. In Dumbarton. I doubt she'll go back to the house."

"That's for the best."

The super looked down. Mo swallowed, suddenly awkward.

"And I doubt she'll be coming back to her job," the super added.

Mo frowned. "I didn't think her injuries were that bad?"

The super's gaze rose back up. He gave Mo a piercing glance, then looked away. "It's not that. Well, it's not for me to say. But either way. The CCU's being disbanded."

"Right." Mo glanced back at Stuart and Patty.

"It's not just because of Jade," the super said. "There've been conversations about restructuring up top for months. But the official line is that we're reallocating resources."

Mo exhaled deeply, nodding. He'd felt this coming since Jade's accident, but hearing the words made it real. "Right."

"I know this leaves you in a difficult position," the super continued. "You've done good work here, Mo. More than that, you've held a team together through chaos. That can't be overstated."

Mo looked past him at the window, where the city sprawled, alive with noise and energy he didn't feel connected to anymore. "And what's next for me, then?"

"You've options," the super said, leaning back. "There's a new position on offer – head of a local CID unit. You'd have some sway over the cases you take on. It's a step up."

For a moment, Mo almost nodded, the instinct to accept a new challenge bubbling up. But then he remembered windswept Arran and the serenity of its quiet roads. The conversations with locals at the community hall. The clear, unpolluted night skies.

"Sir," he began. "I realised something important while I was out on Arran. Being there, surrounded by open spaces, no city chaos... It did something for me." He licked his lips. "I don't want to be in the cities anymore." He met the super's gaze. "If there's a chance to be somewhere quieter, somewhere rural... that's what I need."

A frown. "You're serious about this?"

Mo had talked to Cat, convinced her this wasn't a flash in the pan. He'd never been more serious in his life. "I am. I've got my family to think about. And after everything..." He hesitated, recalling Jade's voice in his ear, her cry of *Christ* as the headlights appeared and bore down on her. "Life's too short to carry on in a place that wears you down."

Fraser nodded. "I can't say I don't understand. The Highlands, maybe, or somewhere coastal – there are posts opening up with this restructuring. I'll make some calls." His tone shifted. "It'll mean stepping away from your comfort zone, but then, maybe that's the point."

Mo allowed himself a small smile. "The comfort zone's already long gone, Sir."

The super rose, shaking Mo's hand. "You've earned this, Mo. If this is what you need, I'll make it happen."

"Thank you, Sir."

It was real. From Birmingham, to Stirling, to rural Scotland. What would Zoe say?

CHAPTER SEVENTY-SEVEN

PETRA SAT at a small corner table in the coffee shop, the kind of independent place that smelled of burnt toast and over-roasted beans. The rain streaked the windows, the glass as blurred as her thoughts.

They were late. She'd checked her watch, her phone, the clock behind her. Were they going to duck out? Put her through all that, and then disappear?

She heard the door open before she saw them. Louisa and Greg Greenwood. She recognised their faces immediately, though in person they looked older than she remembered from the trial. Smaller, too. Grief did that. Louisa's hair hung limp around her pale face, and Greg looked one solid prod away from cracking into pieces.

Petra steadied herself.

"Dr McBride," Louisa said as they reached the table, her voice sharp.

"Mrs Greenwood, Mr Greenwood. Please, sit." Petra pushed her coffee cup aside, making space.

Greg sat heavily, but Louisa stood for a half-second

longer before pulling out her chair. She looked Petra dead in the eye. It took effort not to look away.

"You're braver than I thought," she said.

Petra shrugged. "I got your letter," she said. "That's why I asked to meet."

"So you thought you'd stroll in here, say a bit about why you made the choices you did, and what? Heal us? Fix this? Fix him?" Louisa's voice swung wildly, the pitch alternately high and low, like it was about to crack.

"That's not why I asked you here," Petra said, injecting sympathy into her voice. Today, it felt brittle.

"Why did you ask us here then, Dr McBride?" Greg said, his eyes on hers for the first time.

Petra tightened her clasped hands on the table. "I..." She cleared her throat, started again. "I wanted to hear directly from you. You're angry. I understand why. I thought... I thought it might help us all."

"You understand?" Louisa's voice rose a notch. Heads turned at the nearest tables.

Petra ducked her head, for once wishing she was even smaller than her four-foot-eleven frame.

"You think you understand," Louisa continued. "You don't. You released a monster. You stood there in that court-room, with your fancy title and your cold, clinical analysis, and you told those people he could be managed. That he was safe." She leaned forward, her voice hard. "He wasn't safe, Dr McBride. He killed our boy. He ripped our son out of our lives, and you call that needing *clarity*?"

She wiped away a tear, tutting at herself. Petra fought off her instinct to explain. She pressed her palms against the table.

"I assessed the man based on what I knew then." She

wasn't about to say the name of their son's killer. "Based on the evidence available at the time. I can't foresee what someone will do years later, under different circumstances. I know now that—"

"That's convenient," Greg said. He swallowed. "A convenient excuse for someone like you."

"It's not an excuse, Mr. Greenwood. It's the truth. And it wasn't my decision, when it came down to it. The system weighed my analysis, but didn't rely solely on it." She looked up. "Believe me, if I could do it again, given what I know now, I would have changed my report."

Greg narrowed his eyes. "But you've just told us your report was based on what you knew."

Petra forced herself to meet his gaze. "It was. And now I know more. And I'm sorry for what happened to your son, I truly am. But please, don't make this situation worse. I'm asking you, I'm begging you, to stop harassing me. Persecuting me like this won't undo your son's death."

She looked down. They would never hear what she had to say, never understand what they were doing to her. It was all about what she'd done to them.

But she hadn't meant it. She'd done her job, to the best of her ability, and it had backfired. She'd been beating herself up about it for years.

She looked up. "I think about your son a lot, you know. About David."

Louisa winced. "Don't use his name. You didn't know him."

"I didn't, you're right. But I know how much you loved him. And I know what his death did to you."

"How can you?" the woman asked, her voice full of venom.

She's right. I can't. Not really.

Petra pulled in a long breath. "I don't know how it must feel for you, but I know how angry it's made you, because you've directed that anger at me."

She screwed her eyes shut, waiting for the onslaught.

"How dare—" Louisa began, then stopped.

Petra opened her eyes, just a crack. Louisa was hunched into Greg's arms, shaking. Greg was shushing her. People at the neighbouring tables were trying to hide the fact that they were watching. The café was silent.

"I'm sorry," Petra said. She straightened in her chair. "I'm going to leave Glasgow. You'll never see me again. I hope that will help you find some sort of resolution in all this, and I hope somehow you can forget about me."

"We'll never forget about you," Louisa muttered.

No, and I'll never forget you.

Petra stood up and picked up her bag. She put the strap over her shoulder, determined to be dignified.

"A terrible thing happened to you," she said. "It was partly because of my actions, and I regret that. But it wasn't me who did it to you."

She reached out a hand, then stopped before making contact. Greg was looking up at her. Louisa had gone still.

Greg gave her a nod. "We'll stop," he whispered. His wife whimpered into his sleeve.

Petra swallowed.

"Won't we, love?" he said, addressing the back of Louisa's head. "We'll leave the psychiatrist alone."

Psychologist, Petra thought, but didn't say. She gave him a tight smile. "Thank you. And I'm sorry."

Their pain wouldn't fade. And she'd never forget. But maybe now, she could move on.

She straightened the strap of her bag and made for the door, ignoring the stares as she passed.

CHAPTER SEVENTY-EIGHT

THE WIND CARRIED A SHARP CHILL, cutting straight through Mo's coat. He took a deep breath of the damp air and looked up at the CCU offices.

His last day. Never again would he make the godawful drive to this light industrial estate on the outskirts of Glasgow. Never again sit in that empty space, wondering why their unit was so isolated from the rest of Police Scotland.

He was being moved, temporarily, to an office in the city centre, while he wrapped up the final details of the Haldane case. The trial was due to start in a week, and would be straightforward. He hoped.

He hurried up the steps to the first floor office. Patty had already moved on, to Glasgow CID, and Stuart was heading for Aberdeen. There was very little point in him even being here.

But Mo was expected to be here today, and Mo didn't let people down.

As he pushed the door open, he realised he could hear

voices; not just Stuart's. He pushed his shoulders back, preparing himself.

The super was standing by the door to Jade's office, his back to the door. He turned as Mo entered and smiled.

"Mo."

Mo approached the senior officer, his hand outstretched. But the super didn't approach him. Instead he walked into the office and re-emerged a moment later, pushing a wheelchair.

In the wheelchair, smiling up at him, was Jade.

"Boss!" He cried, feeling warmth soak through him.

She smiled back, then winced. "Mo. Call me Jade now, yes? I'm not going to be your boss for much longer."

He frowned. "Where will you be going?"

She cocked her head. "Come inside."

She turned the wheelchair around, with a small push from the super followed by muttering from her, and wheeled herself behind the desk. He followed her inside, glancing back to see the super, still outside the office, closing the door gently behind them.

The boss's chair had been removed, but the photo of Rory was still on the desk, and the one of Dan. It had been joined by a third: an outdoor shot, of the DI, with Rory and the super.

Mo swallowed and looked down at the carpet. He'd been right.

Jade looked from him to the photo. "I owe you an explanation."

"You don't reall—"

"I'm in a relationship with Fraser, Mo. It's serious. He's a good man."

Mo smiled back at her. Her face was alight, her eyes sparkling.

"That's good news. I'm happy for you."

She pursed her lips. "It's not all good, though. I'm not coming back to the CCU."

He nodded; *no surprise there*.

"Or to Police Scotland."

Mo glanced at Jade in surprise, to see her looking back up at him. He lowered himself into the chair opposite her. "You're not?"

The boss shook her head. "I'm sick. Mo. Not seriously, at least, not yet, but with everything that's happened. And with Rory needing me... Well, I've decided this job isn't the best for me, right now."

"Sick?" he said. "The crash?"

She shook her head. "Not that. The cast's coming off next week. But I have MS."

"MS?"

"Multiple Sclerosis."

"Oh."

He blinked at her, not sure how to respond, trying to imagine what Cat would say. *She'd deal with this so much better than me.*

The DI leaned across the desk. "It's the relapsing remitting type. Means I'm not going anywhere soon, and I should be able to function, except for the times I can't." There was a faraway look in her eyes. "We're still working out how much of the time that's going to be."

He nodded. "I'm really sorry, boss."

"Jade. I'm not your boss anymore."

"Jade. Is there anything I can do?"

She smiled. "You're already wrapping up the Haldane

case. That's plenty. I'm grateful. And I hear you helped Patty and Stuart get through the last few weeks."

"Only doing my job."

She shook her head. "That's you all over, Mo Uddin. You're going to do very well, in your next posting."

He felt his breath catch. "Do you have any news of that?"

She was looking past him, towards the door. Mo turned to see the super, still standing outside. The boss – Jade – beckoned him in.

"Mo," said the super.

"Sir."

The super shared a glance with Jade, whose eyes twinkled as she looked back at him. "It's set. You're moving to Tayside, specifically Perth and Kinross. Based out of Perth, but it's not a large town, you'll be working across a rural area. You're moving in two weeks."

Mo blinked, unsure for a beat if he'd heard right. He hesitated, taking it in.

"Perth," he said. He'd spent time nearby, investigating the death of a man who'd been found on top of Dunsinane Hill. It was beautiful. "Thank you, Sir. It sounds perfect."

The super studied him. "You're sure?"

Mo nodded, his answer firm. "Sure."

"You've done good work, Mo." The super's voice softened. "Jade never stops raving about you."

He looked at Jade. "Thanks," he said, to both of them.

CHAPTER SEVENTY-NINE

PETRA's temporary flat in Ayr wasn't much to look at. The building was sturdy, practical. More secure than the old place, with its new mortice locks, a single reinforced window in the living room, and a bland grey door that wouldn't win any design awards. But it made her feel safe. That was the point, wasn't it?

She ran a hand over the metal edge of the door as she let Aila in, holding herself back from double-checking the latch yet again.

"Tea?" she asked, motioning to the small, functional kitchen. Her voice was thin, an effort at normality she couldn't quite pull off.

Aila stepped further inside, her eyebrows raised. "Petra, do you even want me here? Or are you just playing the host?"

Petra didn't answer. She turned to fill the kettle at the sink, her work outfit still pristine despite the unpacked suitcase in the bedroom. Everything here felt temporary, but she hadn't realised how bleak it looked until she'd been forced to see it through someone else's eyes.

"Well?" Aila scanned the room for something to sit on. There wasn't much. She settled at a modest dining table with two mismatched chairs, crossing her legs.

Petra reached for some mugs. "I'm sorry. I'm... It's been a lot," she admitted, keeping her back turned.

"You could say that," Aila replied. She ran her fingers along the edge of the table, watching Petra as she arranged teabags like it was a military operation. "Why didn't you call me after the break-in?"

Petra set the kettle back with more force than she intended. "I didn't want to worry you."

Aila grunted. "You didn't *want to worry me*? Petra, someone painted *KILLER* on your wall and left you letters. And instead of, I don't know, leaning on somebody, you move into..." She gestured around, "... this bunker."

Petra turned to her ex-girlfriend. "It's not a bunker. It's practical."

"It's lonely. Look, I'm not here to argue with you. I'm here *for* you. If you'll let me."

Petra's shoulders stiffened. "I don't need—"

"Don't," Aila cut in. "Don't tell me you don't need anything or anyone. Not after what you've been through. You do."

Petra fell silent. The kettle clicked off, steam rising in a hiss. Aila stood and joined her by the counter. Petra made no move to acknowledge her.

"I know you're scared," Aila said. "It's written all over you. The way you're gripping that worktop right now, the way you barely blinked when I walked through the door because you were too busy checking out the locks behind me. This obsessing over security... That's not you, Petra. That's your fear running the show."

Petra pursed her lips. She released the worktop to stuff both hands into her trouser pockets.

"I can handle it," she muttered.

"Can you? Honestly?" Aila stepped closer. "It sounds like a load, even for you. And I'm saying this because I care." She hesitated. "Maybe... maybe you should see someone. Get some help for the fear before it eats you alive."

Petra's jaw tightened. *Not this again.* "I don't need therapy, Aila."

Aila let out a long breath of exasperation. "Fine, no therapy. But at least talk to me. Properly."

Petra placed the mugs down without pouring the tea. She turned, leaning on the counter, her expression crumbling just slightly.

"I was... I didn't know how to explain it. The letters, the graffiti, everything... It's not just this bloody investigation getting to me. It's all of it piling up." She swallowed. "I keep thinking about everything I've done wrong. Everyone I've hurt – like you."

Aila blinked. "Hurt me?"

Petra gestured vaguely. "You know, when we broke up. If I'd been better, more stable... it wouldn't have ended the way it did."

Aila shifted in her chair. "Breaking up wasn't just on you. Don't rewrite history."

"It was mostly me," Petra insisted. "I can't hold on to anyone because I don't hold on to anything. I just run. From one flat to another, from relationships, from guilt. And now Jade's sick..."

Aila reached out and took Petra's hand, giving it a squeeze.

"You're not running *now*," she said. "Not if you're here

telling me all this." She smiled. "And even if you're thinking about running somewhere else, it's OK. Maybe you need somewhere new to breathe again."

Petra narrowed her eyes. "What do you mean?"

Aila hesitated. "You mentioned once before that you'd considered more international work. Why didn't you take it?"

Petra straightened slightly. "Because Scotland's home," she said, a little too quickly.

"Is it?" Aila pressed. "Because by the looks of things, it's not helping much. Staying here – surrounded by those letters, reminders of the past, of the Greenwoods, of every-thing – it's wearing you down. Maybe switching focus isn't a bad idea."

Petra considered. Maybe Aila was right. What she was suggesting wasn't just escape. It was opportunity.

As if on cue, Petra's phone buzzed on the counter. She swiped it up, frowning at the unknown number. Her gut tightened, but she answered.

"Dr McBride," she said.

"Petra," came a familiar voice. "It's Susannah Roscoe. From Interpol. I've got something complicated here in Madrid. Might need your expertise. Can you talk?"

Petra resisted a grin. It was like the world knew.

She looked at Aila, her eyes flashing.

"Susannah," she said. "Good to hear from you. Tell me more."

I hope you enjoyed reading my McBride & Tanner series. If you would like to read a novella featuring Lesley and Elsa, why not try *The Lochside Murder*, in which they find themselves embroiled in a murder case while on honeymoon. It's free in ebook and audio, available from: rachelmclean.com/lochside-murder.

Happy reading!
Rachel McLean

ALSO BY RACHEL MCLEAN

The DI Zoe Finch Series – buy from book retailers or via the
Rachel McLean website.

Deadly Wishes

Deadly Choices

Deadly Desires

Deadly Terror

Deadly Reprisal

Deadly Fallout

Deadly Christmas

Deadly Origins, the FREE Zoe Finch prequel

The Dorset Crime Series – buy from book retailers or via the
Rachel McLean website.

The Corfe Castle Murders

The Clifftop Murders

The Island Murders

The Monument Murders

The Millionaire Murders

The Fossil Beach Murders

The Blue Pool Murders

The Lighthouse Murders

The Ghost Village Murders

The Lyme Regis Women's Swimming Club

A Brush with Death

...and more to come